UNEXPECTED LOVE

A MOMENT IN TIME NOVEL

KRISTIN MAYER

Unexpected Love (A Moment in Time Novel) / Kristin Mayer – 1st ed.
Library of Congress Cataloging-in-Publication Data
ISBN-13: 978-1-942910-37-4

VISIT MY WEBSITE AT
http://www.authorkristinmayer.com

This book is dedicated to the most amazing editor,
Jen Matera.
I am so thankful I found you.
Working with you as an editor has been an amazing journey.
Thank you for everything, Jen.

PROLOGUE

Addilyn

My stomach turned at the sound of a key in the lock on the front door. I sat in the dark as unsure of how I was going to handle the confrontation I was about to face as I had been four hours ago. I had been betrayed and lied to by the person I trusted the most.

Hear him out. Maybe you misunderstood.

The evidence was too damning. Deep in my gut, I knew what I had found was the truth, which meant my marriage was over.

Fury surged through me. I clung to that emotion—fueled it, even—so I wouldn't let this be explained away. Too many times in the past, I'd let that happen. I dug my fingernails into the palms of my hands to give myself something to focus on while I waited silently for him to enter.

The door opened, and moonlight spilled into the house. Braden's silhouette appeared in the doorway and then disappeared into the darkness as he closed the front door.

I took a deep, quiet breath to prepare myself, wondering which parts of my marriage had been a lie and which parts had actually been true.

The foyer light flipped on, and he placed his keys in the ceramic bowl we bought on our honeymoon in the Caribbean. Next, he hung his coat in the closet on the third hanger from the left. It was a ritual with Braden.

Everything had a place.

All things were done in the same order.

I considered myself organized, but Braden took it to a whole new level. It had never bothered me because I'd considered it one of his quirks. He never expected the same of me.

The click of the closet door was loud in the silent house. My muscles tightened as I readied myself for the confrontation.

We were supposed to fly to the Florida Keys to celebrate our first anniversary in two days. The plan was to start a family. Or at least start to try. Sitting there, I cringed at the thought of being connected to Braden for the rest of my life. I felt nauseous and slowed my breathing to get that under control.

Braden put his briefcase under the table, to the far left, where it stayed while not in use. I turned on the lamp beside me, casting a soft glow in the living room. I felt like a stranger in my own home—the home I had made with Braden.

Braden loosened his blue pinstriped tie as he stepped toward me. Blue was a good color on him. I always loved buying him blue because it matched his eyes. Those eyes traveled down my body. If I hadn't known better, I would have sworn it was love on his face.

"Hello, my darling. I thought you might be in bed. I didn't want to wake you." He gave me a crooked grin and sauntered a few steps closer. I knew that walk. It was the *I-*

want-to-get-lucky walk. "Maybe we could get an early start on our family planning."

I want to vomit. I stood and shook my head. "No."

He appeared confused, head cocked to one side as he stared at me. "Okay… obviously you're angry. Do you want to tell me why? Because, darling, I honestly have no idea."

The sound of the pet name was like nails on a chalkboard. I grabbed the card from the table and tossed it at his feet. "Care to explain this."

Slowly, he knelt, and his eyes widened when he saw what the card was. Typically, it took a lot to faze Braden. But at that moment, he rose, as if trying to come up with some explanation. "Where did you find this?"

I scoffed. "Where do you think I found it?"

I waited for him to open the card, but he didn't. Because he knew what it said. It was a handmade card, drawn in crayon, that said world's best dad. Inside was a picture of Braden and a child about six or seven. And this kid was Braden's mini-me.

I knew the picture was recent because he had been wearing a blue sweater I'd bought him for Christmas less than two months earlier. And unless Braden had a twin brother I'd never heard of, he had a son with a woman who appeared to be very much a part of his life.

"Addilyn, I can explain." He rubbed the back of his neck, his gaze on the card in his hand.

He would have some explanation. One of Braden's specialties was smooth talking. That was how he got me to agree to date him. Initially, I'd said no. After some time and sweet gestures, I agreed to go on a date with him. From that day, and each day after, Braden had been attentive, caring, and loving.

Lies.

It hurt so much to think about, so I got to the point. "Are you that child's father?"

Braden's jaw flexed, and his response was stern. "Addilyn."

I balled my fists, and tears stung my eyes. I didn't have any other proof, so I bluffed. "Don't lie. I know the truth."

For a second, Braden eyed me. He was of average height, but handsome and well built. I was heartbroken our marriage had come to this. "I will file for divorce from Bridgette tomorrow. We'll go to marriage counseling. We can work this out."

I froze in shock for the second time that day. That was not what I had expected. An affair? Yes. But married to someone else? *How?*

When I remained silent, Braden continued. "I will end things with Bridgette. I'll get joint custody of my son. I want this life with you. I want the family we were planning to start. I don't want to lose you, Addilyn."

Nothing made any sense. *We* were married. Not he and Bridgette. I blinked a few times before I asked, "You're *married?*"

His eyes widened, and he cursed when he realized I hadn't really known the truth. "Fuck."

There was no apology.

No acknowledgement.

Braden was only aggravated because he'd been caught.

And now he realized I had lied.

There was nothing he could say that would matter. It was over; I'd heard enough.

I pointed to the door. "Get out. Get out of my house. This is over."

Braden took a step forward. "Addilyn, be reasonable. Let's talk about this. It was a mistake."

This was more of a mess than I'd imagined. I was the other woman. I wanted to be sick.

Braden mistook my silence and stepped closer. I backed up, pulling my phone out of my pocket. "Get out or I'll call the cops. So help me, if you don't leave this house, I will call them."

Braden stepped back, holding up his hands. "I'll give you some time to cool off and come back in the morning."

There would be no cooling off. *Just keep it together until he leaves.* I shook my head. "No, do not come back. Anything you need to say you can say to my attorney."

Braden grabbed his briefcase and keys. Ignoring my comment, he said, "I love you, Addilyn. Don't give up on me. We'll talk tomorrow."

The door shut, and the dam that had been holding back my tears burst. I dropped to my knees and cried into my hands as my heart broke into a million pieces.

How did this happen?

CHAPTER 1

Addilyn

"Whoa," I muttered as I stared at my computer screen, a picture of Braden's latest wife, Monique, staring back at me. It was like looking in a mirror. His new wife had long, dark hair, chestnut-colored eyes, and was slimly built—just like me.

Three years later, my stomach still got tied up in knots just thinking about the battle it had been to divorce him.

One. Year.

It had taken a full year to get everything sorted from my sham of a marriage.

It was twelve months I would never get back. As it turned out, I was the legal wife. Bridgette and Braden had been married in Mexico and had never gotten a US marriage license. It was a mystery to me why Braden had fought the divorce every step of the way. The judge in our case had been crooked—coordinating with Braden's attorneys at every turn. On my limited budget, I hadn't been able to afford the best attorney.

Braden had three attorneys, which made mine merely a puppet in the show.

I'd had to go through court-ordered marriage counseling.

He contested everything.

I'd even had to spend family time with Braden's son, Devin.

It was the worst kind of hell.

In the end, I offered to walk away from the marriage with only my car, my clothes, and the few things from my grammie. He was welcome to the house, the bank accounts, the investments. I didn't want them, anyway. That had been the only way to get out of the marriage. The judge had been forced to rule after I complied with the other requests although Braden still objected. It had been the best feeling in the world walking out of the courtroom being a free woman, even when I'd had nearly nothing.

After the divorce, Grammie passed away, leaving me a small inheritance, which helped me get back on my feet.

Grammie.

She had been in a nursing home with dementia for a couple of years before I married Braden. It had been a decent place, but I wished I could have afforded the nicer options. Thank goodness, I had been able to keep the divorce from her. During her more lucid moments, it was easier to let her believe I was happy. I hadn't wanted Grammie to stress about me. It was worse when Braden showed up randomly when I was there. It was because of Grammie I hadn't ended up who knew where when my mother dropped me off at her house at three and never came back.

"You are such a bastard," I whispered to the screen.

I wiped an errant tear that ran down my cheek. Those days had been hard in so many ways. There were times I wished I could give her a hug and she'd tell me everything would be okay.

Everything is okay.

I was free from Braden.

I had a successful career.

I was living my best life.

Yep, everything is okay.

The door to my office opened, and I jumped with a little yelp. Ria cocked her head to the side, her latest weave done in long, dark braids, piled on top of her head in an artful bun. "You okay, girl? You're awfully jumpy."

I plastered on a fake smile. "I'm working on my presentation to Black Media on Monday."

She flicked her wrist. "You got this. I've gone over your pitch, and it's spot on."

"Fingers crossed." I held up both hands, crossing my fingers in the air. "And maybe cross our eyes, too."

I brought my eyes to focus on the center of my nose, and she laughed. "Go on, get out of here. It's the weekend. Go be wild. Have fun. Maybe have some hot naked sex with a random guy."

My cheeks heated. I loved my boss, but she was definitely eccentric. "Umm... I think I'll settle for pizza and an old movie."

Ria rolled her eyes. "If I had a body like yours, I would hit the clubs."

I giggled, grabbing my laptop and changing the topic to something more appropriate. "What are you doing this weekend?"

"Chuck's family is in town. So, we're *entertaining* for the weekend." Ria held up her manicured fingers and air quoted. Her in-laws were high maintenance. They needed to have something to do every second of the day. "Let me grab my stuff and we can walk to the subway together."

"Sounds good."

After the year of fighting to get a divorce, it had taken me two more years to rebuild my life. Three years had passed since I found out Braden had had another life with another *wife*. I wondered if he was still with Bridgette. *Poor Monique.* I had no idea who she was, but my heart went out to her, knowing the heartache that would be coming her way if he hadn't changed. From what I knew, he still lived in our old home, still drove the same car, still had the same job. Made me sick.

Shortly after the divorce, I left Virginia and moved to New York City. I had no living relatives, and Wynter, my best friend from college, lived there. She'd begged me to come and start over. It was the best decision I'd ever made. The city that never sleeps kept me occupied. I also felt safer in a city with so many people. It made it easier to blend in just in case Braden tried to find me.

After the divorce was final, Braden had become almost stalkerish. He knew enough about the law to stay out of trouble. So I decided the best thing was to remove myself from the situation. I hoped I never saw him again.

I'd come to New York, and Ria gave me a chance. She owned Impact Marketing, a small firm with only four people. I'd worked in sales before, so it seemed a good progression in my career. Ria was brilliant and an amazing mentor.

Life in New York was exactly what I had needed. And Braden had left me alone. Once I left Virginia, it was like we never had existed. It was hard, but I had consistently worked on making Braden a distant memory.

The crisp October air hit me as we walked outside. I loved New York City in the fall. As we walked on the busy sidewalk, Ria pulled her scarf a little tighter. "If you need anything this weekend while you prep for the meeting, call me."

"I will."

Before Ria continued her pep talk, her phone rang, and she launched into a conversation with whomever was on the phone. My boss could talk a mile a minute.

My plan was to spend the weekend poring over my notes and working on my presentation. Two months ago, Wynter had shown me a posted opportunity online to present a marketing campaign to Black Media for a dating app her company had made. She worked for Keller Industries, who designed the app, but Keller Industries had hired Black Media to distribute the app and handle the marketing aspect. Black Media was looking to expand their current marketing base and get a fresh perspective. By some miracle, they granted us a meeting. Wynter assured me she had nothing to do with it and had only shown me in case I was interested. It would be career-changing if I managed to land the job.

The downside was that it was a dating app. I had zero knowledge about these types of apps. So, I created an account on the site in order to learn the program and present the best marketing strategy. I hoped it worked. The experience so far had been interesting, to say the least. I had received more dick pics than I wanted to think about. If we landed the account, it would be worth it.

As we approached the subway, Ria ended her call, and I said, "Have fun *entertaining*."

She laughed. "I may show up at your place with alcohol if I reach the end of my rope."

We started down the steps, and people rushed past us on both sides. Since it was rush hour on Friday, the subway was a madhouse. "Well, I only have a twin bed, but you're welcome to crash on the love seat."

"Deal! Have a good weekend, Addilyn. Don't stress too much about the presentation. You're prepared. See you on Monday."

Not stressing would be impossible. "See you. Thanks for all the help on the sales pitch."

She flicked her wrist in my direction and hustled down the steps to the right. I headed to the left. Our trains went in opposite directions. I lived toward Central Park and Ria lived in the East Village. I hustled with the group of people to the train. Once in the subway, you learned to walk fast or be trampled.

I'd barely made it before the doors closed. As usual, it was standing room only. I found a little spot to stand next to the door and settled in. My phone vibrated with a text from my best friend, Wynter.

Wynter: *What did you think of the article?*

Me: *Creepy. How did you find it?*

Wynter: *I get alerts for any news regarding that sick bastard.*

Me: *Of course you do.*

I smiled at my best friend's tenacity. She was one of the few people who knew what happened between me and Braden. As well she was a computer genius.

Wynter: *Will you please stop by tonight? I know you keep avoiding the question. Pretty please. You can literally walk here from your subway stop.*

Me: *Won't that be weird since I'm presenting to your company and Black Media on Monday?*

Wynter: *No, not at all. There are other firms here. Just come as my friend, tonight. Kaysen hates these things and refuses to do business at them.*

I wanted to go home, but I needed to support my best friend. Her company was doing a toy drive for a local shelter.

Me: *I'll be there in twenty.*

Wynter: *Good! There are a lot of hot single guys here.*

Oh, good grief. Wynter was fine with unattached sex from what I discerned. She was closed off about the topic, always had been. One-night stands with strangers were hard for me. To sleep with someone, I needed a real connection, not just physical but emotional. Sex was too personal for me. I had only had two partners. One in college that turned out to be a one-night stand and Braden. The one-night stand felt too casual, and I knew they weren't for me.

My phone dinged again.

Wynter: *I'm in the back of the restaurant.*

Me: *Be there in less than twenty.*

Here was hoping I survived the night if Wynter decided to play matchmaker.

CHAPTER 2

Addilyn

"You're here!" Wynter held up her cocktail.

"I'm here." I laughed as I gave her a hug. She was wearing the latest fashion, her outfit edgy as always. Somehow Wynter made black combat boots work with the same colored cocktail dress. Her shoulder-length blonde hair was messy and cut blunt at the tips. Wynter had that look about her that drove guys mad. I was the tame, conservative one; she was the wild, carefree one. Opposites that balanced each other out.

She grabbed me a drink from the tray of a passing waiter. "Drink up."

The restaurant where the fundraiser was being held was hopping. "Where do I put this?" I held up the stuffed giraffe I had picked up in the clearance section of a little shop along the way.

"In this bin. That's adorable. Thanks for the support." There were bins placed around the room along the walls, overflowing with toys. I tucked my little giraffe in on the side.

Wynter worked at Keller Industries, which was a tech company, and she was one of their techies. I honestly did not understand what she did but knew she was good at her job. Her boss allowed her to pretty much do whatever she wanted. Wynter and I had agreed once I put my name in the hat to pitch a marketing campaign for their app to Black Media, there would be no work talk. It made sure everything stayed on the up and up.

I took a sip of the champagne and saw Wynter's wheels turning. "So, at eleven o'clock we have a hottie. He has been watching you since you came in. I can also vouch for him; he's a nice guy."

"Wynter, seriously, I don't want to be set up tonight. I need to get home and work on my presentation."

"Just look."

Casually, I changed my position and saw the guy. He was good-looking. With his glass raised, he nodded our way. My cheeks heated, and I gave a quick nod back. I was sure I looked more like a stiff robot. I was out of practice.

It felt warmer in here. "His name is Andy. Want to meet him?"

Part of me wanted to. It would be nice to go on a date and put myself out there again. It scared me. I had convinced myself that I would know exactly when it was the right time. Or maybe that was an excuse.

Wynter nudged me, waiting for an answer.

"I don't know. Not tonight. I think I'm going to head home."

Another girl came and tapped Wynter on the shoulder before whispering something. She looked torn. I interjected, "Go handle your business. I'm going to go grab dinner."

She looked at her watch and then around the restaurant before sighing. "Thank you for coming. Wanna do brunch on Sunday?"

"It's a date."

Sunday brunch was our thing. We made it a point to get together at least once a week. I hugged her. "Adios."

"Adios, bitchacho."

I laughed and headed to the door. When I was nearly there, someone bumped into me, and I lost my balance. Before I hit the ground, two strong arms caught me from the other direction. I righted myself but had to catch my breath when I looked up at the man who had caught me. Tingles erupted along my skin, and I took a step back.

"You okay?" His voice was deep and gravelly, the kind that affected you bone deep.

"Umm… yes… Sorry, someone bumped me, and, well… the rest is history."

Stop babbling.

He chuckled. "Do you work for Keller Industries?"

For a second, I stared at him, trying to get my bearings. Wait, he asked me a question. *Get it together.* "No, I came to support a friend. You?"

He smiled, and I swore he became more handsome. The smile brought me a giddy feeling. *Stop.* "No. I came to support a friend, too."

I felt my cheeks heat again. *What's wrong with me?* His eyes were a dark golden brown with flecks of black in them. They were stunning. I blinked to break the connection. My lips formed a slow smile. *Say something else.* "Thank you for saving me from complete humiliation."

"Glad I was here to assist. Are you here with someone?"

"Uh… no. I came here to support my friend for the toy drive."

Someone coughed beside us, signaling they needed to pass. The man touched my arm to guide me out of the way three steps to the left. My skin was on fire from his touch. The reaction took me off guard. Was it possible to react this strongly to someone I had never met? Apparently so. "What about you?"

"I came solo as well."

Again, our eyes locked. Was he as affected as me?

"There you are!" a man's voice called from behind me.

He whipped his eyes around and held up a finger, signaling he would be just a minute, before turning back to me. "Would you like a drink?"

I hadn't expected that. "I—"

"I thought you would be here."

This time it was a woman's voice. He looked up again, and his brows pinched. I turned to see a woman staring at him, eyes narrowed. She was a petite blonde with an incredible figure that was showcased in her low-cut dress. She began to make her way toward us. What was that about? Maybe an ex.

From her determined step, it was clear this woman was on a mission. I wanted no part of any drama. I took a step to the side. "I need to get going. But thank you again."

Before he could say anything, I ducked out the door, pulling my coat around my shoulders.

Once I was a couple of blocks away, I slowed my pace. The dark eyes and the feeling of the man's touch stayed with me. I swore my skin still tingled where his hand had been moments ago.

Move on.

I contemplated what was I going to eat for dinner. I was tired and not in the mood to cook, so I popped into a little café two blocks from my studio apartment and sat at an empty table.

The waiter, Chris, came over to take my order. "Hey, Addilyn. You want your usual?"

"Please."

I loved the stromboli there. Chris gave me a sweet smile as he took my order. He was a nice guy around my age. After I'd been coming into the café for a few months, he'd hinted about going out together. I'd still been raw from the divorce, so I'd said no. If he asked again, I might consider going. Maybe. Chris had never given me that toe-curling feeling I hoped for. Neither had Braden, if I was being honest, but I had settled because he'd said all the right things.

No, I wouldn't go out with Chris.

I would never settle again.

The handsome man from the restaurant came to mind. I'd felt those tingles just looking at him. Who had that woman been? The man hadn't been pleased to see her. He said he came alone. Had he lied? None of it mattered; I doubted I would ever see him again. I knew I wanted those types of feelings if I ever dated again. I wanted the tingles.

Wynter might know who he is.

No, no, no. If Wynter caught wind, she would stop at nothing until she figured out who he was and set us up. I wanted it to be natural.

As I waited, I turned to watch the pedestrians as they passed by the café. The wind was blowing, and on the sidewalk, people pulled their coats around them. In a little under seven weeks Thanksgiving would be here. The Macy's Thanksgiving Day Parade was one of my favorites. Then

Christmas was right around the corner, which was a magical time in New York City.

My phone vibrated with a notification, and I smiled. Okay, so I *sort of* met someone on the dating site while I was researching my marketing pitch to Black Media.

Mister_Mystery: *So… I took your advice.*

Well, that was intriguing. I bit my lip as I replied.

Me: *On?*

The three little dots appeared, and I waited for his reply.

Mister_Mystery: *I ate at the hot dog stand on the corner of Madison and 55th. You were right.*

He'd taken my advice.

I looked up as a plate was placed in front of me. Chris gave me a pleasant smile. "It's good to see you happy."

I put my phone away and gave him a polite smile. "Thanks, it's been a good day." Changing the topic, I gestured to the food. "Looks amazing. Thanks, Chris."

Chris nodded, tucking his blond hair behind his ear. "Let me know if you need anything."

"I will."

He lingered for a second before turning and walking away.

Yeah, it seemed crazy I would give anyone online the time of day after my experiences with Braden. But there was something about Mister Mystery. It was hard to explain, but it felt honest.

I shrugged; maybe I was crazy.

We had made sure not to give any identifiable details about each other. And we had no plans to meet. Maybe it was just the fact that there was no pressure... ever. We were just two people conversing. It had been nice to tell someone else about Braden's betrayal. Mister Mystery had also gone through a nasty divorce a year ago. We'd both been betrayed by the one person we should have been able to trust more than anything. In our conversations, I made sure personal details, like locations, names and places, weren't given. He'd been similarly vague. The only thing I knew about his location was that he lived in New York City.

I felt my phone vibrate again, but I ignored it as I ate. Later, when I got home, I would check it. Chris was acting a little weird, coming up to my table, asking if I needed more water, and then walking away again. It made no sense; my water glass was clearly full.

After his third drive-by, I decided that maybe I should take a break from eating here for a bit. Or ever. If he was working up the courage to ask me out, I wasn't interested.

When I dated again, it was going to be for the right reasons. My therapist had helped me break past the thinking that every man who walked the Earth was evil. Over the last two years, I had grown in my thoughts and was ready to tiptoe back into a relationship.

After paying my bill, I left the restaurant with only a quick wave good-bye to Chris. As I walked home, there were clear signs that someone had a fire burning in their fireplace. I loved the smell; it made me think of cozy nights curled up in front of dancing flames. I turned the corner and saw the blue awning of my building.

At first, I'd rented an apartment in a neighborhood in Brooklyn that wasn't the safest. After my first raise, I moved to a studio just west of Central Park, which I loved—all three-hundred and sixty-nine square feet. The building had a doorman, which was a must for me. It added a layer of security knowing someone was watching who came and went. Money was tight, but it was worth it.

I smiled and gave a small wave. "Hey, Clay."

"Ms. DeRoss. Welcome home."

"Thank you. How's your wife?"

He chuckled. "Ready to have that baby. She's ready to just skip over the next four weeks."

"Aww, I can't wait to see pictures."

He tipped his hat, showing the slight bit of gray on his sides. "I'm sure I'll have plenty. Thank you again for the blanket you made. It's special to us."

"You're so welcome." When I was younger, my grammie had taught me to knit. It was something I loved doing in my spare time.

I climbed the three flights of stairs instead of waiting for the elevator. Inside my apartment, I set my stuff on my little table for two just inside the door. It always felt good to walk through the door on a Friday.

I was filled with a sense of accomplishment. My apartment was tiny, but it was mine. The kitchen, living room, and bedroom were all one room. I had a small bathroom, which was its own space, thankfully. There was a closet across from the kitchen. The building had a common laundry area, which was fantastic. No more laundromats for me.

I kicked off my shoes and flopped onto my love seat. Against the far wall, I had a dresser and a twin bed. Since it was just me, there was no need to waste space with anything bigger.

I pulled out my phone, wondering what Mister Mystery had sent me. His last message had been about trying the hot dog stand I suggested.

Mister_Mystery: *Curious… how many hot dogs have you consumed to determine which hot dog cart was best?*

I laughed out loud. That was a random detail only he would ask about.

Me: *Sorry, I was eating dinner. I am ashamed to admit it, but let's say I had to take up walking a few extra blocks every day to stay in my current pants size.*

His response was almost immediate.

Mister_Mystery: *That is impressive. My turn… there's a coffee shop you should try. It's on 10th between 56th and 57th called Rex. Best coffee in town.*

That wasn't far from me. I wondered if Mister Mystery lived nearby. It was oddly exciting that we might be in the same place at the same time without ever knowing it.

Me: *I'll give it a go and let you know in the next week or so.*

Mister_Mystery: *Good. I'll be back shortly. Business calls.*

I wondered what he did. There were a lot of times Mister Mystery had business calls at random hours, so I wasn't sure if he would come back or not. Sometimes he'd disappear until the next day.

I typed out a quick response.

Me: *Have a good night.*

That was most likely a "talk to you tomorrow." I closed out of the *Lots of Fish in the Sea* dating app. First, the name had to go. It was terrible, and I had that noted as part of my presentation. The one feature I enjoyed was that the app allowed for platforms to be created. It was more than a dating network, but that detail wasn't being capitalized on.

I turned on the television, found the original, black-and-white version of *Casablanca* to stream and settled in for the evening.

Will I ever find my one true love?

CHAPTER 3 ♥

Lucian

I hung up the phone and dragged a hand down my face. Expanding the company overseas had taken a toll. There had been more late nights than I cared to count. But it gave me something to focus on besides my crazy ex-wife. I wasn't normally the violent type, but if there was one person I'd ever wish dead, it would be Crystal. She'd done more damage than anything I could fathom in my worst PR nightmare.

My attorney's name flashed across the screen of my phone. "Walt."

"I have bad news, Lucian."

"Shit. What is it?"

"The judge denied the injunction against your ex-wife. He has maintained fifty-fifty custody of your son."

"Fuck."

Crystal had become more and more unhinged in the last few months since the divorce. Each time I saw her out in public, she hadn't been herself. Because of my son, I had been more generous to Crystal's bank account than the divorce decree had mandated. When Remmy had mentioned all the strange men, I knew I had to take drastic measures. I hoped my son came out of this with minimal damage. Crystal had been cut off, and that wasn't going well. The child support was still generous but nothing in comparison to the lifestyle Crystal had enjoyed with me.

I crumpled the piece of paper in my fist while Walt waited for my answer. "Figure out a way to get full custody of my son. You and I both know Crystal is unfit. I would never take a child away from his mother for any other reason."

"I understand. The investigator is working on it. So far, she's kept any suspicious activities under wraps."

If my son was hurt because of her carelessness, there would be hell to pay. The only positive thing from our marriage had been Remmy. It killed me having to give up fifty percent of my time with him.

"Figure it out. That's why I pay you a damn fortune every year."

"Understood."

I hung up the phone, still seething.

My parents had died when I was young, leaving my Aunt Taryn to raise me. She'd been a godsend, taking me in and raising me like I was her own until she passed away four years ago from a heart attack. I wanted my child to have a loving family like I'd had. Instead, he had a psychopath for a mother.

A notification on my phone prompted me to the *Lots of Fish* dating app. My friend Kaysen had signed me up to get my thoughts on it. There was merit to the program, but he had work to do before the official launch. He'd also chosen my screen name, Mister Mystery, which made no sense to me, but he was the creative one. Maybe it was because my life lately had been anything but a mystery. When I opened the app, a little number one appeared in the top right corner. I'd programmed my settings to only allow conversations with another user named Aurora Rose.

The first night I perused the site, I had entered a platform for online dating. The entire concept felt odd, and I had wondered what others thought about the site. Something had drawn me to her comments about the question *"Can you really find true love online?"* There was a candidness I found refreshing, and she shared the same concern I did—would someone really be honest about all their flaws and attributes before meeting? Before I knew it, I was private messaging Aurora, and we started bantering. Of course, I had no way of knowing if Aurora Rose was telling me the truth or feeding me a load of bull. Her answers seemed raw at times—like when she told me about her ex-husband having another wife she knew nothing about.

Sick bastard.

Maybe we connected because we'd both been betrayed. I opened the message to see her last response.

Aurora Rose: *Have a good night.*

I wanted to message her more than I should have. I shoved my phone in my pocket and went into the closet in my office. Sometimes, it was necessary to change there before going to a function instead of going home first. After a dinner party earlier in the evening, I'd come back to work. I had another work function for a local food shelter later that evening.

During the weeks Remmy was with Crystal, I packed my schedule for two reasons: distraction to make the time go by, and it freed up my time when it was my turn with him. I put on my tux, wanting to get the charity event over with as soon as possible. It was important to make an appearance, but I just wasn't feeling it.

My phone dinged with the notification I had set for Aurora. It was odd for her to message me again after she said good night, so I was curious.

Aurora Rose: *I finished the black-and-white version of* Casablanca. *I get why you said it needed to be watched... but still.*

My lips twitched and I fought a smile. One night we were talking about what we did to unwind. I'd mentioned that I enjoyed watching old movies. She had asked for a suggestion on what movie to start with. And every few days, she watched one. At first, I had been skeptical that she was actually watching them. Part of me was still wary, considering my current circumstances. But her answers convinced me that she had.

Me: *But still what?*

Aurora Rose: *The right thing was done, but at the cost of true love. Even though I was scorned—badly—I still hope loves wins one day.*

Me: *Hopefully it will for you.*

Not for me, though. For me, that was over. After the nightmare with Crystal, I was never going to put myself out there again.

Aurora: *How was your conference call?*

Me: *I hate late night ones. They prattle on about nothing.*

It also took twice as long to get things accomplished.

Aurora: *Prattle? That seems like an archaic word. Ha-ha! For some reason I've pictured you in your late twenties, early thirties. Maybe you're actually fifty. No judging.*

Fifty. What the fuck?

I began to type but then stopped. I wanted her to know I was not that old. Then I laughed. She knew I wasn't that old. One night, we'd shared what decade we were born. As it turned out we were in the same decade, which meant we were within ten years of each other. I imagined she was in her mid-twenties, which probably put us about five years apart, as I had just turned thirty.

Sense of humor intact, I played along.

Me: *Sorry, I had to find my bifocals to read your last message.*

Aurora Rose: *Don't forget to recharge your hearing aid tonight before bed. ;)*

I gave myself one last look in the mirror to make sure I was presentable. When I was messaging Aurora, I found my-self not paying attention to what was happening around me. I ran my hands through my dark hair and straightened my bow tie before I headed down to the limo.

"Evening, Lucian."

"Evening, Jim. Thanks for working late."

"Of course."

Jim had been with me for years. He was one of the few people besides Kaysen I trusted, and I insisted he use my first name. In some ways, he was like a father to me. He'd been the one to teach me to drive and had attended all my school functions. Aunt Taryn had tried, but there were things a boy needed a father figure for.

When I settled in the limo, I opened the damn dating app again. I should have been using the time in the limo to send emails, but instead, I wanted to message her.

Me: *Thanks for the reminder. I'll do that when I'm done with this drab function.*

Aurora Rose: *Will you sip tea with your pinky up?*

I laughed, wondering what she really thought of me. Part of me wanted her to know I wasn't some pussy. But there was a line, and I refused to cross it.

Me: *You must think I'm a skinny, arrogant ass with a British accent.*

Aurora Rose: *You said it, not me.*

This woman was pushing all my buttons tonight. *Is she trying to?*

Me: *Well, I can assure you I am none of those things.*

Aurora Rose: *Oh, so you're a pruney old man? Good to know.*

An idea came to mind. I turned on the limo lights and took a picture of my black Ferragamo shoes. Besides my black pants, there were no other discernable details.

Me: *Would a pruney old man have taste this good?*

A minute later, I got a picture of purple furry slippers. There were tanned, toned legs attached to those slippers that had my cock stirring and my brain wondering what she looked like. There was nothing else in her picture except a navy rug.

Aurora Rose: *Maybe not. But I'll match your classy black shoes and raise you a pair of crazy fuzzy slippers.*

Me: *You definitely win this round.*

Aurora Rose: *Have fun at your drab function. I'm going to curl up on my couch. Got any other suggestions?*

Me: Citizen Kane.

A few seconds passed before she responded again.

Aurora Rose: *Good news! It's available to stream.*

Then another one came before I could respond.

Aurora Rose: *Wait! Is this going to be sad? I need an HEA.*

Me: *HEA?*

Aurora Rose: *Happily Ever After. They happen. Not to us, of course, but I won't stop believing they do. My grammie believed in them.*

I dragged a hand down my face as I stared at her message.

Aurora Rose: *I looked up the plot. It says it's a classic, but he dies? Seriously. You have to suggest something happier next go round.*

Me: *You read about the ending? You ruined the movie.*

Aurora Rose: *Or made it amazing.*

Me: *Definitely ruined it.*

Aurora Rose: *Psst… I also read the end of books when the plot gets too stressful.*

I stared at her confession, shocked. And again, I found her candidness refreshing.

Me: *That's just wrong.*

Aurora Rose: *Or perfectly right.*

She was feisty this evening, and I enjoyed her spirit.

Me: *So do you go into Macy's during Christmas and tell all the kids Santa isn't real?*

Aurora Rose: *You know me so well. Go be drab. I need to focus on what this Rosebud business is about.*

Me: *Sleep well.*

Aurora Rose: *You, too. And don't forget to plug in your hearing aid. I heard forgetfulness is a sign of old age.*

Me: *What was that again?*

Aurora Rose: *You're a funny man, Mister Mystery. Night.*

Me: *Night.*

For the first time since we started talking, I wanted her to know my real name. I wanted her to call me Lucian, not Mister Mystery. And I wanted to see the face that went with those purple fuzzy slippers.

CHAPTER 4 ♥

Addilyn

"You'll find the detailed outline in your presentation that dives further into each category." I'd only been allotted forty-five minutes for my pitch, so I had to manage the time effectively.

Kaysen nodded. "Thank you, Ms. DeRoss. Let me take a few moments to look it over and see if there are any additional questions. Wynter, do you have anything?"

"If Black Media decides to go with your ideas, how quickly could you have marketing templates to us?" she asked.

I thought for a second. "From the time we're awarded the contract, I would need seventy-two hours to get you the detailed outline. To give a fully detailed rollout, I would need to better understand Black Media's timing."

"Good to know." A wisp of a smile on Wynter's face told me I'd given the right answer.

Whew.

I took a quiet, calming breath to ease my nerves while Kaysen flipped the pages. At the last minute, the meeting had been moved to Black Media from Keller Industries. I knew Keller Industries was the developer of the app, but Black Media was going to be rolling it out into production. No one had mentioned a reason for the location change, though. Kaysen flipped another page. He was dressed as edgy as Wynter but still looked professional in his fitted vest, skinny tie, and slim pants. His hair was trendy, fuller on the top with closer-cut sides.

Discreetly, I wiped my sweaty hands on my dress. It felt like it had gone well. *Fingers crossed.* For transparency, Wynter had told Kaysen we were friends, but that wouldn't be a factor in who was awarded the account.

Ria sat beside me, all business, with her practiced smile on her face as she patiently waiting for him to say something. She'd toned down her normally bright colors to a forest green today. Inside, I was a wreck but appreciated Ria letting me run the show. If we landed the account, it would be huge for her company and for me. It would mean I'd be able to make all my bills each month without dipping into my inheritance from Grammie when I had unforeseen expenses.

Kaysen was quiet, which made it difficult to read him. I gave him a few more minutes as he flipped through the pages, though it killed me not to say anything.

Finally, he said, "So you believe the product must be re-branded?"

Shifting in my seat, I casually folded my hands on top of the table to show confidence. His comment gave no indication where his thoughts lay, so I stayed my course. "Yes, dating sites are a dime a dozen. While dating is a key attractant, adding the other elements, such as the platforms where users can interact with each other prior to one-on-one conversations, will broaden the horizon. It allows those people who are skeptical about online dating to give your app a try. Otherwise, what makes your product unique to what's currently in the market? You need an edge to get people to try your new app."

He raised an eyebrow to Wynter, who mashed her lips together and said nothing. Her facial expression screamed, *"I told you so."* Or maybe I was just being hopeful.

Kaysen asked, "And do you have marketing concepts if awarded the business?"

It was a gamble to give any more detail than I already had considering we weren't guaranteed the business yet. But Kaysen was interested, so I shared a little more.

"'The world at your fingertips' would be the slogan. From there, you would run different mini campaigns based on the target audience. It would require some restructure on the app, but based on my limited understanding, the expense would be minimal in the scheme of things."

He looked at Wynter, who simply stared at him. Turning toward me, he said, "Yes, the structural components themselves wouldn't be an issue. A few algorithm changes would be key. But all in all, not an unreasonable thing to change."

If they had conveyed all that in a look, talk about impressive ESP.

At that moment another man walked into the room, and the breath was nearly sucked out of my lungs. It was the same guy from the restaurant the other night. The same guy who'd had a starring role in my dreams for the last three nights. The same guy who affected me with just his mere presence.

My memory hadn't done him justice. The tailored business pants and dress shirt fit him just right. The man was slim yet exuded power at the same time. Many times, my thoughts drifted to the way his touch had made me feel.

"Sorry I'm late. Another meeting ran long. I'm Lucian Black."

First, he shook hands with Ria. Then he turned to me. Those dark eyes flared with recognition, and the other occupants in the room faded away. The world stopped spinning as he reached out his hand. "Lucian Black."

Keep it professional.

"Addilyn DeRoss."

His hand caressed mine a fraction too long, sending butterflies to my stomach. "I apologize for being late. A business call ran long."

From the corner of my eye, I caught Wynter as she cocked her head to the side. *Damn it, Wynter can read me so easily.* When Lucian sat, he took one of the proposals and began to go through it.

Kaysen leaned back in his chair. "They're suggesting a complete rebranding."

That was it. After I'd spoken for forty-five minutes, Kaysen gave Lucian a five-word summary.

I added some context. "I would also suggest capitalizing on the other features in the dating site, such as the platforms that allow users to interact in a broader sense. Dating is the key element, but you could gain more market share if you work on reaching those who are single and skeptical of meeting people online. Additionally, I would suggest a new name for the app. Something that isn't so limiting and has those who aren't interested in online dating sites backing away before they give it a shot."

Lucian's eyebrow lifted for a second, and his eyes sparkled with amusement. I kept a straight face, refusing to lose sight of the business opportunity or let Wynter see how much this man affected me. With one hand, Lucian flipped through my proposal before cocking his head toward me. His intense gaze nearly took my breath away again. *How is it possible to feel this pull to a stranger?* I felt as if I was being affected on a molecular level. "You are the only one who has suggested this, Ms. DeRoss. Why?"

The way he challenged me stoked the fire in my belly. "I've been on the site, interacting with it, for the past few months. Maybe the other companies didn't investigate the feature or aren't thinking outside the box about how to make this the most profitable program."

"Did anyone else at your office use it?" Lucian asked.

I took a deep breath. "No, I'm the only single one, so... I became the tribute. It was a great experience. I've enjoyed my conversations on there, which were not romantically inclined... well, besides the inappropriate pictures. I would also suggest a 'report this user' function that's easy to find. The 'report a picture' can be cumbersome."

Mentioning that I had an online friend on the site seemed weird, so I kept everything generic. Lucian stared at me a bit longer before turning to Kaysen. "Do you have any other questions?"

He had begun to jot down some notes. "Nope. I think that's good. Do you have anything, Wynter?"

"No, I don't."

They stood. Kaysen gave me a professional smile. "Thank you for sharing your presentation, Ms. DeRoss, Ms. Charles. I'll go through it in depth and discuss it with Wynter, and then I'll be in touch."

"If there are any questions that come up, my contact information is in the presentation."

Kaysen nodded and shook hands with Ria and me. "Will do. Thank you, ladies."

When I turned back to Lucian, he was staring at me. We shared a smile before Kaysen slapped him on the back and broke the connection. Oblivious, Kaysen said, "Let's grab a quick bite for lunch. Wynter, you coming?"

At the door, Wynter gave me a wink and turned to the guys. "Sure, where are we headed?"

Kaysen turned back to Lucian. It felt weird witnessing this casual conversation. He said, "Something quick; I have another meeting."

From the way they spoke to each other, I was convinced the three of them must have been good friends. Without thinking, I said, "I'd recommend the hot dog stand on Madison and 55th. They have the best hot dogs in town. It's not very far from here."

The men turned my way, their full attention on me. Kaysen grinned. "That's a pretty big statement."

Ria flipped her wrist at him. "I said the same thing. And Addilyn talked me into going. I have to admit, it was a good hot dog."

Wynter had been there, too, but for professional reasons, I doubted she'd say anything. Kaysen nodded. "Thanks for the suggestion. Come on, Lucian, Wynter. Let's go give this hot dog stand a try."

Lucian cleared his throat. "Sounds good." He blinked a few times and his demeanor changed. I wondered what had caused it. "Ms. DeRoss, Mrs. Charles, Nancy will validate your parking. Let her know if you need anything else."

I smiled and nodded, "I will. Thank you. We look forward to hearing from you. I know High Impact Marketing will be a great partner."

For a second, Lucian stared at me as if I were a mythical creature before Kaysen said, "We'll be in touch."

Something had definitely changed.

What happened?

The three left, and we gathered our things. I knew it was ridiculous to focus on my encounter with Lucian Black. Yes, he affected me, but I couldn't stop thinking about the abrupt change at the end of our conversation. Had I done something? Said something wrong? Nothing came to mind.

Move on. This is Lucian Black, owner of Black Media.

He was out of my league. *Way* out of my league.

Once we were back in the office, Ria gave me a hug. "Good job. You nailed it."

We hadn't said much on the way back since Ria had been on the phone the entire time. Her in-laws had decided to stay for the week, and they were quite needy.

"I hope so." I crossed my fingers and my eyes again.

She laughed. "I know so."

I wondered if she had picked up on anything weird between Lucian and me. Or maybe I had overthought it. It seemed like everything had changed when he walked into the room. And still I felt altered inside. "You think they're intrigued?"

"For sure. Lucian Black is a cunning businessman. From his expression, I think he even agrees with you."

That was it. *He agrees with me.* Maybe everything else had been in my head. Ria was the type of person to call it like she saw it. I was being stupid. *Lucian Black is not interested.*

I headed back to my office to sort through my thoughts. Overall, our presentation seemed to be what they were looking for in terms of branding. I tried to work, but my mind meandered to the intensity of Lucian's gaze. There was some strange pull that intensified each time I saw him. And then my brain went back to the restaurant. *Who was the woman at the event?*

Maybe I should search his name online.

No, I wasn't going to do that. That seemed… stalkerish. Lucian Black was a professional man I might have future business dealings with. And that was that. No more.

While I mused, I got a text message from Wynter.

Wynter: *Did you like what you saw?*

Shit, she had noticed. I groaned and decided ignorance was my best defense.

Me: *I have no idea what you're talking about.*

Wynter: *Tall, dark, and handsome seemed to be revving your engine.*

Me: *No revved engine. In fact the engine block is frozen due to lack of use.*

Wynter: *Just do an oil change. Want to go lingerie shopping? My treat.*

Me: *Uhh… my granny panties work great.*

Wynter: *Be ready. We're going after work. A girl needs nice undergarments for when the unexpected happens. Trust me on this.*

I closed my eyes and sighed. I couldn't believe I was about to agree to this.

Me: *Let me know when and where. You are not buying me lingerie, though.*

Wynter: *I'll get you the deets.*

Me: *Sounds good.*

Am I actually going to get lingerie? If I bailed, Wynter would show up with obscene amounts for me. She was paid well and never worried about making ends meet. It really was best if I stayed in control of the situation. A new pair of underwear wouldn't be bad.

The presentation, and now my best friend, had worn me out. I checked my phone to see if Mister Mystery had responded to my message from Saturday night.

Me: *Finished Citizen Kane. Definitely need an HEA next time.*

Still no response. I understood that we were all busy, but it was odd for him not to reply at all.

"Girl, those pieces you bought are amazing."

"Thanks, I like them." Surprisingly, it had been nice to treat myself to a few sexier pieces. I justified them as a reward for how well the presentation had gone. Wynter hadn't given any indication of where things stood, although I knew she wouldn't.

Wynter carried two full bags, and I shook my head, laughing. It seemed like Wynter bought lingerie all the time to the point she must have been swimming in it at her apartment. "What?"

"You have a lingerie obsession."

She raised her eyebrow as we left the store. "I go through a lot. The guy I'm sleeping with tends to be a little impatient."

"TMI. But geez, that has to get expensive."

"It does… for him."

We laughed and stopped at the entrance to the subway. "See ya. Thanks for the evening out. It was fun."

"Good. Hopefully you get to use them soon." Wynter gave me a wink. I shook my head as I walked away. Again, Lucian Black came to mind, and I couldn't help but imagine what his touch would feel like or what he might think of my new lingerie.

Stop. Stop. Stop.

After making it home and letting Wynter know I was safe, I kicked off my shoes and sat on the couch. I checked my phone, but I still hadn't heard anything from Mister Mystery. I sent another message; I was getting a little worried.

Me: *I nailed the presentation today… I think. I'll know soon.*

The message remained unread. Throughout the evening, I continued to check, but there was no response. Something felt off. Hopefully, nothing had happened to him. And if it had, well, I would never know.

Me: *Are you okay? I hope nothing happened.*

No response.
Nothing.

As the minutes ticked by, I continued to check, but there was still no reply. It worried me, but there was nothing I could do. We had been so careful to ensure neither of us had any identifiable information about the other.

Did he just vanish?

I hoped not..

CHAPTER 5

Lucian

I walked into Rex, still staring at the app with the three messages from Aurora.

Or should I say Addilyn*?*

She'd been on my mind all week, and I still wasn't sure how to respond. *What must she think?* It had been four days since I figured out *Aurora* was Addilyn DeRoss, the same woman I hadn't been able to stop thinking about since the Keller Industries toy drive.

They were the same person.

It was a mind fuck. The two women I hadn't been able to stop thinking about were the same person.

What are the chances?

On Monday, we'd made a last-minute decision to change the location for the meeting from Keller Industries to my office. Kaysen had asked me to attend since Wynter wasn't providing feedback on this pitch. Apparently, Addilyn and Wynter were best friends.

Fuck me.

My decision to attend had ruined everything.

Double fuck.

I knew it was a dick move not to respond to her messages on the app. But I refused to pretend I had no idea who she was. The weekend prior to meeting had gone to hell in a handbasket with Crystal, my ex-wife. Remmy had been with our nanny, Jan, thank goodness. Crystal had shown up to the toy event and then later to a charity event, causing all sorts of trouble. And now I understood why Addilyn had run off at the toy drive. Considering her history, which involved another woman, I couldn't blame her for bailing. *Shit.*

Crystal was a psychotic bitch. When I made it home late Friday night, I hadn't been in the right frame of mind to respond to Addilyn about Citizen Kane. And I'd had my son with me Saturday and Sunday, so my focus had been him.

I was worried about Remmy. More than worried, if I was being totally honest with myself. And I felt helpless to save my own son from the one person who should have protected him as fiercely as I did.

Crystal's behavior was taking a toll on him. His schedule had become erratic lately, and there were a lot of random men passing through his life. I hated only seeing him every other week. He'd cried when she'd picked him up today, screaming for me to let him stay with me. It had broken my heart, but I had to stay strong and was forced to send him with his mother. If I'd kept him, she'd have ammunition to use against me in court.

I hated her.

I gritted my teeth, remembering her appearance. The bags under her eyes were more pronounced and told me she'd likely been on another bender. My hands were tied. I fucking hated it.

Shit.

Earlier, Kaysen had told me he wanted to go with Impact Marketing, which only complicated matters. Addilyn DeRoss was going to be in my life, tormenting me, a constant reminder of what I'd done and the unexpected feelings I felt.

Messaging her now, knowing who she was, felt wrong.

I shoved my phone in my pocket, unsure how to handle the situation. When I got to the counter, a brown-haired woman turned my way. *Addilyn.* She was clearly startled, her eyes growing large as she recognized me. They were a gorgeous caramel color. The feelings I'd felt each time I'd run into her intensified. She was beautiful, stunning, exquisite. I was drawn to her like a moth to a flame, but getting involved with anyone would only complicate my life. The tall boots and short skirt looked amazing on her, and my cock stiffened, apparently unconcerned about any potential complications.

"Oh, Mr. Black, I'm so sorry; I didn't see you there. I hope you enjoyed the hot dog."

My tongue felt like it was a lead weight in my mouth. I tried to speak but nothing came out. *What do I say?* I hated lying to her. A nervous smile flitted across her face—I'd been silent too long.

I managed, "It was good. Thank you for the suggestion."

"Good. So glad. Have a good weekend. It was good to see you again."

She ducked away, and I let out a breath. Once again, I had been an asshole.

"Want your usual, Lucian?"

"Thanks, Marty."

It wasn't uncommon for me to come in here on a Friday evening for a cup of coffee and a sandwich when there wasn't some function I had to attend. Remmy loved it here. Over the weekend, I had asked Nancy, my assistant, to clear my schedule for the day, knowing I would need to decompress after Remmy left. After the hellish week of dealing with the fallout from Crystal's bullshit, I needed a break. Walt told me I needed to stay the course and hope that Crystal would hand over custody of Remmy in a settlement.

I heard Addilyn's voice from behind me as she spoke to someone else. "Thank you."

Do not turn around.

It was hard as hell to remain facing forward. After I'd figured out who Addilyn was, I had requested my chief of security to do a full background check. Unsurprisingly, every detail she'd shared about her life had been true.

Cheating ex-husband.

Grandmother who died.

Studio apartment.

In our conversations, she hadn't disclosed where she had come from, but so far everything Aurora—no, Addilyn—had said had been true. I was torn. After Crystal's betrayal, I had sworn off relationships.

"Order up, Lucian."

"Thanks, Marty."

I turned from the counter with my plate in hand and saw her sitting next to the window, staring out onto the street. In one of our conversations, Addilyn had mentioned her love for people watching. As I watched her, that need to be near her intensified. It was unlike anything I had felt before. For that very reason, I should have turned around and walked out the door. But instead, I walked toward her.

I stopped at her table. "Mind if I join you?"

She looked surprised and moved a few things around on the table to make room for my tray. "Of course not. Sorry, I should have asked. I didn't think you'd want to be bothered."

I cocked my head. "Why's that?"

With a smile that almost knocked me over, she replied, "Well, I'm trying to land the account Keller Industries has hired you to manage. I know you work with my best friend, Wynter. I highly doubt you want to be harassed at six on a Friday night about who got the account."

"Are you always this honest?"

Her eyes searched mine probably trying to figure out where that question had come from. "I try to be. I… uh… had something happen a few years back. And because of that incident, I cling to the truth." She nervously tapped her fingers on the table. It was because of her asshole ex, Braden Whitfield. From the information I'd received, he was recently married again and had one child. Talk about one fucked-up situation.

This was the woman I had talked to more than anyone over the last couple of months, and I craved to know more.

Addilyn gestured to the seat. "Did you want to sit?"

Shit, I was acting like a lunatic.

I eased myself into the chair. "Addilyn, we need to talk."

She sat up straighter in her chair. "Okay. I'm not sure how I feel about that breakup line leading into our conversation."

Addilyn laughed, and I assumed it was from nerves.

Double shit. That had sounded bad. It seemed like I stumbled often around her. "No, you got the account."

Her hand reached out and grabbed mine. "Are you serious? We got it. Wow." There was an intense, almost magnetic, connection where our hands touched. Addilyn's eyes shot down to her hand before she frowned and pulled it back. I missed her gentle touch instantly. "Sorry. Umm… thank you. And please say thank you to Mr. Keller."

Double shit. This was going from worse to terrible. I had to tell her. Why was this so damn difficult? "I need you to hear me out, okay? Just listen."

"Okay," she said, her eyes growing cautious.

"I'm Mister Mystery."

She gasped and scooted back as if I'd shocked her. "I… I…" Her lips clamped shut. She stood, so I stood.

She sat, so I sat.

"You're Mister Mystery? How? I mean, I know how. But… I… I don't know what to say."

I took a sip of my coffee, hoping to ease the situation.

Nope. She stood again. This time I remained seated. Slowly, Addilyn sank back into her chair. "H-how?"

"Kaysen set up my account to get my thoughts on the program. This app is his first launch into this area. As you know, his primary focus is security programs. Black Media was looking to branch out, so I invested."

"H-h-how did you find out it was me?"

I leaned back. "That was completely unintentional. I put two and two together with your hot dog stand recommendation at the meeting."

She closed her eyes. "What are the chances?"

"One in almost nine million." I chuckled.

Her eyes met mine, and it nearly took my breath away. "Is that why you disappeared? No, wait… you'd stopped responding prior to that."

I leaned forward to ensure our conversation remained private. "My ex gave me a bit of trouble last weekend. It's complicated. But I assure you, she *is* an ex. Then Monday came.

The morning was chaos, and I'd planned to message you until I figured out who you were. Knowing each other was not supposed to be part of the deal."

"No, it wasn't." She looked down at her plate and then met my eyes. There was something there between us, but neither of us acknowledged it. I was afraid I had already gone too far. "Thank you for telling me. At least now I know. Have a good weekend, Mr. Black."

"Lucian."

She went to stand but stopped halfway. My name was barely a whisper on her lips. "Lucian."

Hearing her use my name was music to my ears. I wanted to respond, but words refused to come out. Addilyn turned and disposed of her trash. At the door, she looked my way before slipping out the door and onto the busy streets.

What was she thinking?

Is there more she wanted to say?

And why did I let her walk out the door?

CHAPTER 6

Addilyn

"How did this happen?" I asked the blank walls of my apartment. I collapsed on my sofa, still in shock from my encounter at the coffee shop. On a whim, I had walked by Rex after work and wanted to give it a try. It was like fate had taken me there and then played a cruel joke on me. All week long, I'd wondered what had happened to Mister Mystery. Now I knew. He was out of my league.

Wealthy.

Good looking.

Polished.

In the same category I'd put Lucian Black. Hell, he *was* Lucian Black. And he had to be worth millions—maybe more. My head was a mess. And he had a child, according to the pictures I'd found when I searched him online while walking through Central Park before coming home.

A child.

Words like "powerful mogul" and "strictly private" were common in the articles I'd found when I'd finally stopped at a bench to sit down. That seemed at odds with what I knew about Mister Mystery.

The articles had confirmed that he was divorced.

His ex-wife seemed to be something of a problem.

My head spun more. Part of me wished Lucian had tried to stop me from leaving. But he hadn't. At least I knew… at least I knew. The conference calls and drab functions from my conversations with Mister Mystery made sense.

But a child. He had a child.

It was like déjà vu from my marriage to Braden, although logically I knew it wasn't the same. But finding out like that was… jarring, to say the least.

Mister Mystery had never brought up a child. Not that he'd had to, of course. In fact, it made sense that he hadn't. Children were precious and needed to be protected. But the news had shocked me. The entire situation shocked me.

I got a pint of ice cream and slipped on my fuzzy slippers before dropping onto the couch and staring at the wall. My phone vibrated. When I saw the name mister mystery flash across the screen, my heart stopped.

Mister_Mystery: *And now that you've had time to think about what happened, what are your thoughts?*

I took a big bite of the cookie dough ice cream and stared at the text. Another message came through. Mister Mystery could tell I had seen the message.

Mister_Mystery: *I understand if you never want to talk to me again. I should have asked you to stay earlier so we could talk more. I haven't handled this well.*

I took another big bite.

Mister_Mystery: *Have a good night, Addilyn.*

It was odd to see him use my real name and not *Aurora*. I set the pint of ice cream aside so I could reply.

Me: *I'm still in shock and I shouldn't have searched your name online. It's very... overwhelming.*

Mister_Mystery: *I'm just a guy, Addilyn.*

Me: *A guy with a lot of... exposure.*

Mister_Mystery: *That's true at times. But my life is also very private.*

Things felt awkward between us. Before, it had been easygoing. I was afraid our time was drawing to an end. I wasn't in the right head space to make any type of decision. But I couldn't get him out of my head, either. And was there really a decision to make? My heart beat a little faster now that I had a name and a face to go with the person I had gotten to know over the last month.

Mister_Mystery: *Night, Addilyn. Sweet dreams.*

Me: *Night. Sweet dreams to you, too.*

I closed out the app, unsure what to make of it all. *I'm just a guy, Addilyn.* What was that about? Had Lucian wanted to continue our conversation? Or was he just being nice? From the beginning, Lucian had been clear he wasn't looking for any kind of relationship.

Minutes turned to hours as I sat on my couch and got lost in another old movie. My mind drifted to Lucian. His lean, muscular body, his dark hair, those enigmatic eyes. At nearly six in the morning, I had only nodded off every now and again for a few minutes each time. I brought out my phone.

Me: *Did you sleep?*

Me: *I mean how'd you sleep?*

Me: *I mean good morning.*

I groaned and threw back my head. *Way to be smooth.* Lucian saw the messages almost immediately.

Mister_Mystery: *Good morning. I didn't really sleep last night. You?*

Me: *Me either. Were you working?*

Mister_Mystery: *No. You?*

Me: *No.*

Mister_Mystery: *I think we both have a lot to say. Why don't we meet?*

I bit my lip. Yeah, I needed to talk to him a little more. At least for closure.

Me: *When? Where?*

Mister_Mystery: *I'm north of Central Park.*

Me: *I'm west of Central Park.*

Mister_Mystery: *How about an hour? Meet me in Central Park at the hot chocolate stand near the carousel?*

I knew the place well. It would be busy as the city had just opened the carousel for a special occasion. I wondered if Lucian picked that place specifically to make me feel comfortable.

Me: *I'll be there. See you soon.*

Mister_Mystery: *Until then.*

I got off the couch, feeling stiff from sitting all night long. My limbs were sore, but the nervous adrenaline helped. We were going to be seeing each other again. I showered, taking too long under the hot spray. It felt good and helped soothe my weary muscles. I kept my makeup light and braided my hair to the side before sliding on a knit cap. My leggings and sweater were casual yet trendy. I grabbed my keys and my purse before heading outside and to Central Park.

I grew more nervous the closer I got. What would we say? Where was Lucian's mind? Was this going to be our final good-bye? By the time the carousel came into view, I was a complete mess. I stopped at the entrance to see the line to ride the carousel already forming. Part of me wanted to flee, but I was rooted in place. The crowd parted a bit, and I saw him. His eyes were trained on me. And once again, my memory hadn't done the real-life version of him any justice.

His eyes were hidden behind a pair of aviators. His stride was confident and somehow made the casual clothes he wore exude power—or maybe it was just the man himself. I had expected him to arrive in a full three-piece suit. But Lucian was a normal guy and not the untouchable mogul I had worked him up to be in my head.

His head cocked to the side, and he picked up his pace, two steaming cups of what I assumed was hot chocolate in his hands.

"Morning." His voice was deep and raspy like he hadn't spoken in days.

"Morning." I took the proffered cup. "Thank you. Hopefully it's loaded with caffeine."

Lucian gave me a smile. "I added a shot of espresso to both of them. I figured we could use it."

I nervously laughed. "True." I took a sip. The espresso mixed with the chocolate created a decadent flavor. "Yum. This is perfect."

"Would you like to walk? Sit? Ride the carousel?"

I took another sip. "If we sit, I might fall asleep. Let's walk."

He gave me a crooked smile. "I have just the idea. Let's go to the zoo."

Zoo. That was unexpected. "I haven't been yet. I keep meaning to go."

"Then it's settled."

We walked for a couple of minutes in silence. People rode their bikes. Dogs played in the open areas. Birds chirped all around us. It was one of those perfect, unexpectedly warm days in October. I took small sips of my hot chocolate but didn't say anything, unsure where to begin. Lucian seemed deep in thought. I finally said, "It's weird, isn't it?"

He looked my way and raised a brow. I continued, "In the chat, we never run out of things to say. In person, it's… harder."

"It is. But I think it's because circumstances forced our hand. If we had decided to meet, I doubt it would have been like this."

True. I took another sip of the warm chocolate, hoping it would help soothe my frayed nerves. It was nice how patient Lucian was, not pushing or demanding my thoughts. "Do you think we would have met eventually?"

Lucian thought for a second. "I don't know."

We came up to the ticket counter, and I pulled out some cash. He looked at my hand, and his brows furrowed. "What?" I asked.

"I'll get your ticket, Addilyn."

"You got the hot chocolate. Let me get the ticket."

He seemed shocked for a moment, and I took the opportunity to step up to the booth. "Two, please."

The lady gave me the tickets with some change. I handed him his, and he just stared at it. I laughed. "It's like you've never seen a ticket before."

"No one has ever bought me one."

I waited for him to make it into a joke, but he continued to stare at the ticket. "Really? You pay every time? For everything?"

"Yeah, I do. It's just… expected."

Lucian looked at the ticket for a second longer before putting it into his jeans pocket. I wanted to reach out and touch his hand. Instead, I looked the other way as we entered the zoo. Lucian seemed deep in thought.

I took another sip of my hot chocolate. "I have a confession."

"What's that?" Whatever had been on his mind was now gone as he focused on me.

"Well, not to sound like a creepy stalker or anything, but I searched you online last night. I was… curious."

He grimaced. "Oh, I can't imagine what you found."

"You have a son with your ex-wife?"

His eyes tightened, and Lucian turned to look at the sea lions. "I do."

There was something else brewing in his expression. Maybe I'd crossed a line. "I'm sorry. I shouldn't have brought it up. It surprised me when I saw it, that's all."

A few seconds passed before Lucian looked my way. "You don't have to apologize. I should have expected it. I'd planned to tell you." That was good to know. As we kept walking, he added, "I searched you, too."

"You did?" For some reason, that shocked me—I was boring in comparison.

"I did. A man in my position needs to be sure he isn't being played. I verified the facts. I had to make sure. I know that sounds terrible, but it's important when you have a child."

It made sense. Good thing I was a nobody, without an agenda, who had nothing to hide. "So, you know I'm from Virginia and relocated here after the nasty divorce?"

"I do." He glanced toward a sign and changed the subject. "Want to feed a goat in the children's zoo?"

"I've never done that."

Lucian put his hand on my back, and I wanted to lean into his touch, but I refrained. "It's a must."

CHAPTER 7

Addilyn

"Are you sure you don't want to feed Ellie?" I held out some food for the black and white goat they called Ellie. As she took a bite, I glanced over at Lucian with a smile. The goat then licked my hand, and I giggled. It was like sandpaper.

"Positive." He watched me intently, and it felt like his eyes were caressing my body. "I've fed Ellie a time or two myself."

I smiled. "Does your son like to feed Ellie?"

"He loves it."

The attendant offered me a wipe, which I happily took. "Thank you. Have a good day. Bye, Ellie."

I petted her neck, and she tried to lick me again. I barely managed to escape and then blew her a kiss good-bye.

Early afternoon was upon us as we walked toward the exit. A photographer jogged up to us and handed Lucian a card.

"Give them this card and take a look at the photo you can purchase as a souvenir."

Lucian took it. "Thank you."

Things were shifting between us, becoming more comfortable. As the day progressed, I relaxed even more. We'd stopped at the Dancing Crane Café within the zoo for lunch after we'd fed the goats. It had been one of the best days I'd remembered having in a long time. I felt giddy and was almost bouncing. I leaned into Lucian without thinking. "This day has been amazing. Thank you."

"You're welcome."

Lucian's arm wrapped around my waist and brought me closer to him. My body danced with excitement, and I wanted to freeze the moment.

We came up on a secluded bench with no one around. The zoo was fairly empty, which was nice. Lucian gestured. "Shall we?"

"Sure."

We sat and watched as a kid played with his balloon across the way. Before I could think about it, I said, "I didn't expect this to be so normal."

"What did you expect?"

The night before, when I searched the internet, my imagination had gone wild. "More cloak and dagger, I guess. People wanting your picture." I shrugged. "After searching your name, I had myself all worked up when you first messaged me. It seems like you've had a lot of pictures taken recently."

He sighed. "My life is a little mixture of both, I guess. I have the exposure, but it's not all the time. A lot of what you saw was because of the divorce and Crystal craving the media attention. Since Sunday, Crystal's disappeared from the media spotlight."

I shivered. When Lucian spoke of his ex-wife, hatred rolled off him in waves. "Well, that's good, right? Why would she want the media in her life? And in your son's life?"

His jaw flexed. I could see the tension growing in his dark eyes like a tempest. "Crystal only cares about one thing. Herself."

"Wow, I can't imagine putting my kid through that."

His eyes tightened. "Well, she and I don't have the same values when it comes to that. But I need you to know something."

"Okay…" That sounded ominous.

"You're going to read articles that say I cheated. I did not. If you do, please make sure to read the latest ones that show proof of Crystal's unfaithfulness. I grew tired of her accusations, so I buried her. Not my finest moment, but her manipulations needed to end."

I was taken in by the fire in Lucian's eyes. "I believe you."

"Thank you."

I chewed on my lip, wondering if I should say any more. "Why doesn't she want the media attention anymore?"

"She's falling apart, and I'm suing for custody of my son. I've cut her off financially, making sure any funds she receives go to my son now. It's caused some rough waters, to put it mildly."

There seemed to be more to his statement.

"I hope it gets sorted soon. It seems like the children are the ones who pay the highest price. My hands were tied with Braden because he had all the money. I was just a pawn in his game until I got out. I walked away from the marriage with nothing but my car and a few personal things I'd had prior to getting married. But still my heart breaks for Devin, Braden's son, because through all the meetings forced upon me by his lawyers, Devin grew attached to me. Braden told Devin to call me *Momma*. His biological mother was *Mommy*. They were of the mind-set that we should all be one big family. Bridgette encouraged it. It was a mess." I shook my head. "Enough about the bad. Let's change the subject."

Lucian nodded. "What are your plans for the rest of the weekend?"

This was where he would see we most likely weren't compatible. "I lead a boring life. I'll walk around the city and clean my apartment. Go grocery shopping and get ready for the week ahead. What about you?"

It was easier to stay to myself. Most of the people I met were into the bar scene. Dealing with drunks and guys who groped wasn't my thing. Wynter was the only reason I would make an exception and go out.

"I want to take you on a date."

I paused and stared at him, wondering if I'd heard him right. *What am I supposed to say?* I wanted to say yes, but there were a million reasons to say no. We weren't the same.

When I did nothing but stare, he continued. "I don't want this to end."

"I... uh... We... uh..." I took a deep breath as I felt myself spiraling more and more out of control. "Lucian, we come from two different worlds."

"Last I checked, this was one world."

I shook my head. "No, no, it's not. I mean, yes, it is Earth, but... I'm not groomed and fancy. I'm just your average girl."

"You are anything but average, Addilyn."

The way he said my name sent goose bumps along my skin. His hand touched mine, and I saw the glint of his Rolex. My watch was a simple Timex that cost me all of twenty dollars. It told me what I needed to know—the time. I pulled back my hand, putting some space between us. "I'm serious. I couldn't tell you what all the little forks are used for at a fancy dinner. I know 'dinner fork' and 'salad fork.' I have no idea how to converse with the people you entertain at functions. I know nothing about wine except if it's red or white. I live in a 369-square-foot apartment. I don't... I just... I..."

I took a deep breath, feeling myself race past the point of return. Abruptly, I stood. "It was so wonderful meeting you. I haven't had this much fun in a long time."

I turned and took off toward the exit. I heard him calling my name, and the logical part of me knew it was childish to run. I wanted the exact opposite; I wanted to be with him and say yes to the date.

I turned right, and before I made it very far, he grabbed my shoulders and brought me to a halt. He turned me around, his breath heaving. "I don't care if you only know what two of the forks are. The rest are a waste, anyway. And I don't care that you know nothing about wine. I could give two fucks that your apartment is 369 square feet. What I care about is the woman I'm holding right now."

I blinked a few times as I let his words sink in. "I don't know if I'll fit into your world. I'm scared to death."

"Then we'll make our own world, Addilyn. I'm not proposing marriage. I'm simply asking you to give this a shot. See where this takes us. You know damn well there is something between us. You've felt it. I've felt it. And if I'm being honest, it was only a matter of time before I asked if we could meet. We know each other. We've shared things about ourselves that neither of us have shared with anyone else. Please just give this a chance."

His sweet words awoke something in me I thought was dead.

Hope.

I laid my head on his chest, and he held me tight.

"Please, Addilyn."

I sighed. "Yes, I want to try, too. I'm just so scared to put myself out there again."

He kissed the top of my head. "Me, too, sweetheart. Me, too."

CHAPTER 8

Addilyn

"Stay calm. Stay calm," I whispered to myself.

I was sitting on the couch, nervously waiting for Lucian to arrive, giddy but uncertain how our date would go. Out of nowhere, I had a quick glimpse of my past self. I used to laugh and have fun. I used to enjoy life. And although I was no longer married to Braden, I realized that I'd given him way too much control of my life.

No more.

I was going to live and take chances. I was not going to let my past dictate my future.

As I was affirming my newfound strength, my phone vibrated with a text.

Wynter: *Girl, you got this. Did you ditch the granny panties for the new undies like I said?*

When I'd returned to my apartment, I had called Wynter, completely stressed about what to wear. Her first statement had been *new lingerie.*

Me: *I'm not planning on having sex tonight.*

Wynter: *Well, I hope you shaved your legs and wore something sexy... just in case. Hairy leg sex... I would imagine that is a total boner deflator.*

Me: *Noted. And yes, my legs are shaved and granny panties are hidden in a drawer.*

Wynter: *Work it, girl. Did my package arrive?*

Me: *Yes. Fifty condoms? That's a lot.*

Wynter: *Trust me, you do not want to be without a large stock when the time happens...*

A knock at the door startled me.

I froze for a second and then typed out one last message to Wynter.

Me: *He's here.*

Wynter: *Then go answer the door.*

Knock. Knock. Knock.

I jumped up and tried to walk calmly to the door. "Coming."

As I opened the door, I stopped breathing for a second at the sight of Lucian. He was wearing dark jeans, a white shirt and a black sports coat. He looked like he just walked off the cover of a magazine.

"Hi. You look beautiful, Addilyn." He held out a bouquet of colorful wildflowers that had an untamed beauty. They were what I always bought at the market when I went. "These are for you."

My breath stopped for a moment. *Flowers*. Lucian Black had brought me flowers. I buried my face in the bouquet to inhale their sweet scent. "Thank you. They're stunning. Come in and let me put them in water."

I walked over to the kitchen counter and pulled out my solitary vase from the back of one cabinet. Lucian watched me but stayed near the door. "Well, I would give you a tour, but it starts and ends where you're standing."

He chuckled. "I like your place. It's homey."

"Thanks. I think so. I miss baking, though. I think when I move again, I'm going to look for a place with a bigger kitchen. Cooking and baking are difficult when your counter space is a two-by-two area."

Lucian leaned against the table and gave me an easy smile. His demeanor had a way of making me feel calm. "What kind of baking do you do?"

I sat the vase on my table and fussed at the flowers. "Oh, I love to dabble in a bit of everything. It's like a stress reliever, I guess."

He took my hand and rubbed his thumb over my palm. "Are you ready?"

"Where are we going?"

"Well, I want to give you a few choices. One, we can go to a restaurant I think you'll like. Two, we have a private dinner at a museum. Or three, we can get takeout and either stay around here or go to my place. I wasn't sure what you would be up for and wanted to take things at your pace."

It took me two seconds to decide. Going out in public, especially to a fancy restaurant, seemed a little too stressful. "Takeout. My place. And maybe we can watch an old movie if you want."

Lucian stared at me. "Is that what you want to do? We can go to any restaurant."

"Yes. Promise. I've always wanted to go to Tavern on the Green, but I doubt we'd be able to talk. This is a perfect night in. We're both exhausted from not sleeping. Next time, we can go out."

"Deal. Now let's decide on what kind of food we want delivered."

We sat on the couch while the movie *Rebecca* played in the background. Our Chinese takeout containers and wine glasses were on the chest I used as a coffee table and storage for my summer clothes. It was a movie we'd already seen. It was poignant; the underlying theme of betrayal by those one should have been able to trust hitting close to home for both of us.

We'd talked throughout most of the movie, and when the credits rolled, Lucian said, "I want to see you again, Addilyn."

It was odd already knowing so much about the person while only having met him a few days earlier. I wanted to see him, too. "I'd like that."

But we were living in a bubble. When Monday came, things would become more complicated. My heart sank, and I focused on my fingers as they played with the fringe on the blanket.

Lucian touched the bottom of my chin, and I looked up. "It all changed when I met you. I was going to stay away. I tried, but I can't. I don't want to."

"How will this affect work? Especially now that I'm going to be working on the marketing account for Mr. Keller."

"It won't. I'll talk to Kaysen. We've been best friends for years. And when we're discussing the account, it's business. If we disagree, we disagree and come up with a solution like in any business decision."

That seemed easier said than done. There were so many pieces in the puzzle, and they would be constantly moving. "I'll need to tell my boss."

"I think that's wise. If you take away the power, the situation becomes easier to control."

That was true. "What if—"

Lucian put a gentle finger over my lips and leaned in a little closer. "We can *what if* this to death. It's what I spend my day doing. Let's take this as it comes and promise to talk about things as they come up. I have my son every other week for seven days, so we'll have to work around his schedule. Given the current circumstances, I think it's best you two didn't meet for a while."

"I agree." I nodded. "What are your plans this week?"

He sighed. "I have to go out of town tomorrow morning for business in Seattle. But I'd like to see you when I get back. Remmy isn't coming over until next Saturday."

"I'd like that."

He helped me clean up the leftover food containers and grabbed his coat from the chair. I hated that he was about to leave. Though I'd told Wynter there were no plans for sex, part of me had hoped for a wild night filled with passion. *All in due time if it's meant to be.*

At the door, Lucian's eyes lingered on my lips. "Good night, Addilyn."

"Good night."

He left and I felt bereft. I had wanted him to kiss me.

As I undressed, I stared at the pale pink lingerie I had worn that night. Part of me wanted him to see it and was disappointed that nothing had happened. There was something empowering about beautiful lingerie. I understood why Wynter enjoyed it. From the hook on the bathroom door, I grabbed my robe and threw it on. A long, hot bath would do me good.

A few minutes later, my phone vibrated. There was a message in our app.

Mistery_Mystery: *I had to leave before things went too far.*

I bit my lip, feeling the desire again. *Maybe I should play with him.*

Me: *Is that why you robbed me of my good-night kiss?*

Lucian: *You wanted more?*

Me: *Yes.*

The dots appeared then disappeared. I started the water, waiting to see if he was going to say anything else. Then his message appeared.

Lucian: *Can you come to the door?*

The message was followed by a soft knock. I giggled as I turned off the water. Did he come back for a good-night kiss? I opened the door. Lucian stepped in, his hands cradling my face. As his mouth claimed mine, I heard the door close behind him with a loud thud.

"Fuck, you taste good."

As I kissed him, his words only fueled my desire. Our hands roamed and our tongues danced. I loved the taste of the trace amount of wine left on his tongue. The kissed slowed, and my back hit the wall. Lucian pulled back to look in my eyes, the desire in his matching my own.

His shirt was half untucked, making him all the more sexy. As his gaze moved down my body, I felt the chill from where my robe had come open. The sides of my breasts were clearly visible. Lucian's gaze moved up to mine, but neither of us said anything. The bulge in the front of his pants told me he liked what he saw. I wanted this. I wanted more.

My finger traced down my cleavage, and Lucian swallowed hard. "You are beautiful. So fucking beautiful." Then he took a step back. "I don't have a condom."

I took a deep breath. I wanted tonight with him even though I wasn't that type of girl to rush into sex. I needed to be consumed by this man, and this time I wanted to give into my desires. "Bathroom, under the sink."

Lucian came back with a jumbo box, a questioning look on his face. I laughed. "Wynter wanted to make sure I was prepared and had these delivered today in case *someone* came over to my place."

"I'm going to send that woman flowers."

I giggled. Lucian tossed the box on the bed before pulling me toward it. "I never thought about the challenges sex might bring when I bought this bed."

He laid me back, and my robe fell open, exposing one of my breasts. "This will do just fine."

I stared up into his eyes. "I need you to know I'm not typically a one-night stand kind of girl."

"Good. Because I'm not a one-night stand kind of guy. But I need you, Addilyn. I can't explain. I can't get you out of my head."

"Me either."

I was so grateful we were on the same page.

His finger traced oh so slowly down my chest, leaving a trail of fire in its wake. As he reached my lower stomach, I felt it pool with desire. "You are perfect."

His fingers neared my core. Breathlessly, I said, "Touch me." Thank goodness I'd shaved my legs.

Wynter, I owe you lunch.

I felt featherlight touches at the top of my folds. My hips moved, searching for any type of friction. "Touch yourself while I undress."

Lucian stood and slowly unbuttoned his shirt while I began to move my fingers. "Touch your nipple. Show me what you like. Show me what you do to make yourself come."

I took my finger and teased my nipple before pinching the tip. I loved the pleasure-pain sensations that moved through my body. My fingers moved lower to my clit, and I closed my eyes and began to rub it vigorously, needing the release. When I was *right there*, his hand came over mine and stopped me.

"I'll take it from here."

My eyes shot open, and suddenly I was breathless. Lucian was naked and was rolling on a condom. He was toned, lean, and powerful, exuding authority even when naked.

He tugged on my belt, and my robe parted completely, fully exposing me to his hot gaze. "Fuck me, you are perfect."

He took my hands and placed them above my head as he hovered on top of me. I felt his dick at my entrance. Warm lips enveloped my nipple, and then he gave it a small bite. I arched into him, moaning. He moved to the other nipple and repeated the same motion. My hands flexed instinctively, trying to move to my clit, but Lucian held them in place. He trailed kissed up my neck until we were face to face. As we stared into each other's eyes, he entered me at an excruciatingly slow pace, making it one of the most intimate moments of my life.

Everything was changing.

Our hands intertwined, and our mouths found each other's as he moved in and out. It started out as a slow burn that turned into an inferno as we found our release.

I awoke to the feel of Lucian's fingers moving along my spine. Before I moved, I wanted to savor the moment. What we shared, the way he felt inside me… I wasn't sure if I'd have been able to put words to it. Whatever it was, it felt right.

"Hey there," Lucian whispered.

"Hey," I shifted in his arms so I could see his eyes.

A man who'd only wanted sex would have left by now. Lucian hadn't lied. He seemed like he wanted something more than a night a pleasure. I shivered thinking about the first time he entered me.

"Are you cold?" he asked.

I murmured, "No, I was just thinking about last night. That was some good-night kiss."

It was more than that, but I was too nervous to say something that forward.

Underneath me, his chest rumbled while he chuckled. "Yes, it was. Feel free to greet me with a loosely tied robe any-time."

I raised my chin and smiled. "Or maybe just my furry slippers."

"I can guarantee you the result will be the same. You'll be ravaged, and I'll be inside you."

I giggled. "I'll have to remember that. Maybe I'll come to our next meeting in my favorite wrap dress with the tie at the waist."

In a flurry, Lucian flipped me over and hovered over me. There was a teasing glint in his eyes. "I dare you."

I couldn't help but laugh.

He kissed my neck, and I closed my eyes to savor the feel of his stubble against my skin. His lips left a wake of fire as he moved toward my breast. "What time do you have to leave for your trip?"

"My flight leaves at seven."

That was only nine hours away. I hated that he was going to be gone.

He kissed his way back up, and I arched for more. The slow, delicious torture was perfect. As he made it past my jaw, his warm breath tickled my ear, and I felt his dick harden against my leg. "Then we better make the most of the time we have left today."

He grabbed another condom from the box and rolled it on. Again, as he entered me, our eyes stayed connected.

I knew I would never be the same.

CHAPTER
9

Lucian

"Walt, do you have anything for me yet?"

"No, not yet. You'll have Remmy to-morrow. Hopefully next week, we'll be able to find something."

"Let's hope." I hung up the phone and muttered, "Shit."

Nothing was going according to plan. What was supposed to have been a three-day trip had turned into a five-day one. It was Friday, and I hadn't seen Addilyn all week. Business with the foreign investors on the West Coast hadn't gone as well as I'd hoped, and I was about two seconds away from pulling the plug. Needing to be home for Remmy on Saturday, I'd taken the red-eye back to New York. Crucial matters needed to be handled before the weekend, and I wanted some time with Addilyn before my son arrived and I wouldn't be able to see her for most of the week.

At least I had been able to hear her voice every night.

I was in deep. Deeper than I wanted to admit. And though I sensed Addilyn felt the same way, neither of us said anything about it.

The elevator opened to the Black Media offices. My shoes clacked against the black marble floors as I walked straight toward my office.

"Morning, Mr. Black," Janine, the receptionist called.

"Morning."

My head was throbbing. I still hadn't told Kaysen about Addilyn, and she hadn't spoken to her boss yet either. I'd asked her to wait until I told my best friend. Blindsiding Kaysen wasn't on my to-do list. It was unlikely Kaysen would care, but I wanted to avoid any drama, nonetheless.

Heaven knew I had more than my share of it to handle with Crystal. I rubbed my temple, thinking about her slurred speech on the phone the night before. Crystal wasn't budging on letting me have more time with Remmy. I knew she was doing it to be difficult. It was a delicate manner, considering that offering her money for sole custody wasn't allowed. Walt was working on a legal way to present it.

Then there was the issue with my son that I discovered on my own. It sat in my stomach like a stone. I still wasn't sure what to do about it.

I turned the corner and saw Addilyn standing in the door of the meeting room, laughing.

Fuck, I had missed her. I fought the urge to pull her into my arms and forget the world for just a bit.

"Yes, yes, I promise I'll be there," she said.

Who is she talking to?

Addilyn stepped to the side. *Wynter.* "Good morning, ladies," I said as I got within earshot.

Addilyn whipped her head around. A beautiful smile greeted me, and I saw more than just happiness in her eyes. It was desire to be together again. Clearly surprised, she asked, "You're back?"

"I took the red-eye this morning."

The day before, I'd thought I'd arrive either late afternoon or early evening. But I'd been able to power through some issues and leave Thursday night.

With wide eyes, Addilyn glanced at Wynter and then back to me. Addilyn had told me that Wynter knew, but I'd also been assured Kaysen wouldn't find out until I was able to speak with him. It was ironic how intertwined our worlds were.

With a wink, Wynter said, "I'll catch you later."

"Bye," Addilyn responded.

I nodded to Wynter. "Is Kaysen here?"

"Yeah, he's on a call in the conference room. After our meeting with High Impact, he got an emergency call from China regarding some software and took over your conference room. I was about to let him know I was heading back to the office. Want me to ask him to come see you?"

"That would be great. Thanks, Wynter." I turned to Addilyn. "Walk with me?"

"Of course."

We kept a professional distance, but it was hard as fuck. A couple of people tried to flag me down, but I dismissed them with a quick wave of my hand. This morning was not the time for mundane shit. Near my office, Addilyn said, "Wynter invited me to a work function with Keller Industries tonight. I thought it would be nice to meet the team I'll be working with. It was one of those things I couldn't say no to."

Damn it.

That was right. Each quarter, Keller Industries had a team-building event. My guess was that it was more Wynter's doing than Kaysen's. He hated events more than I did. Fuck, there went my plans with Addilyn. We entered my office, and I closed the door.

I didn't say anything, and Addilyn touched my arm. "Are you going?"

Going mentally through my schedule, I knew I could move some things around to be done earlier. I said, "Yes, I'll be there."

Addilyn licked her lips, and I couldn't stay away. I was on Addilyn in a matter of seconds, crushing my mouth to hers. "I missed you."

"I missed you, too."

Nancy's voice came over the intercom. "Mr. Black, Kaysen Keller is here."

I dropped my forehead to Addilyn's. "Can I see you after the function?"

"Yes."

Before I lost my will, I took a step back and pressed the intercom button on the phone. "Send him in."

The door opened, and Addilyn gave a polite nod and a professional good-bye before passing Kaysen as he strolled in.

"The new version of the app is ready for beta testing," he said.

"That's what I saw in the email recap. That's good. I think the changes will help the marketability. What did you decide about the name?"

It was hard to get Addilyn's taste out of my mind. *Tonight. We have tonight.*

Kaysen put his hands in his pockets. "Socialite."

"I like it."

"Addilyn pitched it, and it stuck."

She was smart, more so than I had realized at our initial meeting. The concepts had been solid, but Addilyn hadn't let on how much further she'd thought the marketing through without any guarantees of winning the pitch. "I think it's a wise choice. Much better than the fish name."

Kaysen held out his hands to the side with a smirk. "Man, that was a classic."

I raised my eyebrow. "No. It was cheesy and dated."

He rolled his eyes. "Wynter said the same thing. She's hated the name from the get-go."

I took a seat behind my desk. Kaysen sat in one of the chairs and threw his arm over the back. Now was the time to let him know. "I need to tell you something."

"Okay." Kaysen cocked one eyebrow. "I'm not sure if this is a good 'tell you something' or a bad 'tell you something.'"

Hopefully good.

"I'm seeing Addilyn. It's complicated, but I want to continue seeing her."

I wasn't asking for permission, but it would make things easier if everyone was okay with it. Kaysen looked at me like I'd grown two heads. "Wait, you're dating someone?"

"Yes."

Kaysen nodded. "'Bout fucking time." Then a cocky smirk appeared. "I guess I walked in on more than a business meeting."

Ignoring that comment, I said, "Thanks, man. I appreciate your understanding."

"Crystal know yet?"

Through all the shitstorm, Kaysen had been there for me. Remmy loved him like an uncle. "No, and I'm hoping she doesn't find out for a while. We're keeping it low key. With everything Remmy has going on, I don't want to add more stress to his life by introducing another woman."

"Fuckin' hate her. That bitch is crazy."

I sighed. "You have no idea."

"What's going on?"

The headache pulsed behind my eyes. "Later. It's too much to go through now."

"I'll bring whiskey over, and we can catch up. On another note, you coming tonight?"

I let out a frustrated breath. "Yeah, it seems Addilyn is."

Kaysen gave me a knowing smile, but he kept his thoughts to himself. Instead, he said, "Wynter organized this stupid shit, and now I have to be there. Team building and networking, for fuck's sake. It seems like a way to spend a hell of a lot of money and make me do stuff I hate."

For some time, I had suspected there was something going on between him and Wynter. They were professional and kept things low key. The only reason I knew was because one time, Kaysen had taken a call on his cell in my office and then left his phone on my desk. When I'd sat down in my chair, a message from Wynter, asking for a "tune-up" had flashed up on his screen. Reading between the lines had been pretty easy with that one.

I raised my eyebrow. "You could always say no."

"And deal with hell at the office. No, thank you."

Yeah, it was these little subtle moments that confirmed they were sleeping together. Kaysen hated being out in public. He was more of a homebody.

I waited, but he didn't say anything else. Kaysen had it worse than I ever did when it came to getting involved with the crazy bitches. His story was… well, tragic. Which was why I never asked about his relationship with Wynter. When Kaysen was ready, he'd tell me.

I brought the conversation full circle. "Thanks, man, for understanding."

"You deserve it, Lucian. I'm not saying you guys are going to ride off into the sunset or anything like that. But you deserve to be happy."

One thing sorted.

"Now if Addilyn's boss calls…"

"It's a non-issue as long as she can keep it professional. But you wouldn't have let it get this far if you didn't believe that was possible."

"True."

Kaysen stood. "Well, I guess I'll be seeing you tonight unless there's something else."

"No, nothing else. Thanks, Kaysen."

"Of course." Kaysen waved good-bye and I grabbed my phone.

I texted Addilyn:

Me: *I told Kaysen. Probably best to inform your boss.*

Addilyn: *I'll do that as soon as I get back to the office. Was he concerned at all?*

Me: *Not at all.*

Addilyn: *Good, that's a relief. I'll let Wynter know that Kaysen knows.*

Me: *What a small world we live in. Who would have thought when we met at the toy drive that we'd have best friends who worked together? See, we don't come from two different worlds, Addilyn.*

Addilyn: *So what time are you coming tonight?*

Apparently, Addilyn wanted to change the subject.

Me: *I'll be there hopefully around six.*

Addilyn: *Good. Can't wait.*

Now I had to figure out how to keep everything going without it imploding. I also needed to contact my PR team about the best way to handle it when our relationship became public, especially with the latest information on Crystal. I figured it would be sooner rather than later.

CHAPTER 10

Lucian

"Your coat, Mr. Black?"

"Thank you."

Once I had my coat-check ticket, I made my way into the restaurant. It was almost eight, and I was late. I hated that I'd lost two hours with Addilyn, but meetings had run longer than I'd expected. As I looked around the room, it wasn't long before my eyes landed on her. She was beautiful, and some asshole was hanging on her every word, of course. *Andy fucking Barnette.* I hated that people weren't aware she was taken.

Addilyn's boss, Ria, stepped in front of me. "Mr. Black, do you have a second?"

"Sure."

We stepped to the side, and Ria gave me a sugary sweet smile laced with arsenic. "Addilyn informed me you and she were in a relationship."

"Yes." I had to tread carefully. Addilyn had said the conversation with her boss had gone well, but maybe it hadn't gone as well as she thought.

She leaned in closer. "May I speak off the record?"

"Yes, of course." I kept my face as expressionless as possible.

She motioned with her finger in the air. To anyone watching, it probably seemed like a harmless enough conversation. "You hurt her, it won't be pretty. She's a good person—one of the best I know. Protect her from your world, Lucian. The vipers will chew her up and spit her out."

Her comment stopped me for a second. This woman was willing to put her company and the account on the line for Addilyn. I respected her even more. "I can promise you I won't let that happen."

"Good to know. Then we're clear. I look forward to working with Black Media."

I chuckled. "Likewise."

She patted me on the shoulder. "Nice talk."

As she walked away, my focus darted back to Addilyn. Andy was interested. Before I approached them, I needed to calm down. So, I made my way up to the bar to get a bourbon. What Ria said had struck a nerve because it was true. I needed to ensure that I protected Addilyn from the wolves.

Wynter walked up to them. Andy moved a little closer, and my blood began to boil. It wasn't like me to lose my cool, which told me I needed to stay put for a little longer. I took a sip and let the alcohol burn my throat. In my life, I had dated just a handful of women. This possessive, territorial behavior wasn't like me. The only reason Crystal and I had gotten married was because she became pregnant.

I took another sip before I walked toward Addilyn. It was hard to not claim her with a kiss in front of everyone, but that would be the asshole move. She was at a dinner party, mingling. *Trust her.* If I made Addilyn pay for Crystal's sins, it would doom our relationship from the start. Addilyn was beautiful. Men naturally wanted to talk to her. I needed to grow the fuck up.

When Andy moved closer yet again, Addilyn changed position to put more distance between them.

Trust her.

My eyes drifted down her body. My cock stirred, enjoying her little skirt and blousy top.

As if she sensed I was near, she turned her head and our eyes connected. I'd missed her, more than I should have at this point in our relationship. We shared a secret smile.

"Ladies. Andy."

Wynter gave me a knowing smirk before saying, "I need to go mingle. You boys play nice." She winked at Addilyn, who blushed. That woman was hell on wheels. Poor Kaysen had his hands full.

Andy reached out his hand. He was one of the accountants at Kaysen's company. "Mr. Black. It's good to see you."

"Likewise." *Not really.* I wanted to strangle the fuck out of him.

"I'd like to introduce you to Ms. DeRoss."

The way he stepped closer to her was a douche move on his part. Andy was trying to mark his territory.

Game on, motherfucker.

"Good to see you again, Addilyn. Would you like to join me for a drink?"

The relief was obvious on Addilyn's face. "I'd like that." She turned to Andy. "Nice meeting you, Mr. Barnette."

He looked crestfallen. *Good. Take that, asshole.* My nerves were stretched too thin to deal with his childish bullshit.

We walked up to the bar. "What would you like?"

"Red wine."

I smiled remembering her words about wine. The bartender waited for our order. "A glass of pinot noir for the lady. I'm still good."

The bartender nodded and grabbed one of the nicer bottles before pouring a glass. "Here you go, sir."

"Thank you."

Addilyn took the wine glass from me, whispering, "I have no idea what you ordered."

"Let me know if you like it."

She took a hesitant sip. "I like it. I'll remember that for the future."

"Good. I like that as well."

Addilyn gave me a concerned look. "You look tired."

"I'm exhausted. It's been a long week, and nothing has gone according to plan."

That asshole came up behind Addilyn. Andy looked at me, as if waiting for me to leave, but I took a sip of my bourbon instead. He pressed on. "I hope I'm not interrupting, but I wanted to introduce Addilyn to some people."

Addilyn turned his way, surprised to see him standing behind her. "That's kind of you, but I'm actually about to leave. It's been a long day."

"Can I get your number?"

Addilyn pulled a card out of her clutch. "Here's my office line and email. If you have questions regarding work, please let me know."

His eyes shot to mine, clearly irritated, and I casually took another drink. *She's not interested, prick. Take the hint.*

She turned back to me and put out her hand. "It was good seeing you, Mr. Black."

I held her hand. "You, too, Ms. DeRoss. Let me get your coat."

Finally, we were leaving. Soon I would have Addilyn all to myself. She handed me her coat-check ticket. "Thank you."

With my hand on the small of her back, I guided her to the coat check, glad to be rid of Andy for the night. The stout man behind the counter took our tickets. When he returned, I slipped him a twenty-dollar tip. "Thank you, sir."

The air was crisp when we slipped out. I asked, "Have you had any dinner?"

"No, I'm starving."

We waited for Jim to pull up. "Would you like to go out to a restaurant or get some takeout?"

She gave that some thought. "Definitely takeout. I've had enough socializing for the evening."

Me, too. And I want you to myself. But if she'd wanted to go out, I would have. "How about Italian?"

"Perfect. The more carbs, the better." She pulled her jacket tighter around herself.

Jim, my driver, pulled up with the limo with blackout windows. Normally I had the town car for the city, but I wanted my drive home with Addilyn to be private. "Where to, sir?"

"My place." Jim opened the door, and I guided Addilyn in. "Will you call Tony's and have an assortment of Italian food delivered? And can we drive through the park on the way home?"

"Yes, sir."

As soon as the door closed, I made sure the privacy screen was up before we were on each other like wild animals. "Fuck, I missed you."

Her reply was breathy. "Me, too."

I yanked her onto my lap and ran my hands up her bare legs.

I needed her.

I needed this.

Addilyn worked furiously at my zipper before freeing me.

She stroked my cock once, then twice. Suddenly, Addilyn froze in my lap, her eyes wide. "He'll know we're having sex."

I grinned. "Maybe, but we're going through the park to buy us time. Jim won't say anything. He's been with me since I was a kid."

This didn't seem to reassure her, and I sensed she was growing more nervous. I was desperate to have her. I ran my fingers up further to tease her core. The fire came back in her eyes. With my free hand, I unfastened one button at a time while her eyes fluttered close when my fingers danced along her sensitive spot. When I reached the top button, I stopped short at the sight of her lacy cream bra that pushed up her breasts. "Fuck me."

The rose nipples puckered under my stare.

"That's what I plan to do to you, Lucian."

Hell, yes. I raised her skirt to find matching lacy boy shorts. "Definitely worth the wait."

Addilyn looked outside as the traffic passed us, worrying her lip. I assured her. "They can't see you. I would never let anyone see you like this."

With my words of encouragement, she relaxed and trusted me, letting the shirt fall off her arms. Addilyn reached for her clutch, pulled out a condom, and ripped open the package with her teeth.

She shifted off my lap and slowly took off her skirt and panties. "Leave on your heels and bra," I instructed.

On her knees, she rolled the condom onto my cock with her mouth. I slipped my fingers inside her and felt her walls clinch in anticipation. This image of her head bobbing over my lap was a sight to behold. When I was almost to the point of coming, I pulled her up to straddle my lap and hover over my dick.

"Do you want my cock?"

"Yes."

"If I let you have it, you can't move until I say so."

"I won't."

Her eyes were glazed over with lust. I let her sink down, and her mouth dropped open and her eyes fluttered closed. She began to move, and I grabbed her hips. "No moving until I say. I want to savor you and make this last. Lean back."

She put her hands on my knees and arched back, giving me a fantastic view. Seeing where my dick disappeared into her was the hottest fucking thing ever. I flexed it to make it jump and she squirmed.

My fingers roamed over her tight, perfect body. Her tits were small and perky, just the way I liked them. I kissed up her body, moving my hips just a little to give her some friction. I pulled back and brought us face to face. Her face was glowing and her breathing was becoming more labored.

I moved my hips again, sensations spiraling through me. "Can you hold your orgasm?"

"I-I-I don't know."

"Put your hands on the ceiling. Fight it." She did as I asked. "Now ride the fuck out of me."

She positioned herself and began to move, increasing her speed as she found her rhythm. The muted glow of the city beyond the tinted windows illuminated her body. Her tits jiggled, and I thrust into her every so often. This was incredible. I had never felt this connected to a woman in my life.

"Lucian…"

"Keep holding it. Do you feel it building?"

"Y-ye-yes."

She moved harder and bit into her lip.

"Look into my eyes, Addilyn."

She did.

"Let go now."

We erupted, and it was the most power orgasm I'd ever had in my life. She kept riding me as the tremors raced through our bodies. As we finished, she collapsed against my chest. "I don't think I'm ever going to be able to move again."

I twitched my still semihard dick buried inside her. "I don't think my dick would mind."

She giggled. I grabbed her face and brought her lips to mine, tasting her while still buried inside her.

"I keep thinking this is a dream."

"No, sweetheart. And I don't plan on letting you go."

CHAPTER 11♥

Addilyn

"**D**on't touch me, you bastard!"
I awoke with a start to the sound of a female screaming from outside the door. For a second, I had no idea where I was and I had to get my bearings.

Lucian's.

"You are such a motherfucker!"

What's going on?

That was the same female voice. Anxious, I threw on my skirt and blouse before putting my hair up in a messy bun on top of my head. It was still dark outside. *What time is it?* My watch said just after two in the morning. *What's going on?* Alarmed, I cracked open the door to hear Lucian speaking in a tone I hadn't heard before.

"Get out, Crystal."

Crystal. Oh my gosh. The ex-wife. She's here.

"Who is she? I want to know who she is!"

Is she talking about me?

Another door across the hall opened, and a pair of blue eyes stared at me. He had to be Lucian's son. I quietly approached him, hating that he could hear them fighting. "Hi, you must be Remmy."

"Who you?" He seemed apprehensive yet curious.

Shit. I had to improvise and hopefully steer him away from the yelling. "I'm your daddy's friend, Addilyn. Can I come in and play?"

"You play cars?" He was wary... and rightly so.

"I love cars. Once your daddy finishes talking, he'll come here."

He opened the door to let me in, and then he ran to the closet where there were so many cars. I quietly closed the bedroom door behind me. The woman's yelling was much more muffled.

"Addawin, you play dis one."

"Oh, I like the blue color on this one. And it has sparkles."

I heard something crash in the other room. Remmy's head shot up. "What dat?"

"I think something fell. Why don't we keep playing? As soon as your daddy is done, he'll come in here."

For a second, Remmy stared at the door, his mouth pulled down. "I don't wanna go with Mommy."

"Does your car go fast?" I asked, hoping the distraction got his mind off the racket.

Remmy raced the car along the track rug in the middle of his room. "Vroom. Vroom. Look at how fast."

"Oh, that's super fast. Let's see if mine goes that fast, too."

We raced our cars on the rug in his bedroom, making the screeching tires and loud engines noises.

"Hey, buddy, you hungry?" Lucian called from the hallway.

The door opened, and Lucian stopped short when he saw me sitting on my knees, racing a car. I knew he hadn't wanted to introduce me to Remmy this soon because of the complications with Crystal. The plan was to wait four to six months, depending on how things progressed.

I set the car down and stood.

"Addawin, race cars with me! Vroom. Vroom. You wanna race, Daddy?"

Lucian's face was tense. "Just a second, buddy. Let me talk to Addilyn."

"'Kay. Is mommy gone?"

With a few steps, he knelt in front of Remmy. "Yes, she's gone. You're staying with me."

Remmy threw his arms around him. "'Kay, Daddy."

Once we were out in the hallway, I could still hear Remmy continuing to play. "Vroom. Vroom."

For a second, Lucian was quiet. Too quiet.

"I'm so sorry. I woke up and heard yelling. When I came into the hallway, Remmy had his door open and was listening to his mother yell. He looked scared, so I tried to distract him." I looked down. "I know you weren't planning on us meeting for a while. I didn't know what to do. He thinks I'm your friend."

When Lucian remained silent, I looked up nervously. He grabbed my face and kissed me hard. I was shocked, and it was over before it began. "Thank you."

"Why is he up this late?"

"Crystal. I need to get him fed and to bed."

I touched his arm. "He hasn't been fed?"

"No. And he hasn't been to bed, either."

That was terrible. I was speechless. "Okay, I'll head home."

"Please stay. Listen, I know things haven't gone to plan. But I don't want to worry about you getting home, and... I need to tell you some things." There was something in his voice—a vulnerability I hadn't heard before. I knew Lucian needed me tonight.

"Okay, for sure. Whatever you need."

The door opened. "Daddy! Can I come out?" Remmy rubbed his eyes. That poor child. It was amazing he wasn't cranky and crying.

Lucian let out a breath and then flipped a switch into daddy mode. "Yes, I have missed you so much."

He ran out of his room, and Lucian picked him up. "Missed you, Daddy. Don't wanna go back with Mommy."

"I know. I'm working on it. You hungry?"

He nodded and sniffled. "I asked Mommy for dinner. She said no."

My heart broke, and my throat grew thick. His hair was greasy like he hadn't been bathed in a few days. "Why don't I make something to eat while your daddy gives you a bath? My grammie always said we sleep better if we're clean."

"Bath! Yes! Can I have bubbles?"

Lucian held Remmy close to him—it was obvious he loved his son. "For sure. Let's go take a bath in my bathroom."

The pair disappeared down the hall, and I made my way to the kitchen. The place was spacious and huge, but the furniture was sparse. From what Lucian had told me, after Crystal had left, he'd wanted to start fresh. I hadn't realized how literal he'd meant it. Last night when we'd gotten here, it had been straight to the bed and more sex, so I hadn't looked around. Now I had the chance.

As I rooted around the kitchen, opening cabinets and searching the refrigerator, I realized I was sore.

We had sex in the car.

Sex in the shower.

And sex in his bed.

I touched my tender lips, remembering each time.

Food. Focus.

I found pancake mix and fresh strawberries. About fifteen minutes later, Remmy came running into the kitchen dressed in Superman pajamas. Lucian was not far behind him. "Addawin, I clean!"

"Oh, and you smell so good. I made you some pancakes. I hope you like them."

He vigorously nodded as he climbed onto the barstool. He grabbed his fork and took a big bite.

I asked, "Are those good?"

"Umm-hmm."

Lucian sat next to his son and gave me a smile. I took a minute to really look at Lucian and Remmy. They both had brown hair and similar coloring, but Remmy must have inherited more of his mother's features.

I handed Lucian a wet cloth, and he cleaned Remmy's face when he was done eating. The little boy yawned.

Lucian picked him up. "Let's get you to bed."

"'Kay."

I patted his back while Lucian held him. "Night, Remmy. It was nice to meet you."

"You, too. Dank you for pancakes, Addawin."

"You're so welcome."

I got myself a glass of water and sat at the bar while Lucian put his son to bed. A few minutes later, he came into the kitchen. "He fell asleep fast."

"What was she thinking having him up this late?"

Lucian sighed. "I don't know."

I sympathized with him. To have a child but not be able to protect him—especially from his own mother—had to be the most helpless feeling in the world. I hadn't met Crystal officially, but she was obviously more of a mess than I'd imagined if she kept her three-year-old son out until four in the morning.

He looked deep in thought, so I stayed quiet.

"Thank you for tonight, Addilyn. For the entire night." My cheeks grew warm, and I looked away. Lucian put his finger underneath my chin. "I mean it. You are exquisite in every way. And helping with Remmy... well, it meant a lot to me."

"Thank you. And you're welcome."

Lucian leaned his forehead against mine. "I need to tell you something." Inside my chest, my heart beat double time. He whispered, "Remmy's not mine."

I gasped, shocked. When he pulled back, the mixture of hatred and utter devastation broke my heart. I had no words. Lucian walked us to his couch in the living room, where we sat as he continued his story. "I found out three days ago; he's not mine."

I had so many questions. My mind whirled with this information. Lucian always talked about Remmy as though he were his own. "What brought this on?"

"Well, I have come to find out Crystal had affairs throughout our marriage. It got me thinking. When she got pregnant, it was a shock. I was on the verge of divorcing her. We'd had sex maybe once or twice in the month prior to her getting pregnant. But I was busy running my company, and she convinced me the baby was mine. Looking back, I realize I was a fool, but I wanted to do the right thing."

He paused, gathering his thoughts. "At our last court hearing, Crystal told me she had information that would make me pay big. It made me realize the only hold she had over me was Remmy. So, I had a DNA test done. Crystal has no idea I did this. The thing is, I think of him as my son. But as it turns out, I have zero parental rights. Well, I won't if she files any motion against me."

I wrapped my arms around him. He put his chin on my shoulder and whispered into my ear, "Please don't run. I know your ex-husband did all sorts of fucked-up stuff when he brought his kid into the picture, but please don't run. I want to figure out what this is between us."

It was my turn to cup his face in my hands. "This is nothing like that situation. You are not Braden. I was forced to spend time with a little boy who was told I was his second mother and we were going to be a happy family. Devin called me Momma. It was hard keeping myself emotionally detached in order to save the little boy."

Lucian stood and cursed. "Fuck, your ex was an asshole."

"Yes, he was. He's married again. Wynter tracks him—I saw pictures. His new wife looks a lot like me."

The similarities were actually a little unnerving.

Lucian said, "I saw in the report I received that Braden was remarried. And this time, it seems the new wife is friends with Devin's mother."

Then his words sank in. "Wait. What? Monique and Bridgette are friends?"

He nodded. "Yes, it seems like they're all living together in a polygamous lifestyle."

"Oh." Then the meaning hit me. "Oh. Well, I'm glad she's aware of the situation or knowingly went into it." I touched his hand. "Braden is out of my life. Regardless, he no longer controls my decisions. I do. He has no power over our situation."

"Good to know." Lucian was still tense and worried.

My mind was still whirling at the fact that Remmy wasn't Lucian's child. "Why did she show up to give you Remmy in the middle of the night instead of tomorrow morning?"

"Crystal has friends in the same social circles I do. She was with me for several years. One of them probably texted her saying I was leaving with a woman. Crystal showed up here in order to ruin my night. She wanted to know if you were still here. I think she's doing drugs. Her behavior was erratic."

Drugs. Oh no. My mind raced with possibilities that Lucian had probably already considered regarding Remmy. There was no need to voice them. "Why do you think drugs?"

Lucian paced a few times. "This week, she called several times while I was out of town. There was something off about her voice, her breathing, her mood. She wasn't acting right. Tonight, it was clear she was on something. From what the front desk said, a man in a red car brought her here. Remmy said he's been sleeping on couches." He put his hands behind his neck. "I never wanted this for my son. All this money at my fingertips, and I can't save him." Then he gave an ironic laugh. "And fuck, he's not even mine."

I stood and put my hand on his heart. "Don't say that. He's yours, Lucian. In here, Remmy is yours. Don't forget that. Don't let yourself think you are any less important to him than you are. That little boy loves you. You have to stay positive for his sake. What's your next move?"

He dropped his head with a sigh. "I don't know." Rubbing his hands over his face, he looked me in the eye. "I understand if you need time to think about whether this is something you want to be involved in. I have no idea how things will go or what will happen. And I can already tell that Remmy is connecting with you."

"I—"

He placed his fingers against my lips. "Just think about it. I know you went through hell. And Remmy is a permanent part of my life. But it may require a fight I will most likely lose. And if I lose, I'm not sure where that will leave me."

My throat tightened. I knew what he was saying. Because of genetics, he might lose the little boy he loved as his own.

CHAPTER
12

Lucian

*C*hoose me. Choose us.

That was what I wanted to say as Addilyn stared into my eyes, but it had to be her choice. Our relationship was so new, and the amount of stress in my life might be catastrophic to it before it had time to grow. But if it wasn't, we might have a shot.

I was about to tell her that Jim would take her home if she wanted time to think when she grabbed my hand. "I want to be part of this, part of *us*. I know it's not a promise of forever. And if things end… well, then I'll make sure Remmy is as unaffected as possible. All I need is honesty."

She was unreal. I had only dreamed of finding someone like Addilyn. I took her by the hand; I had to make sure she understood. "If this gets to be too much—"

It was her turn to touch my lips. "I'll tell you and we'll figure out what to do next."

Nodding, I closed my eyes. It still hurt like a motherfucker to know Remmy wasn't mine.

Crystal was a piece of work.

She'd used me.

The legal system was fucked up. One would have thought I'd have had the upper hand, but Crystal knew my weakness was Remmy. And she'd played the judge like a fiddle. Even though he wasn't mine, I loved Remmy, and it would devastate me to lose him. As Crystal lost touch with reality more and more, I feared she would use the fact that Remmy wasn't mine to demand a large payout.

And ultimately, Remmy would pay the price. Tonight, in the bath, he'd told me his mommy stayed in the beds of boys who tickled her when they needed something. I wanted to punch the bitch. I needed to contact my lawyer. By some miracle, Remmy was physically unharmed. I had one week before Crystal had custody again. Time was of the essence.

Addilyn asked again, "What are you going to do? Are you going to tell anyone about the paternity test?"

That was the big fucking question of the day. "Not yet. And I shouldn't have put that burden on you. I'm sorry."

But I needed to confide in someone. Maybe it wasn't wise telling Addilyn, but my gut told me she would never tell a soul.

She touched my cheek. "Anything you need to talk about—I'm here. I won't tell anyone."

"Thank you. I need to work out a few things with my lawyer. Do you want to get some sleep?"

At the word *sleep,* she let out a great yawn. "Sure. I'll head back to my place."

Selfishly, I wanted her next to me. "You can sleep in my bed, sweetheart."

She bit her lip, uncertain.

"If Remmy wakes up, I'll tell him you were helping me and got sleepy."

"I think it's best if I head home."

Fuck, I wanted her with me. From the hallway, I heard, "Daddy?"

Addilyn put a respectable distance between us before I called out, "Yeah, buddy?"

"I had a nightmare. Is Addawin here?"

Remmy came into the living room, and Addilyn smiled. "Hey there. I was about to go home. Do you want to know what my grammie always did when I had a nightmare?"

He cocked his head. "What?"

"She would hum to me. It was a magical song that helped me go to sleep, and the bad dreams never came."

Touching my hand, Remmy asked, "Can Addawin sing to me?"

Addilyn's eyes rounded a little; clearly, she had not been expecting that. I said, "I can hum."

Remmy shook his head. "I need her grammie's song."

I nodded to Addilyn when she silently asked if it was okay. "I'll hum my grammie's song if you want me to."

"Yes! You need 'jamas. Borrow Daddy's."

She looked at me, silently waiting for my response. *Of course, I'm saying yes.* This was working out perfectly. "There's some in the top left drawer."

Addilyn raised her eyebrow, and I smiled. We both knew I'd gotten my way in the end. I wanted to lose myself in her and pretend none of these problems existed.

I picked up Remmy and held him. *He's not mine.* The reality of it was devastating. I wanted Remmy as my own. If it cost me my fortune, I would pay it to keep him. Addilyn's words came back to me. *He's mine. He's mine. Blood doesn't matter. I am his dad.* Yeah, I would fight for him and never give up.

I tucked the little guy into bed and gave him a kiss.

"I like Addawin. She nice."

I kissed his forehead. "I like her, too."

"Is she your girlfriend?"

For a second, I wondered if I should deflect or tell the truth. Lies surrounded Remmy, so there was only one option. "Yes, Addilyn is my girlfriend."

His brow furrowed. "Mommy's boyfriends don't like me."

I bit my cheek and balled my free fist. *Son of a bitch, I'll kill anyone who hurts him.* "What did they do?"

"They say mean things. One spit on me. Mommy just told me to go 'way with my toys."

Over my dead body would he be left with Crystal again.

I gave Remmy another kiss. "Did anything else happen? Did anyone touch you, Remmy? Like your privates?"

"No, Daddy. You said don't let anyone."

Thank goodness. I breathed out a huge sigh of release. "You don't have to worry about your mother, Remmy. I'll figure it out. And I know Addilyn likes you."

He hugged me, and I held him tighter. Why the fuck Crystal would hurt this little boy was beyond me. "Wuv you, Daddy."

"Love you, too, son." I choked on the last word. Biology didn't matter. I loved him like my own.

Addilyn came into the room, swallowed up in my pajamas. "You ready for the song that is so amazing it guarantees good dreams?"

"Yes, yes!" Remmy clapped.

She knelt next to his bed, grabbed his hand, and began to hum. After the fifth verse, and seeing that Remmy was asleep, I whispered into her ear, "I'm going to go make some calls."

"Sounds good. I'm just going to hum a bit longer."

As I left, a soft, sweet sound filled the room. And with it, I fell harder. This was the type of mother my son deserved. It was hard to believe how fast Crystal had gone downhill in the last two weeks. I needed documented therapy meetings with Remmy and whatever else the lawyer suggested, and I needed them immediately.

"Sounds, good. Thanks for working on this, Walt."

There was a rustling on the other end of the line. "Anytime. I understand tonight's the exception, but I wouldn't have your girlfriend over past bedtime anymore. Or, hell, at least let Remmy see her leave and sneak her back in."

"Understood." Basically, I was going to have to live my life under a microscope.

"I'll get these motions filed for an immediate injunction and keep you posted. Based on the footage from your apartment, I believe the judge will demand drug testing."

"Thanks. And if Crystal shows up?"

"Tell security not to let her through. If she won't leave, call the cops and then me. We need everything documented. By the time she's supposed to have custody again, hopefully we have this handled."

"Will do. Walt, I'm not giving him back."

"We'll cross that bridge when we come to it, Lucian, but I hear you loud and clear. Let's focus on getting through the motions."

"Thanks, Walt." I hung up the phone with my lawyer, sat up, and scrubbed a hand down my face. "Fuck."

If the judge rejected my injunction for full temporary custody, then he needed his head examined. *No way Remmy is going back.*

I walked into his bedroom to find Addilyn sitting on the floor, her head leaning against the bed while she held Remmy's hand. They were fast asleep.

I carefully took her hand out of his before I picked her up. She snuggled against my chest, and I felt empowered by her trust. I brought her into my bedroom and locked the door behind us. Carefully, I laid her in the bed and for a moment, just watched her sleep.

She stirred and her eyes fluttered open. "You done?"

I pulled the shirt over my head. "Yeah, it's finished."

"What did he say?"

I ran my fingers up her stomach to find her breasts. She arched at the touch. "Later. Right now, I want to bury myself inside you."

"Please."

CHAPTER
13

Lucian

"Thanks for coming over tonight." I held up my tumbler to Kaysen, who held up his, as well. The Pappy Van Winkle was smooth as it went down.

Kaysen tilted his glass to one side, swirling the golden-brown liquid around. "I missed the little squirt. I can't believe the shit Crystal pulled. I knew she was a piece of work, but I never thought she'd be neglectful."

"Neither did I. I mean, she would never have won Mother of the Year, but she never mistreated him."

It was nice catching up with Kaysen about what had happened this week. There weren't many people I trusted. Still, I kept the paternity news to myself; I didn't want to add more to his plate.

"Remmy seems taken with Addilyn," Kaysen said.

"He is. That happened sooner than I'd originally planned. But it's happened, and I don't regret it. She's been good for Remmy, I think."

I hadn't expected Remmy to get attached so quickly. But like I told Kaysen, it had happened. Our relationship was so new, and it made me nervous if we were to go our separate ways.

"And you're still good with Addilyn meeting him so soon?"

I thought about this for a second. "I am. No, it wasn't my first choice. But I also trust her. It's hard to explain, but Addilyn isn't like the others."

"Just be careful."

When I had proposed to Crystal, Kaysen had been against it. He'd said he thought it was too soon and a baby wasn't a reason to get married. I understood his reasons, but at the time, I thought I was doing the right thing. "I am. Addilyn is not Crystal."

"Money changes people."

I appreciated that he was looking out for me. "I know. I appreciate the warning. Things are different with Addilyn than they were with Crystal. But I will be careful."

"Good. Wynter says the same thing about her, but it's better to be safe than sorry." Kaysen finished his drink. "I need to head out. Let me know if there's anything I can do to help."

"I will. Thanks for stopping by."

I stood and walked Kaysen to the door.

"Anytime. If you need something, let me know."

"I will."

When the door closed, I dragged a hand down my face. *Am I making the right decision about Addilyn?*

Yes, I was. She was the only thing going right in my world.

I pulled out my phone and sent her a text.

Me: *What are you doing?*

Addilyn: *I just finished Alfred Hitchcock's* The Birds.

I chuckled, knowing it probably wasn't the HEA she was looking for in an older movie.

Me: *And? I hadn't suggested this one so I'm definitely interested in what you think.*

I had never enjoyed *The Birds*.

Addilyn: *Okay, it's confusing. And a lot creepy. Of course, I got nervous, so I looked up if Melanie and Mitch lived.*

Me: *You ruined the movie.*

Addilyn: *Or made it better.*

I laughed out loud.

Addilyn: *Anyway, I've read critics' interpretation about how the birds really represent the women in Mitch's life.*

Me: *Really?*

I'd watched the movie a long, long time ago but hadn't put much thought into it.

Addilyn: *Yes, it's just… I better not start having birds attack now that I'm dating you. Ha-ha!*

I grinned from ear to ear.

Me: *If they do… I promise to protect you.*

Addilyn: *You better!*

Addilyn: *But seriously, I need a* happy *old movie. I need something that isn't depressing, sad, cryptic, or creepy.*

Me: *How about* Meet Me in St. Louis.

Addilyn: *Does it have an HEA?*

Me: *Will it really matter what I say or will you just look it up?*

Addilyn: *Good point. Good night, Mister Mystery.*

Me: *Night, sweetheart.*

CHAPTER 14♥

Addilyn

"So, I've been testing the new app this week, and I think it's great," I said to Wynter in her office at the Keller Industries office. Thank goodness it was Friday. It had been an exhausting week of trying to get all the marketing stuff settled for the new app, *Socialite*.

Wynter leaned back in her chair. "Good. I'll let Kaysen know we're ready for rollout."

"Black Media has the marketing packet ready to go. I sent an email with a link to all the materials that need to be reviewed. Once we have the okay, we'll launch."

"You are rocking this shit."

That meant a lot coming from Wynter.

"I'm trying to."

Working with her, I had learned how particular she was. She was a perfectionist when it came to her job, which I not only respected but appreciated. But since we were friends, I wanted to make sure she never regretted telling me about the opportunity.

"Well, you are. Kaysen is impressed, too. Keep doing what you're doing." Wynter changed subjects. "Girl, I gotta tell you—hot sex looks good on you."

I blushed. Somehow, I thought I'd avoided this topic. Looked like I was wrong. "I don't think this is the time or place."

She shrugged and laughed. "Everyone ducked out early for the day. Seriously, you have been holding out on me and not telling me *anything*."

She was right. I hadn't said much because I didn't want to betray Lucian's trust. While I was avoiding looking at her face, I noticed the bottom buttons on her shirt were askew. I quirked a brow. "And it looks like you have a few secrets of your own."

Her eyes widened for a second but just as quickly re- turned to normal. If I hadn't been watching, I might have missed it. "Why would you say that?"

"Your blouse." I pointed to the haphazard buttoning job.

She looked down and fixed it. "Oh, damn it. He's a nipple man."

I nearly choked on my tea. "*Nipple* man?"

Leaning in, she gave me a mischievous smile. "Well, I go braless and crank the air conditioning down in my office be- fore a meeting with this *client*. It ensures a good ravaging. The office was empty, and I had a lunch meeting with said client."

"At work?" My eyes widened.

"Desk sex is amazing. You should try it."

I shook my head, unable to imagine Lucian having sex in his office while people were around. "Who's the guy you're seeing?"

The office had been empty when I arrived. Wynter gave me a wink. "Don't worry; it's just a fun time."

That was Wynter's personality. "Give me a hint about who he is?"

She took a pretend key and locked her mouth.

"Well, I guess the same goes for me, too." I mimicked her motions which caused us to giggle.

On a more serious note, she added, "I'm happy for you. Things seem to be going well with Lucian."

"They are. Meeting Remmy so quickly nearly threw a wrench into everything, but I think we've managed that. He's a cute kid."

"Super sweet. Kaysen loves him to pieces."

I knew Kaysen and Lucian were best friends, but we hadn't really gotten to know each other. "I feel badly for them."

"Me, too. But I think you're good for Lucian and Remmy."

Hugging her, I said, "I hope so. I'm heading out. Chat later."

"For sure. Let's do a girls' night soon."

"Perfect."

As I left, it was hard not to worry about Wynter and her extracurricular activities. Mixing business and pleasure always complicated things. I expected at some point we'd have to deal with some sort of issue of mixing the two now that I was sort of working with Lucian. Maybe Wynter cared about this person more than she cared to admit. I hoped Wynter found happiness, too.

Lucian: *You still good to watch Remmy Sunday?*

His nanny, Ms. Jan, couldn't watch Remmy due to a prior obligation. Lucian had taken a lot of time off work this week to be with his son. Sunday was going to be his catch-up day at the office, so he would have a lighter work load the following week.

Me: *Yes, for sure. We're going to bake.*

Lucian: *He'll love it.*

Crystal hadn't made further contact after being served with legal papers the day before. Remmy was safe for the time being. I loved spending evenings over there. I pretended to leave at bedtime and snuck back in later for time with Lucian. Things with him had only intensified. We couldn't get enough of each other.

I returned to my office for my laptop only to find a big, white box on my desk. "What's this?"

Ria poked her head in. "Beats me, but I bet it's from lover boy."

I shook my head, laughing. My boss had been amazing about who I was dating. "Are you sure it doesn't bother you I'm seeing Lucian Black?"

"As long as he treats you right and I don't have to go bust the balls of one of our biggest clients, yeah I'm good with it. And girl, I'm glad you're finally sowing some oats with a good-looking guy like Black. When I was your age, I was setting the world on fire with all my oat sowing."

I put my head on my desk. "Between you and Wynter, I think I'm doomed to embarrassment all day."

Her laughter filled my office. "It's good for you. Well, I'm off. Chuck and I finally have a weekend to ourselves. He told me we have a no-clothes policy this weekend."

Lifting my head, I raised an eyebrow. "I swear, everyone has lost their filter today. There are images a girl doesn't need to have in her head."

Ria left, still laughing. "Go home. Be wild."

"Thanks! I will. I was thinking of eating ice cream and wearing purple slippers."

Ria poked her head back in. "He better be dripping that ice cream on you, then eating it."

Shoot. Me. Now.

Sex talk with my boss about my boyfriend eating ice cream off my body.

No. No. And no.

I gave her a sweet smile. "I'm pretending you said, 'Sounds great, Addilyn. You sure know how to be wild. Enjoy your slippers.'"

"That, too." Ria laughed her way down the hallway.

Every single woman in my life was crazy.

Every. Single. One.

Now, what's in the box?

I opened the lid to the white box to find a beautiful yellow dress. On the top was a card.

Will you be my date tomorrow for dinner?

I want to show the world you're mine.

Yours entirely,

Lucian

I stopped and stared at the note again. Lucian wanted the world to know I was his. *He's ready to announce we're dating?* I smiled at the thought. *Yes, I am ready.* The past was the past, and I was ready for what the future held.

I grabbed my phone and opened my text messages.

Me: *I got a pretty package.*

Lucian: *Oh, yeah. What was in it?*

Me: *A beautiful dress from an amazing man. There was a note with a question.*

Lucian: *And...*

Me: *Yes, I want the world to know I'm his.*

Lucian: *I need you.*

Me: *I think I need to wash my goldfish tonight.*

I giggled.

Lucian: *The hell you do. Get your ass over here.*

Me: *I have on black lacy panties and my black heels to-day.*

Lucian: *Bra?*

Me: *You'll have to find out.*

Lucian: *Gladly.*

CHAPTER 15

Addilyn

"Is this one of your favorite places to eat?" I stared at the cavernous room filled with fancy furniture and chandeliers. Long red velvet drapes adorned the windows, and tall bouquets of champagne-colored flowers sat in the center of each table. It was a far cry from my hot dog stand recommendation.

Lucian led me toward the hostess with his hand on the small of my back. "No, but I know in this place, we will make the paper."

The hostess recognized him and led us toward a table.

"Paper?" I nearly stumbled as we made our way through the dining room but managed to remain upright.

Paper? We're going to be in the paper.

As we sat, it felt as if all eyes were on me. Lucian ordering something to drink barely registered. "Addilyn."

"Yes," I answered almost robotically.

The pressure on my hand made me focus on his words. "We can leave. I thought you were okay with everyone knowing we were together."

The waiter filled our water glasses and brought champagne. Lucian watched me closely. It was clear if I wanted to leave, he'd take me. "I do. I hadn't associated that with newspapers or having our picture taken. It's fine. I want this." Lucian watched me closely, obviously weighing my words. My word, Lucian in a tux took my breath away. I placed my hand on his. "I promise. I'll never be the type to seek the papers, you know that. But I get that there will be times we're in them."

And tonight, I felt decadent. The pale-yellow dress dipped low in the back and the front. It was elegant and made me feel like I belonged in Lucian's world even if it was a fairy tale.

We ordered, and I sipped my champagne. The waiter had called it an aperitif. "Where are all the forks?"

"They'll set the table between each course." Lucian winked at me.

I took another sip. "That's handy."

"I thought so."

The meal progressed, and I managed through everything fine with Lucian's expert guidance. During dinner, we drank a red cabernet. No one would have guessed I'd never eaten at a fancy place before. Dessert arrived, and I took a bite of the chocolate cake. "I don't think I'll ever be able to eat again."

Lucian reached his hand out to mine. "This place does have great food as well as the social advantages."

"Do you eat here often?"

"No, not really. When I have clients in town, sometimes I'll bring them here. I've attended events occasionally. But I try to avoid the papers when I can. There's a certain amount of exposure Black Media must procure to ensure we stay at the forefront of the industry, but personally, I couldn't give two fucks. The only reason the media currently cares about my personal life is because they want a good story. Drama sells. And Crystal has tried to use the drama to hurt Black Media."

I imagined having strangers in your personal business all the time would be exhausting. Lucian had normal days without the media like we'd had at the zoo. "How have you stayed in front of it? I saw mentions here and there, but it's not *everywhere*."

"I pay my PR team well to make sure Black Media isn't marred by her drama. And given proof of Crystal's cheating, those news outlets had to publish retractions. So, it's all about managing them."

The professional side of me loved hearing Lucian talk business. He was smart and cunning. "Still no word from Crystal since she was served with the judge's decision?"

The judge had ordered drug testing based on the evidence Lucian's lawyers had provided. He shook his head. "No, she was served with the judgement and has since disappeared. Which is fine with me; the longer she goes without contact, the better. Dance with me."

That was a swift change in subject. "What?"

Lucian stood and held out his hand. "Dance with me."

My eyes went to the open floor in front of the three-piece band. "Lucian, no one else is dancing."

"I know."

This was how Lucian planned to get our photo out there. An out-of-character action to draw attention. I put my hand in his as he led me to the dance floor. Lucian brought me close to him. I caught a quick glimpse of a camera. I murmured, "They're taking pictures."

"Good. That was the plan."

Lucian expertly spun me around the dance floor. "Does this benefit me more than you? I mean, I imagine all the women want to be on your arm." I laughed. "I don't think my bank account is nearly as attractive."

"Andy Barnette will see this."

Confused, I asked, "Andy?"

The sweet music filled the air, keeping our conversation private. "Yes, the man drove me insane trying to claim you that night at the function. It took everything in me to not act like an immature prick."

His possessiveness sent a shiver down my back. There was something attractive about a man staking his claim. "Well, Andy Barnette can't compare to you."

"Good."

As the song ended, there was a light applause. He leaned in to give me a sweet, innocent kiss. When he pulled back, he said, "See, there's only one world and you fit perfectly in every aspect of the world we make for ourselves."

CHAPTER 16 ♥

Addilyn

"Addawin, do you wuv my daddy?"

I stopped icing the cupcakes. Lucian was at his office working while I was at his apartment, watching Remmy. We were baking cupcakes before he took his afternoon nap.

I touched his cheek, unsure how to navigate his question. At the same time, I wanted to be honest. "I care for him a lot."

"Good." Remmy smiled at me and we returned to decorating the first batch of cupcakes. It was messy, and Remmy had consumed more icing than he'd gotten on the cupcakes, but we were having fun. It broke my heart at how much he craved female attention. "He wuvs you."

I stopped icing again and swung my head toward Remmy. "Why do you say that?"

"He giggles a wot."

It was sweet to see the perspective of an almost-four-year-old. But when I was here, the house was filled with laughter.

From what Lucian had said, everything had been tense when Crystal had lived there.

Whether it was the truth or something a child had made up, my heart sped up in my chest. Again, Remmy asked, "Do you wuv him?"

The timer went off for the next batch of cupcakes. Internally I sighed, grateful for the distraction. I turned with the cupcakes in hand and immediately dropped them at the sight of Crystal standing in Lucian's kitchen. The loud clang made Remmy jump.

Crystal stepped closer, her arms outstretched. "Remmy, baby, come to Mommy."

I dropped the potholders on the floor and dashed to Remmy, who had scrambled off his chair and run to me. In one swift movement, I picked him up and held him close, turning my body to shield him from her. His small frame shook, and he clung to me.

"Give me my son, you bitch," Crystal spat.

I held him closer, refusing to let go. "Let me call Lucian so you two can talk."

"Give me my son, damn it!" She was swaying and itching her skin. The woman was on something.

Remmy tightened his arms around my neck. "I'm scared, Addawin."

"I'm not going to let her take you. I promise, Remmy."

His fingers dug into my neck, and his legs locked around my waist. Crystal took a step around the counter, and I mirrored hers to keep the wide island between us. "Like I said, I'll call Lucian and you guys can talk. But you are not taking Remmy—there's a court order. I'm watching Remmy for Lucian."

"He's mine!" she screeched, pulling at her hair. "He's mine! Not yours! He will never be yours."

Her erratic behavior was beginning to scare me. I kept my voice calm while my heart was about to be beat out of my chest. "I know you're his mother. I have no intention of taking him from you."

Remmy began to sniffle, his head buried in my neck.

"You're in the papers! You're on his arm in all the papers! He has that look with you. I want that look!" Her volume rose with each sentence. "You will not take what's mine!"

Crystal's movements were jerky and she moved toward the knife block on the counter. She pulled the chef's knife out of the holder. That wasn't good. "You are scaring Remmy. I need you to leave now and wait in the lobby until Lucian comes home."

"I want Remmy! Remmy, come to Mommy! Don't you love your mommy?"

She was so cruel. His body shook with fear, and he held onto me like his life depended on it.

Crystal moved again, and I angled my body toward Lucian's bedroom as a possible escape. There were several doors I could lock if necessary. I remembered my cell phone was in my back pocket. With one hand I pulled it out. "I'm calling Lucian, and you two can sort this out as his parents."

I pushed the Send button on my phone as Crystal became more agitated. She was chanting *My son* repeatedly while dragging the knife along her skin.

"Hey, sweetheart."

I cleared my throat, trying to sound calm. "Crystal is here, and she's trying to take Remmy. I have him in my arms and told her no, but I assured her you wanted to talk about it with her."

"Don't let her take me, Addawin."

I kissed Remmy's head and whispered, "I won't let her take you, Remmy. I promise. You're staying with me. Your daddy is going to get us help."

"My son! My son! My son!" Crystal chanted louder, and things only grew more chaotic. "My son! My son! My son!" Crystal moved, and I shifted, too, unable to pay attention to what Lucian was saying. "I want my son! She's taking it all from me!"

"Addilyn, did you hear me? Security is on the way." Lucian's concerned voice drew my attention back to him.

"Y-yes. Okay." *Stay focused.*

Lucian asked, "Is she on something?"

"I think so. Looks like it. We're in the kitchen."

"My son! My son! Give me my son!" Crystal moved again, and I countermoved, making sure the large island remained a barrier between us. Crystal screamed, "Lucian, I want my FUCKING son!" and Remmy began to cry.

"Sweetheart, security is coming up the elevator. They're almost there. As soon as they get there, take Remmy to my room and lock the door. I'm already on my way."

The elevator door dinged, and I kept moving around the kitchen as Crystal picked up her pace. There was blood trickling down Crystal's arm from where the knife had penetrated her skin.

Two men came in the room, their weapons drawn. She looked at them, her head cocked to one side. "Who are you?"

The taller one said calmly, "Ms. Black, we're here to take you to Mr. Black. He wants to talk to you."

She shook her head. "No, no, no! It's a trick! It's a trick! He took everything away from me! EVERYTHING!"

Crystal shook her head and moved about erratically. The men approached from different sides. The taller one whispered to me, "Go!"

I dashed for the bedroom, Crystal's screams piercing the air behind me. After locking the door, I took Remmy to the couch on the far side of the room. He was bawling. "Don't wet her take me. She's mean to me. She's so mean. She wet her fwiends spit on me. Don't let me go, Addawin."

Tears gathered in my eyes. "Shh, you're not going anywhere. Remmy look at me." His tear-streaked face and turned-down mouth were so sad. "You're not going anywhere. I will not let her take you; do you understand? We're safe. Your daddy is on his way. I promise you, she is not taking you. Do you hear me? You're staying right here with me."

"Pwomise?"

"I promise."

Remmy hugged me, and I rocked him while I hummed. A short time later, there was a soft knock at the door. "It's me, Lucian."

I got up with Remmy and unlocked the door. Lucian looked at Remmy and touched his back. "Hey, buddy, I'm here."

Remmy reached for Lucian. "I don't want to go, Daddy. Pwease don't make me go."

"You're not going anywhere. Your mom left. She won't come back." He stroked Remmy's back and looked at me. "The police are here. They need to ask you some questions for the record."

Remmy reached for me. "Don't go, Addawin. Don't leave me. Pwease."

I caressed his cheek. "I'll be back. I need to talk to the police. It helps keep your mommy from trying to come see you again. Okay?"

He nodded and then reached for me. Hugging me again, Remmy whispered, "I wuv you, Addawin, just like my daddy."

My eyes jerked to Lucian's; there was so much emotion in his dark eyes. The black flecks seemed to glow. I kissed Remmy's cheek, knowing it might be too soon, but I had to let this little boy know how I felt. "I love you, too, Remmy."

I left without looking back, unsure what else to say, but knowing my heart belonged to Lucian and Remmy Black.

CHAPTER 17 ♥

Addilyn

Lucian and I tiptoed out of Remmy's bedroom after humming him to sleep. We were exhausted. It had been a long day. The police had questioned me for quite some time. After they'd left, Remmy had been glued to us, switching between Lucian and me. I was in deep, deeper than Lucian or I had yet to put into words. Those precious words, *I wuv you,* from Remmy today in front of his dad were the sweetest I had heard in my life. Before he'd fallen asleep, Remmy had asked if I would stay the night to make sure I was safe. The images of Crystal haunted me. The truth was, I needed Remmy and Lucian tonight, too.

We walked into the front room, where Kaysen and Wynter were sitting at the kitchen island. "I think this tech show would be worth attending, too. It has some great panels, and we might be able to look at it for our future programs."

"I agree. Send the details to Erma, and she'll set us up."

They stopped talking when they saw us. Kaysen asked, "How is he?"

Lucian dragged a hand down his face. "Asleep for now."

"Any updates on Crystal?" Wynter asked.

"Not yet. She's been detained and placed under evaluation since she physically harmed herself today."

Watching her dragging the knife across her skin had made me sick.

Lucian said, "Walt said we would have more updates in the morning, but there was no chance of her getting out tonight."

"Good. How did she get up into the apartment?" Kaysen asked.

"They're looking into it. Our best guess is someone gave her the new code; it's the only way. Everything was changed after she left."

"I hope they lock that bitch away." Wynter stood and yawned. "I'm heading out—unless you need anything else. Do you want to stay with me tonight, Addilyn?"

I cleared my throat. "I'm actually going to stay here tonight. Remmy asked if I would. I'm torn about it. Lucian's assured me it won't hurt his chances in court, but I don't know."

Kaysen watched our exchange without saying a word, and I wondered what he was thinking. The room fell silent. *Maybe I should go home or to Wynter's.* Lucian put his arm around my waist. "It will be fine."

Standing, Kaysen said, "I'll see you guys later."

There was a chill in his voice I was sure Lucian picked up on. "I'll see you out."

The two walked toward the elevator in a hushed, heated discussion.

"Wynter, what do you think?"

"Don't mind Kaysen. He's very protective of Lucian and Remmy. Always has been."

"But what do you think?"

She sighed. "I know you guys are beat and may not be thinking clearly. And I know things are going well between you and Lucian, but…" I hated the pause. "Think about how it will look, from a judge's perspective, with you dating for all of two minutes and staying the night."

"I know."

Wynter put her hand on mine. "I'll support you either way, but I won't lie to you. Hell, if I'd gone through what you went through, I wouldn't want to be alone either. Come to my place. Then get up early and be here before Remmy wakes up in the morning."

Lucian walked toward us, and I asked, "Can we talk?"

He hesitated for a moment. "Of course."

Wynter stayed put, so I knew she would wait for me.

We walked into his office. "I need to go stay with Wynter." Lucian started to object, and I rushed to speak. "Kaysen and Wynter are right. I don't want to leave you, either, but Remmy's welfare has to come first. I know you think that, too."

Lucian released a long breath. "I know he's right, but it pisses me the fuck off. He's offered to stay with Remmy and me, though."

I leaned up and kissed him. "Let him. I'll be back first thing in the morning."

He nodded but didn't verbally agree. "I will. I want you guys to take a car to Wynter's and let me know once you get there." He kissed me again and then put his forehead against mine. "I want to be the one who comforts you tonight."

"I know. And I want to be there for you, too." We needed each other. Crystal, strung out on whatever drugs she was taking, was a sight I'd not soon forget.

Lucian cracked his neck, tension radiating from him. "I should have been able to protect you both from her. If something had happened to Remmy or you... I don't know what I would have done."

This was not the time for him to get worked up again. "We are safe. She may have scared us, but she never put a hand on Remmy."

He stroked his thumb along my cheek. "I have you to thank for that." Lucian touched his nose to mine. "Will you go furniture shopping with us tomorrow? Remmy mentioned tonight how empty the house was. He's afraid I'm going to disappear. I think it will be good for Remmy to see the house filling up with things."

I bit my lip. "Are you sure you want me to go?" It scared me how fast I had gotten attached to Remmy and vice versa. *What if things go south between Lucian and me?*

"Yes, this may seem fast to everyone else, but they weren't part of our conversations over the last few months. I get that we need to be cautious, and I appreciate Kaysen speaking out because we weren't thinking. But we have to move forward with our lives." I looked down for a second. His finger touched my chin and lifted my face. "You are the only thing that is going right in my life. My son is in love with you... and I am, too. I need you to know that before you leave tonight."

My world shifted at the sound of those sweet words. He loved me. His son loved me. "I love you, too. And Remmy. It scares me how fast I've fallen for you."

Lucian pressed his lips to mine, and I melted into him. "Hurry back."

"I will."

I left in a daze, Lucian's words on repeat in my head. When we were in the car, Wynter touched my hand. "He's a good guy. I'm so happy for you. I knew you guys were meant to be."

"Thank you. I'm so happy, too. I never dreamed I'd get a second chance at love."

Once we arrived, I texted Lucian.

Me: *Made it to Wynter's.*

Lucian: *Good. I wish you were in my arms right now. I should have waited to tell you I love you until I could make love to you.*

Me: *I'm glad you didn't wait. It helps while I'm away from you.*

Lucian: *I agree. Can you accompany me to a business function next Friday? I understand if you're not ready. It's a charity fundraiser for a local children's hospital Black Media supports.*

Me: *I'd love to.*

Lucian: *I'll make the arrangements. Night, sweetheart.*

Me: *Night.*

I put away my phone. Wynter had a substantially bigger apartment with two actual bedrooms. They were small, but there were two. Some of her furniture had a very modern look. The hand chair with its thin, cradling fingers, always freaked me out. Being an executive tech for Keller Industries paid well. Wynter also had a trust fund she'd inherited when she turned eighteen. The details were vague, and Wynter always changed the subject when it came up.

One of her earlier statements registered with me. "What did you mean you knew we were meant to be?"

Wynter stopped midstride on the way to the kitchen. "Shit." That made me feel uneasy, and that feeling only grew as she slowly turned around and held out her hands. "Hear me out."

"Wynter." It was definitely not the night to play games.

She sighed. "Okay, but please let me explain. I was analyzing conversations. Aurora Rose and Mister Mystery were constantly at the top of one of the interaction reports for *Lots of Fish*. It showed the usage by user, and I saw your name. Kaysen had set up Lucian's account as a ghost account so no one would know it was him. I moved you to a ghost account, too."

The blood drained from my face, and I became lightheaded. "And?"

"I knew Lucian was coming to the toy drive. So I asked you to be there. I wanted you to have a chance to meet him in person. With the interaction report, I saw you guys messaged a lot. I couldn't see your messages, by the way. The night of the toy drive, Lucian was running late, so I figured that night was a bust. Then luck was on my side when he arrived as you were leaving. You guys connected. I could see it from across the room. It was insane how lost you became in each other. But then Crystal ruined it. That's why I changed the meeting location from Keller Industries to Black Media and requested Lucian's presence at the last minute for your presentation."

I plopped down on the couch as I tried to wrap my head around this news. "Does Lucian know?"

"No, and neither does Kaysen. I only provided you two a platform to meet. Your connection did all the work."

I massaged my temples, unsure what to make of the situation.

Wynter pleaded, "Don't be mad. Please. I wanted you to be happy. You deserve happiness, Addilyn."

It was still hard to process. Wynter sat next to me and hugged me. "I know it was a little sketchy as a friend, but after I saw you interact at the toy event, I had to try one more time."

What would Lucian think? It felt like we'd been manipulated, but I knew Wynter hadn't meant to be deceitful. "Thank you for always having my back, but I need to tell Lucian."

"I know. Will you come talk to me afterward?"

"Yes, of course."

I dialed his number and proceeded to tell him everything. Once I finished, I waited for his reaction, biting my nails. "Tell Wynter to choose a spa; she has a day on me."

"You aren't mad?"

"No, I'm thankful."

That wasn't the response I'd expected. "You are?"

"Yes, because of her, I have you. And like I said before, it was only a matter of time before I manned up and asked to meet you."

I smiled even though he couldn't see it. "Thank you. I know she's worried. I need to tell her."

"Okay. Good-night, Addilyn. I love you."

"I love you, too."

When I was done, I found Wynter was sitting on the couch, clearly worried. "Lucian wants you to pick out a spa for a day on him. He said thank you."

"Really?"

"Really."

She stood on the couch and danced. "Hell yeah!"

"Thanks, Wynter. You are the best friend a girl could ask you."

Wynter continued to dance, singing, "I'm good. I'm good. I know it. Woo!" Then she hopped down off the couch. "Now, let's have a drink and celebrate."

CHAPTER
18 ♥

Lucian

"**M**r. Black, Ms. DeRoss," the hostess said, welcoming us into the event.

We nodded and thanked her. I had my hand on Addilyn's lower back as I led her inside. The dress she wore that night was cut to the lower part of her back like the yellow dress. I loved having my hand on her bare skin. If I placed my hand just right, the tips of my fingers could slip slightly underneath the sides of her dress.

It was torture knowing she wasn't wearing a bra. The emerald dress had a diamond-studded halter with fabric that hung in layers. Earlier that week, I'd had several different gowns brought to my place for Addilyn to choose from. If she was going to come to events with me, I wanted her to feel like she belonged. I knew the difference in our finances bothered her, and she was nervous about tonight. I wished I could make her see that money wasn't happiness.

A performer was spitting fire as we approached the doors. "Wow," Addilyn murmured. "I thought this stuff only happened in the movies."

It was a circus theme this year. "The bigger the show, the larger the donations. People want to feel like they got their money's worth."

"That's so backward. The amount of money spent tonight would help so many."

"True, but that's not how it works." I'd often thought that myself, having attended these over-the-top charity events for many years.

The Martins were the hosts this evening. Dr. Dwayne Martin was an older man who had invested well in the stock market. On top of being on the board of directors of this charity, Dr. Martin headed up one of the children's hospitals here in New York. Remmy had been there when he had RSV as a baby. Dr. Martin's wife of twenty years, Teresa, seemed like a nice woman from the limited interactions I'd had with her through the years.

Addilyn's hand squeezed mine tighter, most likely due to the nervousness she'd admitted to before we arrived. I doubted she realized she was even doing it. It was important that tonight was a success so Addilyn could see that she fit in perfectly at these events. And after this hellish week, I was ready for a night out with her. Remmy had needed my full attention, and Addilyn had been there through it all, never asking for time alone together. Her primary concern was Remmy. The therapist seemed to be helping Remmy, which was a relief.

Kaysen had offered to watch Remmy for me tonight. I loved my son, but I wanted to steal away some time with Addilyn. Thankfully, Remmy had been excited about having

Uncle Kaysen all to himself. One day, Kaysen would make a great dad.

I leaned in to her. "Have I mentioned how beautiful you are?"

Again, I was awarded with a brilliant smile. "You might have mentioned it a time or two."

"Well, you are."

A man touched my shoulder, interrupting us. "Lucian, it's a pleasure to see you here."

I turned to see the douchebag owner of a local art gallery. Crystal had been one of his biggest clients at one time. Word was business was slow and he was in trouble. "You, too, Charlie."

"Do you have a second to discuss a business venture? I have something that might interest you."

My money. I kept my face neutral. "Not tonight. I promised my girlfriend no business. It was good seeing you, Charlie."

I hadn't promised Addilyn, but I knew the women were salivating to get their hooks into Addilyn. That wasn't going to happen. As we walked away, Addilyn looked at me. "If you need to talk business, I'll be fine."

I brought her a little closer. "He needs money to bail out his failing business. No business tonight. I want to spend it with you. And I'm a selfish bastard."

"How are you selfish?"

"I don't want to leave you alone and let another asshole move in."

Addilyn blushed. "That wouldn't happen."

I saw the pricks eyeing her from a distance. She was beautiful, innocent, and sexy. "Oh, but it would. And tonight,

I'm not in the mood to fend them off. It's been a shit week and I just want to be with you."

She kissed my cheek. "I feel the same way." Thank goodness she hadn't bailed on this fucked-up situation with Crystal.

Dr. Martin appeared up on the balcony. "If everyone could take their seats in the dining hall, we have a short video for you before dinner is served."

Addilyn and I made our way toward the banquet hall, where our seats were at a table set off to the side as I'd requested. And hopefully a friend of the family would be seated with us, which I believed would help Addilyn feel more comfortable. I hated being in the front or the middle. Those seats were for the individuals who wanted to be seen. I'd never been that type of person, but I'd frequently been seated there with the hosts of various events.

People filed in, and I watched Addilyn's eyes widen a little as people discussed their houses in the Hamptons, arriving on private jets, and elaborate vacations in the Mediterranean. The Davidsons, longtime friends of my family, walked toward our table. Good. Nancy had made it happen.

I was about to make the introductions when Harriett beat me to it. "I don't think we've had the pleasure."

Addilyn extended her hand. "I'm Addilyn DeRoss."

"Harriette Davidson. We're friends of Lucian's and his late Aunt Taryn's."

"I've heard so many wonderful things about her. She sounded like an amazing woman."

Harriette put her hand to her heart. "Oh, she was. We miss her dearly. She was quite the spitfire, but she loved Lucian more than anything."

She had. If Taryn had even sensed someone was taking advantage of me when I was a child, heaven help them.

"That is so wonderful. My grammie raised me from the time I was about three, and I don't know what I would have done without her. It takes a special person to raise a child they weren't expecting to."

Harriette nodded. "Yes, it does. Bless their souls."

Dr. Martin stepped up to the podium. "My wife, Teresa, and I would like to thank everyone for coming. We're going to start with a fifteen-minute video about how last year's funds were used. After dinner—and, of course, some after-dinner drinks—we'll ask you to open up your checkbooks and get those donations flowing again." Laughter filled the room. "In all seriousness, thank you for all you've done and continue to do. *Bon appétit.*"

The video started and ended rather quickly. Dinner went by in a blur; sitting with the Davidsons had made the time pass almost too quickly. It was the best time I'd had at one of these events for as long as I could remember. It was easy and the conversation was real. When dinner came to an end, Addilyn leaned in to me. "I survived. And I love the Davidsons."

"They loved you, too. Ready for the circus?"

She smiled. "Absolutely!"

CHAPTER 19

Lucian

"I won! I won! I think Remmy will love this." Addilyn held up a stuffed bear she'd won at ring toss.

She was excited at winning a bear for my son. It was hard not to take Addilyn in my arms and kiss her senseless with how much love I felt for her in that moment.

"He will love that. You ready to go?" I asked.

We'd mingled and seen the different acts. I'd dropped off my donation pledge, too. My presence had been noted enough to benefit Black Media, so we were free to leave.

She laced her arm through mine. "Yes, my feet are killing me."

"Well, those heels make your legs look gorgeous."

She laughed, shaking her head.

I nodded toward the side of the room where the Martins stood. "Let's say good-night to our hosts."

"Sounds good."

As we approached Dwayne and Teresa, I noticed an odd look on Teresa's face the moment she looked our way. Not quite startled, not quite confused, but definitely uncomfortable.

"Dr. Martin, Mrs. Martin, lovely event as always. This is my date, Addilyn DeRoss."

I shook hands with Dwayne. Teresa stared at Addilyn, frozen in place. Dwayne narrowed his eyes and then they flared wide as he seemed to realize something. Addilyn was stiff as a board and white as a ghost. There was something wrong here and we needed to leave. "Thanks for the evening."

Teresa's head whipped over to look at me and then back to Addilyn. I took Addilyn's arm, and she jerked before looking at me, barely managing to whisper, "I… uh… Thank you for the event. It was lovely."

What the hell is going on?

I tipped my head toward them before putting my hand back on Addilyn's waist to lead her out. As we waited for our coats, I sent a text to Jim to say we were coming. I needed to know what was going on, but I'd save that until we were in the car. We were waiting for Jim, who was about four cars back, and Addilyn's face was blank. My nerves were on edge, but I said nothing, wondering what had happened.

When I handed her into the car and we were on our way, she dropped her head back against the seat, closed her eyes, and let the first tear fall.

"What's wrong? Sweetheart, what happened?"

She swallowed hard and shook her head. "I can't believe it. I just can't believe it. I hadn't really paid attention to her through the night, just him," she sobbed.

"What, sweetheart?" I began to worry. "For fuck's sake, what's going on?"

"Teresa Martin is my mother! I know it's her. I have one picture that Grammie kept. She threw out all the other ones when my mom abandoned me. She recognized me, too. But she said nothing! She only stared at me. I-I... I didn't really look at her tonight because I was so nervous. Then when we went to say good-bye, something clicked. I don't know how I missed it."

It took me a minute to process this. I knew about her mother and the solitary picture Addilyn had of her, but I'd never seen it. I muttered, "Fuck," holding her close and rubbing my hand up and down her arm. "We'll figure this out."

On another sob, Addilyn said, "She's been in New York all this time, married and wealthy. She left me in Virginia. Do you think she knew where I was?"

The Martins were very wealthy. I gritted my teeth. If Teresa and Dwayne had kept tabs on her, they could have helped Addilyn out of the terrible situation she'd been in with Braden Whitfield as opposed to letting her suffer for a year. *Did they keep tabs on her, though?* Addilyn had no idea who her father was and neither had her grammie. "Stay with me tonight at my house."

Something about the way Dwayne Martin had eyed me at the benefit bothered me. It was the calculated look of someone who had a loose end. I'd have bet money they knew about Addilyn and had kept track of her all along. I needed to go home in case Dr. Martin decided to stop by my place tonight. Kaysen would be blindsided, and Remmy was there. But I didn't want to leave Addilyn alone at her place in case they went to see her. And this wasn't really a time for her to be alone. *Shit, what a mess.*

She shook her head. "Lucian, we can't. We talked about this. I thought we were going to a hotel."

I took her face in my hands. "If it makes you feel better, we can stay in different rooms, but we should be home. If either of them wants to talk, the first place they're going is your apartment or mine. I can't leave Kaysen to deal with that."

"Remmy." She gasped. "I don't want him involved in any of my drama."

"He won't be, but I need to be there." The city lights illuminated Addilyn's face just enough to see her worry her lip. I held her closer. "I promise it will be fine."

"I trust you."

Best fucking words I'd ever heard.

It was nearly midnight by the time we got home. The tension was palpable, and Kaysen set his laptop to the side as we walked in. "Everything okay?"

On the way, I'd asked if Addilyn was comfortable letting Kaysen know what was going on. She had agreed.

Addilyn said, "I'm going to change."

She walked out of the room without saying anything else. We couldn't seem to catch a break lately.

Kaysen asked, "What's going on?"

I loosened my necktie. "Addilyn's mother abandoned her when she was a child. She never knew who her father was. Her grandmother raised her. Tonight, Addilyn found her mother. It's Teresa Martin, Dr. Martin's wife."

"Fuck. You're kidding me. And she had no idea?"

I slipped off my jacket. "None. When I did my background check on Addilyn, there was no data on her mother. Someone paid a lot of money to have her identity erased. To make matters worse, Addilyn had a marriage that ended badly. The guy had another wife and a kid, and it was a really bad scene. The husband had all the money and dragged her through the ringer in the divorce. And since she couldn't afford a decent attorney, Addilyn was her ex's puppet until the judge had no choice but to sign off on the paperwork."

From his shocked reaction, it was clear Wynter had never filled Kaysen in on Addilyn's past. I respected her all the more for having kept Addilyn's trust. "Now imagine Addilyn's surprise when she finds her mother is married to a very wealthy and powerful doctor in New York City. And I'm sure they've kept a close eye on Addilyn all her life. There is no way they allowed this type of situation to go unchecked over the years."

"What a piece of shit," he spat.

"I imagine Dr. Martin is going to show up at her place or mine because he recognized Addilyn, too. It might not be tonight, but I'm certain he's going to reach out. And I don't feel comfortable with Addilyn being there alone right now until we can figure out our next move."

Kaysen dragged a hand through his hair. "I wouldn't either. What are you going to do?"

"See what I need to do to keep the judge off my back if the situation with Crystal goes to court. Addilyn's number one concern is Remmy. And he's mine, as well, but I'm not leaving her out there to fend for herself against those wolves."

"Fuck. Want me to stay over tonight, too?"

"That would be great. I need to go check on Addilyn."

"I'll be out here."

Over this past week, Walt had been reviewing custody cases where there was a girlfriend or boyfriend involved. Recent rulings showed that when there wasn't a string of girlfriends and the relationship was steady, it wasn't a huge issue.

But there were still some risks that neither of us was willing to take.

I checked on Addilyn in the guest bedroom. She was curled up on the bed, still in her dress. "Hey, sweetheart."

"Hey."

It broke my heart to hear her so sad. I got into bed and curled against her back. After a few minutes, she murmured, "It's crazy to think she never thought to reach out to me. After all these years, she never came for me. I wouldn't have wanted her money. I just wanted a mother."

"I know."

"But she let me suffer. She had to know what was going on in my life, right? From the looks on their faces tonight, they're worried about what I'm going to do or say. I wonder why they seemed so surprised. Wasn't my name on the guest list?"

Not much of this made sense. "It was added in the last few days. Maybe they didn't check the revisions. They'd have a team for that. And your name was most likely not on any list that would have alerted anyone to tell them. They may have known we were together or maybe they didn't, but I originally only had one ticket. They probably thought I wasn't bringing you."

At some point, their paths would have crossed. If they were keeping track of her, they had to have known this was coming.

My phone rang, and I gritted my teeth when I saw the name that flashed across the screen. "Let me get this. It's Dr. Martin."

I sat up against the headboard before answering. "Hello?"

"Mr. Black, it's Dwayne Martin. We need to talk. I'm in the lobby."

We were in the dark about their intentions, so it was best to see what we were dealing with. "I'll let them know to buzz you up."

I hung up the phone. "Do you want to come out there?"

Addilyn twisted her fingers. "What do you think?"

"Well, you can listen to the entire conversation. But if it's just me, there's a chance we'll get more information. I'll leave that up to you."

"Let's do that. I'm not ready to face him or my mother."

CHAPTER 20

Addilyn

"**P**ut these in when I head into the living room. You'll be able to hear." Lucian handed me and Kaysen a pair of wireless headphones.

The entire living room was on a surveillance system. This surprised me. A little shocked, I asked, "Does this record everything all the time?"

There were times Lucian and I had done *things* in the living room.

"When I enable it, yes. But that's rare. Typically, it's only on when there's a new nanny we're still getting to know. Nothing is more important than the safety of my son. There is also a camera in his room. My ultimate job as Remmy's parent is to ensure he's safe. With my schedule, people's words aren't enough."

I placed my hand on Lucian's and nodded, feeling better. Lucian was letting me know without words that he hadn't recorded us. This was important, considering Kaysen was standing just a few feet away.

He kissed the top of my forehead. "Let's see what this visit is about."

Lucian was still dressed in his tux pants and shirt, with his sleeves rolled up to his elbows. Out in the living room, I watched as he poured himself a drink and stared at the elevator doors. I could see the whole room from the video feed, and it hit me how the new furniture created a warm, homey feel. This place looked alive with the deep, warm colors. Together we had created a home, and I loved being part of it.

"I misjudged you, and I'm sorry."

I turned around, shocked at Kaysen's words and unsure how to respond.

Kaysen seemed contrite. "I want to apologize for misjudging you. It worried me how fast you came into their lives, but I was wrong. Wynter was right about you; you're good for Lucian."

"Th-thank you. That means a lot."

The opening of the elevator doors brought my attention back to the screen. My palms were sweaty watching Dr. Martin enter with my mother on his arm. They were still in their clothes from the function, as well. It was odd seeing her alive—older but alive. So many times growing up, I'd wondered where she ended up and if she ever thought of me. I knew Grammie had been heartbroken that her daughter left me. Slowly, anger replaced the shock. I was angry with her for abandoning me. So angry. I'd never wanted a dime of her money, but she apparently had resources that could have stopped the insanity with Braden. *What kind of mother would let her child go through that? What kind of mother would leave without a second glance back?*

Lucian nodded. "What do I owe the pleasure at—" He checked his watch. "—one-o'clock in the morning?"

"Addilyn. Where is she?" Teresa asked. The voice was so familiar yet different, more mature, more polished. It brought back clips of memories I had of us together when I was a child. One was of eating an ice cream cone on the steps outside a house. From what I remembered, she had never been mean.

"No."

I jumped a little at Lucian's tone, having been lost in my memories. His answer was brutal and final, and it seemed to echo through the room. Lucian's strength awed me at times. I usually saw the softer side.

He took another drink as if the entire conversation bored him.

Teresa looked at her husband, who spoke next. "That's it? Just no?"

"You asked a question; I answered it."

"Is she here?" Teresa stepped into the living room. "It's imperative we speak with her."

Lucian took a few steps to the new, oversized, brown leather chair and gestured to the couch. "Have a seat."

They exchanged a look before sitting.

"Why are you interested in speaking to Addilyn after all this time? Why now?"

"So she told you." It didn't sound like a question.

They weren't making much progress. Lucian cocked his head. "How long have you known she's been in New York City?"

"What does that have to do with anything?" Dr. Martin snapped back.

Another look was exchanged. They'd known I was here.

Lucian waved off that argument with a gesture of his hand. "It has everything to do with why you're here, and you know it. And I wouldn't say this is the most proper time to call on your daughter after having abandoned her twenty-three years ago."

"Now would not be the best time for the news that I have another child to come to the surface," Teresa answered. "There are situations we are dealing with, and this isn't something we need to come to light."

That was vague. What were they talking about?

Lucian stayed quiet for a moment before responding, "I'll communicate your sentiments to Addilyn. However, I believe she has the same concerns of being linked to you."

Not that I had communicated that, but yes, I wanted nothing to do with the media finding out I was not only dating Lucian Black but also the long-lost, abandoned daughter of Teresa Martin. I shuddered at the thought. Words like *scandal* and *shock* would dominate the headlines.

"If she needs money, we'd be happy to help," Dr. Martin offered.

I gasped. It sounded like they wanted to buy my silence.

"Addilyn manages fine on her own. She doesn't need anyone's money, including mine. And I assure you, she'd rather live on the streets than take a dime from you."

I smiled at that. Supporting myself financially was important to me. Lucian understood me.

They stood, and Dr. Martin turned to Lucian. "Well, I guess there's no reason to continue this. We'll be in touch."

Lucian tipped his glass with an arrogant nod. "I'm sure you will."

They walked to the elevator and left. Lucian punched a code into the keypad to lock the elevator and block any further attempts to reach his apartment.

I walked out into the living room, shaking, and shook my head while Kaysen headed toward his bedroom, giving us some privacy. "So they want to keep me quiet?"

"No, I think there's more."

There's more they want from me? This was giving me a headache. "Why do you think that?"

"Just a feeling I have—intuition, maybe. If Teresa wanted to reconnect with you on a personal basis, she could have chosen a different way to do that. Coming to my home at one in the morning isn't a way to win over the daughter you abandoned. I suspect they wanted to assess our relationship, see if you were more than a random date. Second, I think they were determining how money hungry you were. And third, they're probably trying to get a sense of whether they'd be up against me in this fight, too."

Braden had been this kind of manipulative, but I'd never understood it. "And what do you think they assessed?"

"Well, I'm certain they're fully aware that I'm committed. So, they know if they fuck with you, they fuck with me. I don't think that's something either of them wants."

Whoa. I was speechless at his possessive tone. "Oh."

"Yeah, sweetheart."

My head was reeling. "So what do we do? What do they want from me?"

"We'll try to figure out what their intentions are."

I shivered. "I wish I knew. I googled them earlier while you were talking to Kaysen. They have two kids together. Boys. I wonder if my half brothers know about me." My entire life, I've wondered what it would be like to have a sibling. All along, I'd had them. One was eighteen years old and the other was sixteen. I was eight years older than my oldest brother.

"I don't know. If they start coming around, we'll have our answer. I doubt they will, but I may be wrong."

I leaned my head on his shoulder. "It's weird knowing I have a family, but they're complete strangers. For so long, I thought I only had Grammie. I wrote off my mom long ago. But when I dared to think about her, I always imagined her as a type of gypsy—someone with no stability. Never a socialite with another life, another family."

It hurt deeply.

Braden had had another secret life.

My mother had had one, as well.

If I hadn't been involved with Lucian, would they have come looking for me? I doubted it. Deep down, I knew it was only a matter of time before they reached out now that their secret was out. Lucian was right; they wanted something from me.

CHAPTER
21

Addilyn

"My lips are tingly," I said with a giggle. I was feeling warm and fuzzy from the vodka and cranberry juice. Tonight, Wynter and I were having a desperately needed girls' night.

Wynter laughed. "Mine, too."

We'd decided on a girls' night in at my place filled with laughter and, of course, alcohol. Lucian and Remmy were having a boys' night. After I'd told Wynter about my mom, she decided we needed drinks.

Lucian sent me a text.

Lucian: *Having fun?*

Me: *The bestest. My lips are tingly.*

Lucian: *When is she leaving?*

Me: *You coming over after?*

Lucian: *Without a doubt.*

Me: *I'll let you know.*

Lucian: *Perfect. Make sure you have on your purple fuzzy slippers.*

Me: *Already on.*

Lucian: *Tell her to hurry. The nanny's here to watch Remmy.*

I looked over at Wynter. "Lucian wants to know when you're leaving?" I laughed.

She took another drink. "That man has it bad." She looked at the clock. "I bet he's put Remmy to bed and now little Lucian wants to play."

"*Little* Lucian?" That made me giggle more. "How about your guy?"

She picked up her phone and sent a text. It vibrated with a response almost immediately. "Oh yeah, Vlad the Impaler wants to play."

"Vlad the Impaler?"

She shook her head. "His idea. I was thinking something like Princesa Isabel."

We were in a state of hysterics. "You wanted to name his penis Princesa Isabel? Why?"

"I saw it on *How to Lose a Guy in 10 Days* and thought it was funny. However, Kaysen did not play along like Matthew McConaughey did in the movie. So, we went with Thor."

I laughed. "How long have you guys been sleeping together?"

"Four years."

I gasped. "Wow. Four years. How did I not know this?"

"I'm good. It's unattached, exclusive sex. And he's definitely not in the right head space to have a relationship in the foreseeable future. So, yeah, it works."

Four years. That seemed more serious than I'd thought. "Do I know him?"

Wynter winked. "Maybe. Maybe not."

Now I was fascinated and intrigued. Four years. It would be hard not to have feelings after being together that long. "Aren't you afraid about one of you falling in love and not the other?"

"We've got more combined baggage than an airline. It's why the arrangement is so perfect. We're exclusive. And when one of us needs to bump uglies, we do."

Maybe it was my drunken state, but it sounded like that would work. "It seems so simple."

"It is. But we keep it on the down low so people won't try to make more of it than it is. Having people try to make it into a happily ever after isn't what we want. So, yeah."

There was a knock on my door. Wynter looked at me. "You expecting someone?"

"No."

I made my way to the door a little haphazardly and peered through the peephole. I gasped and whispered, "It's my egg donor."

"What the fuck?" Wynter whispered back.

There was another knock, and this time she called through the door, "Addilyn, please. I'd like to talk to you."

I walked back to my couch, the buzz from the alcohol starting to wear off. Wynter looked at me. "What are you going to do?"

"Ignore her. She had nothing to do with me all those years, and now I want nothing to do with her. And it's weird how she shows up less than two hours after I got home today."

No, I wasn't going to answer the door.

We heard another soft knock at the door. "Addilyn, please. I'd really like to talk—just me and you."

Wynter stood and put her phone away, looking completely sober. "I'll get her gone."

I flicked my wrist her way. "Have at it."

Wynter swung open the door, her hands on her hips. "You're a bitch."

My mother looked taken aback at Wynter. "Excuse me?"

"You heard me. You abandoned your daughter, leaving her to be raised by your mother. Then things got bad, but you were too busy playing socialite wife of the year to bother with your firstborn. So, you can turn your skinny ass around and march out the door you came through."

Wynter slammed the door in her face, turned the lock, and marched back. "After seeing her, I'm even more pissed."

I leaned my head on her shoulder. "Thanks for being such a good friend."

"Any time." Then she laughed. "Did you see her face?"

"She was not expecting the gale storm of Wynter Sykes."

"Damn straight she wasn't, and she'll get a boot in the ass if she comes back. What a bitch."

Just thinking about her leaving me twenty-three years ago and never reaching out again made my chest ache. Grammie had never healed from the betrayal, either. "I can't imagine how a mother could do that. And you know the crazy part? I only have good memories. I don't remember her being mean, being angry, or abusive. I remember laughing and loving her. It's odd."

"Yeah, for sure. I agree with what Lucian said... something is weird."

There was another knock on the door, and I froze.

Wynter stood to answer it. "Don't worry. It's Lucian. I texted him in case she came back."

That was smart. She opened the door, and he was immediately at my side. "Jim will take you wherever you need to go, Wynter. Thank you."

"Thanks." She hugged me, whispering, "You are so much stronger than you give yourself credit for. Don't ever forget that."

"I hope so."

The door closed behind her, and I was relieved to have Lucian there. It scared me how much I wanted him with me.

"You okay?"

"Yeah. She just took me by surprise."

"We're going to sort this out."

And just his presence helped ease my nerves. I knew we would find out the answers.

CHAPTER 22

Lucian

After brewing coffee, I sat at the dining room table trying to come up with a solution to keep Addilyn safe and not cause issues with the court. Teresa showing up at Addilyn's place so soon after she arrived meant someone might be watching her.

What the fuck are they up to?

I wondered what my investigation into the Martins would pull up. Keeping Addilyn a secret all these years made little sense. Why not have her part of their lives?

Kaysen walked out with his bag, wearing running clothes. "I'm heading out." He stopped and asked, "Did they ever find how Crystal got in?"

"I found out yesterday. I meant to tell you and Addilyn. We found footage of her in the service area. She used someone's keycard. It appears she charmed her way into it. The guy's been fired, and there's an additional layer of verification added to get to my floor. Fucker."

With everything we had in place, Crystal was smart enough to figure out the weakest point. It was how she'd snuck her boyfriends up here and remained undetected for quite some time. Pissed me off that I'd missed it. I was typically a very thorough man.

"Shit. I'm glad you were able to figure it out."

"Me, too. Thanks for everything last night."

"Of course. Let me know if you need anything else."

Kaysen left and I took another sip of my coffee, still not any surer how I should handle it. An alert vibrated my phone. *Remmy's door open.*

Last night, I'd brought Addilyn back to my place since it was more secure. Kaysen had stayed the night as well. Since I'd slept with Addilyn in the guest room, I wanted to make sure I knew when Remmy got up so he wouldn't see us in the same bed together.

A few minutes later, Remmy walked, rubbing his eyes. He had the stuffed animal Addilyn had won for him at the charity circus.

"Do you like your bear? Addilyn won that for you."

Remmy squeezed it tighter. "Yes. Where Addawin?"

"She's asleep in the guest room, and we are not waking her up." I raised my eyebrow.

Remmy jutted out his lip in the most adorable way. "I want Addawin to live here with us."

Me, too. "Maybe someday, buddy."

"Why not now?"

I loved how much my son loved her, but it scared me shitless at the same time. "Well, we're not married, so Addilyn has her own place."

I got out the bowl and cereal for his breakfast before turning back to Remmy. His brow was furrowed. "Then marry her, Daddy. Then she can be here all the time."

That was the plan at some point, but neither of us was ready… yet. "Patience, Remmy. Things like that require patience."

After a second, Remmy said, "Mommy never nice like Addawin." He crawled into my lap at the table, ignoring his cereal for a minute. "Where mommy go?"

I kissed the top of his head. "She's sick, so the doctors are seeing if they can make her better. But you get to stay with me."

"After medicine, will she be nice like Addawin?" That broke my heart. Addilyn was more of a mother to my son than his biological mother had ever been. It had to be confusing for him why a woman who was not his mother showed him more love. "I hope so, Remmy."

He turned his face up to me. "If you marry Addawin, will she be my new mommy?"

"Your mom will always be your mom, buddy, but you can love Addilyn, too. There is enough room in your heart to love as many people as you want."

Remmy thought about that for a second. "Do I hafta see Mommy again?"

"I'm trying to make it so you only have to see her if you want to."

Remmy furiously shook his head. "I don't wanna see her. Never, ever. She mean to me, Daddy."

Damn Crystal for all she's done. At least I had full custody for the time being, and Remmy was safe. The judge wasn't going to rule on permanent custody until a thirty-day evaluation on Crystal had been completed.

At this point, it felt promising that the judge would sign off in my favor.

Knowing that some other prick was Remmy's actual father was never far from my mind. There was only so much this little boy could take.

He was mine.

Mine.

And I would do whatever it took to keep him.

"Why don't we make breakfast for Addilyn?"

Remmy jumped off my lap and ran to the kitchen, his cereal forgotten. "Pancakes! I wanna make pancakes."

I took the last pancake off the griddle as Remmy finished his after deciding against the cereal. "Now, we wake Addawin up?"

"Let's get her plate fixed, and we'll bring her breakfast in bed."

Remmy added the syrup, drowning the poor pancake. "Addawin wuvs syrup. She told me so."

Once we had her plate ready, Remmy ran to the door and threw it open. "Addawin! Addawin! Wake up! We made pancakes."

Addilyn stretched and sat up. "Oh my. You made me breakfast in bed? You are the sweetest boy ever."

I put the tray on her lap and Remmy sat next to her, still holding his bear. Addilyn took a bite and started making noises of appreciation. "Oh my, these are the most delicious pancakes I have ever tasted in my entire life. Remmy, did you make these?"

Remmy beamed. "I helped Daddy. I stirred like you showed me."

Addilyn took another bite. "Well, these are the best. And I love breakfast in bed. Thank you so much. Did you decide on a name for your bear?"

"Mister Teddy."

"Oh, I love that name. It's perfect."

I leaned against the dresser and watched them together, more determined than ever to make scenes like this our norm and not the exception.

CHAPTER 23

Lucian

"Sir, here are the latest numbers from Kaysen."

I perused the report; the usage numbers were impressive. As I grabbed a highlighter from the drawer, I caught sight of the picture of Addilyn feeding Ellie the goat on my desk. That had been our first date.

I loved her.

And I continued to fall more in love with her every day.

Throughout the week, she'd stayed with Wynter, and I was growing tired of not being with her to make sure she was okay. I hoped she liked the suggestion I planned to present to her today.

Kaysen came into my office and dropped into a chair. "Have you seen the latest numbers?"

"They're impressive. I think you can officially say you have a success on your hands. Congrats."

"Thanks. With these number, we'll beat the full-year projections in the first quarter alone."

This was Kaysen's first venture into apps. But apps were the way of the future, and he knew this. His primary business structure was security programs for banks and medical facilities like hospitals, clinics, medical practices and groups. It was always smart to diversify. I leaned back in my chair, needing a break from the project to expand the company I was working on. "What's next to keep the momentum?"

"Wynter and I brainstormed some other app ideas. We're in the beginning phases. I'm in talks with Ria to handle this next rollout, too. I think her company is a good fit."

"That's wise and I agree. Are you going to use Black Media again for distribution?" If the projections became reality, Black Media stood to make a pretty profit by simply providing the platform.

"Yes, I've decided to stay focused. It'll be more profitable for both parties."

"Agreed."

Nancy's voice came over the intercom. "Mr. Black, your next appointment is in conference room four in ten minutes."

"Thanks, Nancy."

Today Kaysen, Wynter, and I were meeting with Ria and Addilyn to go over the initial impressions from the marketing campaign.

I hung up and gathered up the reports. Kaysen said, "So, seems like things are going well with Addilyn. Your picture has been splashed all over the paper more often. From the headlines, it seems like they're trying to cause trouble again."

Fucking vultures. Crystal had been moved to a psych ward for evaluation, and suddenly my life had been getting more attention the last few days.

"Ex-wife Committed so New Girlfriend Can Take Over."

I gritted my teeth at the latest headline. Addilyn had been shocked and then mortified yesterday morning when she saw it. It had scared me shitless she might be too worried to move forward with our relationship. But Addilyn had surprised me, as usual. She was strong and determined not to let the sharks interfere with our lives.

"Yeah, I'm not sure how it got out that Crystal was being evaluated. Nevertheless, it's out, so we're managing. But overall, things are going well. The Martins have thankfully stayed away since Teresa paid Addilyn that surprise visit."

Kaysen shook his head. "Bastards. I got an invite to another one of their charity events. Wynter was ready to respond with the word *no* carved into it with a knife."

"You've got your hands full."

"Tell me about it." Kaysen dragged his hand through his hair, and I sensed there was more to that statement than he would admit. "Let's go to this meeting, and then I'm ducking out early for the weekend."

We walked into the conference room, and there she was, beautiful as ever. She stood, exchanging pleasantries. The first thing I noticed was her dress—it wrapped around her like a robe and was fastened with a belt. My dick hardened instantly at the reminder of our first time together and how I'd dared her to wear her robe to my office. After this meeting, I planned to follow through.

Yes, Ms. DeRoss, we'll be having a private meeting after this.

"Thanks for meeting with us."

Ria sat at Addilyn's side. Wynter was there, too.

Addilyn leaned forward and began the meeting, addressing Kaysen directly. "I'd like to discuss with your team about stepping down from this account and handing it off to Ria."

"What?" Kaysen asked, clearly perplexed. Wynter's eyes widened in surprise, mimicking my reaction. I hadn't known about this either. My first instinct was to ask what was going on. But there was a reason Addilyn hadn't mentioned it to me beforehand, so I remained quiet.

Kaysen asked, "Why would you want to step down?"

"I'd like to speak frankly, if that's okay."

"Of course," Kaysen responded.

"My dating Lucian is causing negative press for the company and for the app. Your competitors are using it to their advantage, and I can't be the cause of that."

I had seen the report this morning, and she was right.

"This will blow over. The numbers still look good," Kaysen argued.

"Yes, it will blow over. But it shouldn't be at the expense of your app. This is my decision. Ria wanted me to stay on the account. However, we know your PR teams would agree with me. It doesn't mean I won't have any involvement, but it will be behind the scenes from now on. I'm going to be working from home for the foreseeable future. It will give the media the impression that I've quit, and they will assume they've won. And I'll still be working and assisting in other ways that can be beneficial to both companies. But I need to take a step back."

I gritted me teeth but kept quiet. Stepping in at that point would only undermine her authority and her decision.

Ria took up where Addilyn left off. "Addilyn will still be an employee. I want to assure you that this is her idea and not mine. I say fuck the media, but we need to respect Addilyn's opinion. We've discussed this at length."

Addilyn added, "This is my decision. Completely."

Kaysen nodded. "I respect your decision, but this was not and never will be an expectation."

"I know. And I appreciate that more than you'll ever know."

He sighed. "If this is what you want, I'll support you."

He looked to me and Wynter. I nodded, and Wynter responded, "If this is what you really want, I'll support you. But I don't want you doing this because you feel you have to."

"I promise that's not the case."

"Then it's settled," I said. I wasn't okay with it, but whatever I had to say to Addilyn was personal and not for the rest of the group.

I saw the tension leave Addilyn's shoulders. "Good. Then let's go over the latest reports." Addilyn launched into the meeting. "The numbers out of the gate are encouraging. It appears most users range from ages twenty-four to thirty-five, which is great since those are the segments we intended to target to begin with. Based on the feedback from users over forty, they want an intellectual platform to pose topics—more like a discussion board. My suggestion would be to poll topics and put questions up for discussion. That creates user engagement and would help with expanding the target audience."

"I like that idea," Kaysen said.

"That would be easy to implement. Make basic respect rules and allow users to report violations of those rules," Wynter added.

"Yes, so far the report functions seem to be working well. Those who have arranged dates have mentioned in the initial reports they are nervous about their first dates. I would suggest having a tips screen for conversation starters and the like. If you like the concept, Ria will submit the pitches from marketing we created."

"I like them all." Kaysen looked at Ria. "Get with Wynter, and we'll work on the rollout schedule to coordinate."

Within minutes, the meeting came to a close. Addilyn grabbed her things while Ria and Wynter arranged the next meeting.

I stood at the door, waiting for Addilyn, and Wynter stopped as she was leaving. "I hope you realize what an incredible woman she is."

"I do. More so every moment she's in my life."

"Good. Because what you saw right there was nothing but selfless. She's walking away for the sake of everyone else in that room."

Yes, and it pissed me off that Addilyn had been forced into that decision. My shit wasn't supposed to affect her life. I turned my attention back to Addilyn, who was speaking with Ria. "I'll be back to the office in a bit to pack up my stuff."

"Okay." She hugged Addilyn. "I'll see you soon."

Ria paused at the door. "She assured me you had nothing to do with this."

"I just found out myself. If I'd known I would have tried to talk her out of it."

Ria gave me a wink. "I like you, Lucian. And you better keep taking care of our girl."

"The feeling is mutual, Ria. And I plan to."

At the end of the day, we each had Addilyn's best interests at heart. There was a room full of people willing to ride out the storm with her. Yet Addilyn had sacrificed herself for the good of others. Unbelievable how I had ended up with such an amazing woman.

Finally, it was only Addilyn and me. "I'd like to talk to you in my office."

"I figured you might." She winked. There was no sadness or regret in her eyes, which helped.

After I closed the door to the office, I turned to her. "What happened?"

"The media is everywhere, including in front of my office. You and I both know they're getting worse. And the battle with Crystal is just beginning."

I rubbed my forehead. "You are not supposed to pay the price for my sins."

"I'm not losing anything, Lucian. I still have my job. I still have my paycheck. I've just eliminated the stress."

"Fuck." I ran my fingers through my hair. "I hate that you have to do this."

She wrapped her arms around my waist. "I was upset when I first saw the headlines the day before yesterday. I still don't like it. But it's like what you said before... take the power away. I'm taking the power back for my life."

It was true. She was brilliant.

Fiercely, I kissed her. "You are unlike anyone I have ever known."

"Good."

"Do you realize what you're wearing today?" I saw the glint in her eyes. She'd done it on purpose to make me think about the robe.

I locked the door.

Addilyn took a few steps back to lean against the small conference table in my office. She loosened the tie around her waist. "Don't you have another meeting?"

I stalked toward her. "I think one just popped up on my calendar."

"Oh yeah? What's it about?"

"Acquisitions," I growled.

Slowly she unfastened the single button on the side that kept her dress together. A little of her lacy, red bra showed.

Coquettishly, she asked, "And what is Black Media acquiring?"

"This is a sole venture." My fingers traced down her cleavage, causing the dress to fall open. "Black Media has nothing to do with this. What I'm acquiring I don't plan on sharing." Addilyn shivered. "Drop your dress."

Addilyn stood and let the dress fall to the floor. She stood before me in nothing but lacy, red lingerie and black heels that emphasized her legs. I touched her panties and rubbed her clit. She gasped.

"It's time to finalize this deal, sweetheart."

CHAPTER
24 ♥

Addilyn

"Do you need this?" Lucian dangled my dress off one finger while he watched me in the mirror of the bathroom that connected to his office.

I turned around in my bra and panties. Lucian's eyes roamed my body; the appreciation in them was obvious. With a confident stride, I swung my hips as I walked to him. "That might be helpful unless you plan to keep me here as your sex slave."

With his free hand, he trailed his finger along the top edge of my panties, causing my stomach to quiver. "I think that could be arranged."

His hand dipped in a little more, and then it was gone. I closed my eyes and felt his lips on the swell of my breasts. Then that touch was gone, too. "Your dress, Ms. DeRoss."

"Why thank you, Mr. Black."

Lucian kept his stare trained on me while I dressed. "Are you coming over tonight? I have something I want to show you."

"Yes, I'll be there." I'd been staying at Wynter's house, which I knew he hated. We also knew the few times I had stayed the night at his apartment had to be the exceptions. "I'll see you later."

He kissed me good-bye. "Bye, sweetheart."

I returned to my office. The media was waiting for me. They threw out many questions, which I ignored.

Ria was in my office, holding two glasses filled with wine. "I figured you could use this. Screw the office policies." She tapped her wineglass against mine. "Let's have a drink on your fake last day."

Swirling the glass, I smiled to myself as I recognized the smell of the cabernet. Lucian had taught me well. "To fake last days." I toasted and took a sip. "Thank you for working with me, Ria."

"You're a damn good associate. I don't want to lose you, but I see the writing on the wall, so I'll take what I can get."

"Writing on the wall?"

Ria raised an eyebrow. "That man will propose at some point because he's so head over heels. But I have to give him props for letting you do your thing today. He supported you even in a blindside."

He had, which meant a lot. "If I'd told him, he would have tried to change my mind."

"Because he cares. I like Lucian Black."

I smiled into my glass. It was a little bittersweet. and I wondered if I would ever return here to the office. *Is there writing on the wall?* I wasn't sure.

I didn't have much to pack. When five o'clock arrived, I knew it was time. I had my box ready to face the piranhas. I'd pay the money for a cab on my fake last day. Having them chase me through the subway while holding a box sounded like anything but a good time.

As we came down the escalator, Lucian walked in. I hurried to him. "What are you doing here?"

"Facing this with you. I've caused this. I'm not letting you do this alone."

If that wasn't a sign of love, I wasn't sure what was. He loved me. Lucian Black loved me.

Ria hugged me. "I'll see you soon."

"For sure."

Lucian took my box and my hand. "You ready for this?"

I took a deep breath and walked out of the building with Lucian standing beside me, supporting me in every way he could. Outside, it felt like the photographers had multiplied upon Lucian's arrival. Cameras flashed, and people yelled.

"Addilyn! Addilyn! Were you fired?"

I had gotten used to walking by them, but this time we stopped to address them directly. Lucian looked to me, and I answered, "No, I wasn't fired. I have decided your presence is too disruptive, so I've taken another opportunity."

The crowd erupted in questions I couldn't understand. Jim and a couple of security guys were able to clear us a pathway into the car. Before we got into the car, Lucian turned to face the crowd. "There's no story here, guys. Addilyn and I met after my divorce. Last time you did this, most of you ended up having to print a retraction. Do you really want to have to print another? I doubt two retractions in such a short amount of time would be good for your career. Have a good day."

Lucian got into the car. In just a few seconds, we were pulling away from the curb. I leaned back in the seat. "I'm glad that is over. Thank you for coming."

"I will always support you. Always."

"After today, I know that. I'm sorry I didn't tell you before I did it, but I needed to make this decision on my own."

Lucian kissed my hand. "There's nothing to be sorry about. I get it."

The drive to Lucian's place was relatively short. But when we got into the elevator, Lucian hit the number of the floor below his massive penthouse.

"Where are we going?" I asked.

"Indulge me."

"Okay."

We rode up to the floor, and when the doors opened, we stepped into a moderately furnished apartment that felt sterile. *What is this place?* I looked at Lucian, who took a deep breath. "Will you hear me out?"

I knew where this was going, and I wasn't sure how I felt. Cautiously, I responded, "I'll hear you out."

"We both agree that staying overnight at my place isn't a good idea, given the situation."

Slowly, I said, "Yes."

Lucian was building his case, which meant he'd put a lot of thought into it to make sure I said yes.

"And you also know I worry about you being at your apartment by yourself considering we still don't understand what the Martins want, which has resulted in you staying at Wynter's. I know Wynter doesn't mind, but you said you feel like you're cramping her style."

Oh, it was starting to make sense. "What are you asking me?"

"Move in here for the time being. If we have a custody battle with Crystal, we are not cohabitating, and it keeps you safe. I want you to keep your apartment—I know you need the independence—but just stay here. You can use my office to work."

This place had to cost a fortune. "Are you renting this out?"

"No, I own the building. It needs a remodel, and I've been thinking about expanding my place to take up both floors. So, it's been vacant for about two weeks and will stay that way until I decide what to do with it."

It made sense, and there wasn't any additional cost Lucian wasn't already spending. "Yes, I'll do it for the time being."

"That easy?" He smirked. "I thought for sure I was going to have to work for days to convince you."

I gave him a kiss. "I like to keep you on your toes, but yes, I will stay. You've supported me through all this, I want to support you, too. When do I move in?"

"Tonight."

CHAPTER 25

Lucian

"Walt, what's going on?"

I was on my office line. It was early—not even six in the morning on Saturday. Addilyn was in her new place, which made me sleep a hell of a lot easier. Remmy was in his bed. But I knew whatever my lawyer had to tell wasn't good news. No one called at six on a Saturday morning with good news.

"Crystal committed suicide."

Did I hear that right?

I sat down on my couch, shocked. "What? Crystal?"

Walt cleared his throat. "Yes, they found Crystal in her room. She had hung herself with her sheets."

I leaned back in my chair. I didn't know what to think. "What are they saying? Was she not on suicide watch?"

"Not much. She didn't leave a note. Police have ruled it as a suicide. Of course, now full custody reverts to you."

I sagged with relief. It was over. I'd hoped Crystal would get the help she needed. But suicide? That wasn't something I'd even considered. In the end, the best solution would have been for her to get better and be a mother to our son. *Remmy.* I shook my head. This was one more thing he would have to deal with. At some point, it would have consequences for Remmy. *Fuck.* "Thanks for the phone call. Let the hospital know I'll pay for the funeral and all the other expenses. Crystal's parents are gone. She didn't have any siblings, just some extended family we hadn't seen in years."

"You're a good man, Lucian. Want my office to handle it?"

"That would be appreciated."

We hung up the phone. I wasn't sure what to think. Relief I wouldn't have to worry about Remmy's custody. The funeral. *Fuck.* How would he take that?

She'd been sick, and I'd hoped she would get help. I knew what it was like to grow up without a mother, and I never wanted that for my son.

Addilyn stood in the doorway and yawned. She had access to my place from hers with a code, but I hadn't heard the elevator. "Is everything okay?"

"Crystal committed suicide." The words sounded foreign, wrong.

She crawled into my lap. "I'm so sorry. I know you wanted her to be there for Remmy once she got help."

Without me having to say a word, she got me. I wrapped my arms around her. "What can I do to help you, Lucian?"

"Just let me hold you. I don't know how the fuck I'm going to tell Remmy."

There was so much to process and still so many unknowns—like Remmy's biological father. Addilyn snuggled closer, and it was like everything fell into place. "Tell him she was sick and now she will sleep with the angels. She wanted to get better for him, but her body was just too weak. And that when he sees her in heaven, she'll be the mom he remembered and loved."

"Thank you."

"There's no reason for his memories to be any more tainted than they have to be. She's gone, Lucian. Let the good part of her live on in Remmy."

I kissed the top of her head, and she said, "I love you."

"I love you, too."

We held each other for a while. Soon Addilyn's breathing was even and I knew she was asleep. I sat on the couch, holding her, thankful I had my son and this woman.

She was the missing piece I had been waiting for my entire life.

"So… Mommy in there?"

"Yes, she is."

I had brought Remmy to the funeral home a few hours before the funeral. After a lot of thought, I decided Remmy would not attend the actual funeral. One, there was the press. They had been like maggots on shit. And two, I wasn't sure if some of Crystal's friends were going to be able to control themselves. If they came up to me, spouting obscenities about my cutting Crystal off, it wouldn't be good for Remmy to be present. Walt had done well with the funeral arrangements. Everything was nice but not extravagant.

Out of respect for Crystal, Addilyn had stayed home. She was going to hang out with Remmy while I attended the actual funeral and made a statement as to why Remmy wasn't there.

Remmy let out a big sigh. "Why the doctor not make her better?"

"Sometimes people are too sick, and the doctors don't have the right medicine."

He thought about that for a moment. "Will you get sick and die, too? I don't wanna lose my daddy."

This was breaking my fucking heart. "I'm not that kind of sick, buddy. You'll understand when you get a little older."

Remmy's mouth turned down. "My mommy really loved me?"

"Yes, she did. She was sick and didn't know how to get better."

Scrambling on my lap, Remmy cried into my chest. I felt completely helpless.

"I don't wanna lose you, Daddy. Don't die. Pwease don't die."

"I'm right here, Remmy, and I'm not going anywhere. I promise."

The sniffles were tough to handle, but I held my son and looked at the casket. Crystal and I might have never been in love, but she had given me Remmy. Setting aside all the shit we'd had between us, at least I had Remmy. He was what I lived for every day of my life.

CHAPTER
26 ♥

Addilyn

"A ddawin! Wake up."

I woke from my nap on the couch to a little boy poking my shoulder. It had been two days since Crystal's funeral, and my heart ached for Remmy. He was scared Lucian was going to get sick like his mommy. Then he was afraid I would get sick. The therapist had said we just needed to give him love and constant reassurance. There wasn't much else to do. I pulled him close and kissed the top of his head. "I'm awake."

He hugged my neck. "Will you hum to me and Mister Teddy tonight before you leave?"

Remmy gave me puppy dog eyes, so I gave him another hug. Since I'd given him the bear from the charity auction, he carried it around almost all the time. "Of course I will." The scents of garlic and oregano filled the air. Suddenly, I was ravenous. "Did you cook with your daddy?"

"Yeah, we made you sgabetti."

I stretched. "Yum, I'm starving."

"Come see."

Remmy grabbed me by the hand and dragged me to the kitchen. Lucian turned our way. There was something innately sexy about him standing barefoot in the kitchen, wearing jeans and a T-shirt. "Hey, sleepyhead. You hungry?"

"Yeah."

Lucian frowned at me. "You still feeling bad?"

For the last few days, I hadn't been feeling the best. It was like I had a lingering cold. "Meh."

"I think you need to go to the doctor. With Thanksgiving next week, you don't want to be sick."

Remmy pulled my arm to get my attention, then motioned for me to pick him up. He sat on my lap and played with my hair. "I'll make an appointment tomorrow with the doctor."

When he heard the word doctor, he stiffened. "Wait, you sick? Are you gonna die?"

I sat him on the island and turned him to face me. Lucian came to stand by my side. Remmy started bawling, and I placed my palms against his cheeks. "Look at me, Remmy."

He looked at me, his eyes swimming with tears.

"I'm not that kind of sick. I have a cold."

"Do you remember when your throat hurt real bad and we had to go to the doctor?" Lucian asked while I continued to rub Remmy's back.

He nodded. "She that kinda sick?"

"Yes," we said in unison.

"The doctor is going to give me medicine. I'll be fine."

Remmy grabbed my cheeks like I had his. "Pwomise?"

"I promise."

He threw his arms around my neck, and I sighed in relief. Lucian patted his back and his eyes met mine. This was tough.

I held Remmy tight and worked on changing the subject. "Are you excited about putting up the tree next week?"

"Yeah," he said with a hiccup.

I started rocking him side to side. "What are you asking Santa for this year?"

Remmy looked at me. "A f-f-fort."

"Oh, that sounds like so much fun. We can play cars in the fort. And read books in the fort."

I could tell he still was worried. "Remmy, do I look like I'm sick?"

"No."

"Then you don't have to worry, okay?"

"Okay." He held out his hands to Lucian, who held him tight and closed his eyes. This entire situation had been so hard, but things were calming down. Remmy asked to sit back on my lap. "What do you want, Addawin? From Santa?"

"Hmmm... I'll have to think about that."

Lucian set out three plates of spaghetti. Remmy sat to my left and Lucian to my right—just like every night. Lucian put his hand on my thigh and gave it two squeezes. We were going to make it through this.

CHAPTER 27

Addilyn

"You're pregnant."

The doctor looked up from my chart. It was like he was speaking another language. No way he said what I thought he said. My ears must have been clogged or something.

I shook my head in disbelief. "Wait… what? Can you repeat that?"

He set aside his clipboard. "Ms. DeRoss, you are pregnant. Your bloodwork came back positive."

I let out a nervous giggle. He had to have the wrong person. It was the wrong chart. Something. No way was I pregnant. "That's not possible."

"Have you been sexually active?" His brows creased in confusion, and he checked his clipboard again.

What kind of question is that? My mouth grew dry. "I… uh… yes?"

"Then it's possible, Ms. DeRoss."

But I was on birth control. And we used condoms every time. *Didn't we?*

From that point forward, I was on autopilot. Pregnant. I was pregnant. The doctor gave me prenatal vitamins as well as a slew of other information I only half heard, but my purse was overflowing with pamphlets to read later. I felt like I was in a tunnel with a thick fog surrounding me. I tucked the vitamins into my purse and hailed a cab.

Where am I going to go?

Thank goodness the media wasn't around. A movie star had fallen off the wagon with some hooker, and that was the media's focus. I hated it for the guy but was glad they were leaving me alone.

"Where to, lady?"

I spurted out an address and sat back, trying to process the news.

I'm pregnant.

A baby.

I am pregnant with Lucian's child.

When the cab came to a stop, I paid, took the elevator to the sixth floor, and banged on the door. "Wynter, it's me. Please. It's urgent."

There was a noise behind the door before it cracked open. "Addilyn, now's not—oh my, what's wrong?"

I started crying. "I'm pregnant. And I'm not supposed to be. And… I don't know what to do."

"Oh, fuck. Come on in."

As I walked, Kaysen came out of the bedroom, half-dressed, and my eyes bulged out of my head. He stopped midstride when he saw me.

Wynter walked over to him. "Nice meeting and strategizing. It was invigorating to see what you have in mind. Gotta spend time with my girl now. Chat later about the new coding."

Kaysen said not a word as Wynter basically pushed him out the door. When she turned around, I pointed to his shoes. Wynter picked them up and opened the door, where Kaysen was holding up his fist, preparing to knock. "Here are your shoes. Anything else I'll bring to the office. And if you tell Lucian Addilyn's here, imagine a cigar cutter heading toward Thor. I'll make sure she gets safely to Lucian, and I will know if you snitch. Remember—snitches get stitches. Thanks again for the creative session."

The door closed, and she pointed at me. "Not a word."

What just happened?

Cigar Cutter?

Thor?

Wynter was crazy. I pressed my lips together. "But *your* drama would take my mind off of *my* drama."

She held up her hands. "Okay, fine. I'm fucking my boss. I have been for four years. Happy?"

"So, he's nipple man?" I giggled.

Wynter started laughing. "Oh yeah, he is. That's why I got them pierced."

Whoa. The conversation turned TMI on a dime.

"You guys hide it so well." After all the time I'd spent with them, I never picked up on anything sexual between them. "You aren't afraid it will complicate work?"

"Nope. Neither of us wants a relationship. We've managed it for four years. No one knows or suspects—that I know of. Lucian might because he's Lucian, but he keeps his thoughts to himself."

"I won't say a word." I shook my head. "Well, that definitely made me forget my issue."

Wynter sat beside me. "Does Lucian know?"

I gasped. "No."

"Umm, sweetie, he's the father. He kind of needs to know." She patted my leg, comforting me.

I put my head in my hands. "I know. How did this happen? I'm on birth control. We used condoms. Can we get more tests and make sure the doctor wasn't wrong?"

Wynter stood. "Of course. Be right back."

I was still on the couch when Wynter came back from the pharmacy with a bagful of tests. "Drink up." She tossed me a huge bottle of water. "We'll verify the doctor's findings."

About twenty minutes later, I finished the bottle and Wynter lined up the tests on the counter for me. "Pee on this part and put them on the plastic over here. I'll be outside, ready to start the timer. You're not alone in this, okay?"

I nodded. After the door closed, I peed on the fifteen sticks she'd laid out, then came out to the living room and watched the timer count down. It went off and I stayed put. "I'm not pregnant."

Wynter looked around. "Uhh… are you The Flash, who can zoom in there to check the tests and come back here without me noticing?"

I chuckled. "No."

"At any time over the last six weeks, did Lucian stuff your muffin?"

I giggled. "Yes." It was time to find out. "Go check. Just tell me what it says."

"You sure you don't want to?"

My legs weren't moving. "I'm sure."

Wynter returned from the bathroom in no time. "It's conclusive… all fifteen tests. You, my friend, are preggers. It seems Lucian filled your muffin when he stuffed it."

I threw a pillow at her, thankful for the comic relief. "You're crazy."

"And I'm going to be an aunt! Oh, I will love this baby so much."

A baby. I touched my stomach. "I can do this."

Wynter held my hand. "Of course you can. You're going to be an amazing mother."

It still didn't feel real. "Do you think I should do more tests to make sure?"

"If you want me to go get more, I will."

That was stupid. I dropped my head in my hands again. "How am I going to tell Lucian? How will he take it?"

She sat back on her heels. This was the reason I had needed to come here first. Wynter was calm and supportive. "Do you expect a proposal?"

I shook my head. "No. Never. This isn't some sort of trap."

"Did you do it on purpose?"

I reared back. "Of course not. I was totally shocked myself."

"Do you want to keep the baby?"

Without a pause, I said, "Yes. Of course."

"Then it was a risk you both took when you tickled his pickle." Wynter sat on her ottoman and leaned forward with her elbows on her knees.

I threw another pillow at her, laughing. My phone started to ring, and I dropped it on the couch like it was on fire. "It's him."

"Okay, so pick up. And if it sounds like Kaysen told him something was up, let me know because… I'll snip his tip."

I giggled because Wynter might actually go through with it. His name flashed again on the screen. Another ring or two and it would go to voicemail. "What do I say?"

"Hey, Lucian. Remember that time we sowed some wild oats? Well, the oats took root and sprouted."

I rolled my eyes and put my call on speakerphone. "Hey."

"Hey, what did the doctor say?"

I panicked. "I'm... healthy."

Wynter slapped her forehead. Yeah, that was a bad cover-up. But when I told him the news, I wanted it to be face to face, not on a phone call.

"Good. I have a sitter tonight. I was hoping I could take you out on a date."

Wynter started sliding her index finger in and out of her fist. I swiped her hands away.

"Sounds great. What time?"

"Be at your place at six. That should give you time to do whatever stuff you needed to do at your apartment today."

Six would give me time to get my thoughts together. "That's perfect. I'll be ready."

"I miss you. Love you, sweetheart."

Wynter put her hand to her forehead and pretended to faint on the couch.

"Love you, too."

I hung up the phone and laid my head back. "I have no idea how I'm going to tell him without freaking him out. Crystal trapped him by getting pregnant before they were married."

"One, you are not Crystal. Two, Lucian is a good guy. He'll know the difference. Just be honest with him. But don't compare yourself to Crystal. You are nothing like her."

I sighed. "I hope he sees that."

"He better, or I'll maim him so bad his snake can't hide in a bush for a while."

I stood, laughing. "I'm going to go get ready. Thank you. And I'm sorry I interrupted you and you-know-who."

"Oh, it's fine. Trust me. He lives on the top floor. If either of us wants more, it's easy to get."

It was hard to picture Kaysen as Mr. Nipple Man. He hadn't made my list of suspects. Well, to be honest, no one had been on my list. They controlled their feelings so well in public. "Thank you for everything. I appreciate it, Wynter. I need to go shower or maybe take a long bath."

"If you take a bath, just make sure it's not too hot."

"Why?"

Something passed over her face. "I had a friend who was pregnant in college—her doctor told her that. Just check the temperature and make sure it's not too hot."

I knew when not to push Wynter. And I also knew there were things she kept hidden. I nodded. "No baths. I'll search online for other no-nos."

"Good. I'll check on you later to see what happened and if I need to get my cutter before visiting Mr. Black."

CHAPTER 28

Lucian

"Sir, everything is set."

"Thank you, Jim."

The car pulled up to the small house on Long Island. Before I picked Addilyn up, she'd texted me to let me know she was off through Thanksgiving, which was nice. I'd changed our plans to something more of a night to ourselves. Kaysen was watching Remmy for me again. I owed my best friend big time.

Addilyn fell asleep again on the ride here. Lately, she'd been sleeping like the dead. Maybe she needed a second opinion. I hoped to hell something wasn't wrong.

Please let her be okay.

We had enough going, considering the new information I had received about the Martins. I needed to tell Addilyn, but tonight I wanted to focus on us.

I touched her cheek. "Hey, sweetheart, we're here."

She stretched, revealing that small strip of skin below her shirt. "Where are we?"

"The house I inherited from my parents."

The sun had already set by the time we'd arrived at the small white house on the ocean. The porch lights illuminated the property. Addilyn stopped and stared. "I love this place."

I put my hand on her back and guided her toward the rear of the house. "After my parents became successful, they bought a home in the city but always kept this place as a memory of where they'd come from. This house has been passed down through my father's family. Right before he made it big, they thought they might lose the place."

"How did your dad become successful?" Addilyn asked as I pulled back her chair at the kitchen table.

"He made a few smart investments, started a business, and worked tirelessly to grow it. He saved this house. My Aunt Taryn made sure I understood how important this place was to him."

Addilyn touched my hand. "That's a beautiful story." She looked at the mantle. "Are those family pictures?"

"They are. You can see me in my younger days."

Addilyn walked around, taking it all in. Aunt Taryn had made sure this place remained full of family memories. Addilyn picked up a frame and smiled. "I love this place. It feels like a home."

"Remmy does, too. The three of us will make a weekend out of it soon."

"That would be fun."

I leaned against the bar as she looked at the family photos.

She picked up a picture of me in my mother's lap, napping on the beach. "This is you?"

"Yes."

She leaned over to look at the other pictures on the shelf, which gave me a fantastic view of her ass. As she rose, I slipped my hands underneath her shirt. "I've missed you."

"You've had me every night when I've come up to your place."

I kissed her neck. "I know. I can't get enough."

What we had wasn't enough anymore. I wanted more of her. I wanted her in my life as more than a girlfriend.

She moaned. "Where's the bedroom?"

"Right this way."

We walked into the bedroom, and she touched the gauzy canopy. "This is beautiful."

"Not half as beautiful as you."

She blushed, then turned my way.

"Lucian, I—"

I cut her off with a kiss, needing to taste her. She moaned into my mouth. "Lucian, I need—"

Against her lips, I whispered, "What do you need, sweetheart?"

"Lucian, I need you. Just you. Please make love to me."

I laid her back on the bed. "With pleasure."

The next evening, we headed back to the city. There was something growing between us, a drive to be closer, to be more. When we arrived at my building, the concierge met us at the door. "A package came for Ms. DeRoss."

She frowned but took the envelope with a shrug. "I wasn't expecting anything. Maybe it's from Ria."

Remmy was waiting for us when the elevator opened into the apartment.

"Addawin! Daddy! You're back!" He ran straight into Addilyn's arms. "I missed you. Did the doctor make you better?"

"I missed you, too. Yes, he did. I'm all better. Did you have fun?"

He nodded with his whole body. "Ms. Jan played with me lots. And she let me eat a bowl of popcorn with my movie."

That morning, Kaysen had to go work and Jan came over to watch him.

"Hey, buddy, where's my hug?"

Remmy jumped into my arms, and I gave him a kiss.

Jan came out with her bag. "Bye, Remmy. Thanks for all the fun."

"Bye, Ms. Jan. Come on, Addawin, I wanna show you the tent I made."

Remmy pulled Addilyn down the hallway as she laughed. "I'm coming. I'm coming."

Jan shook her head with a smile as she watched them go. "That boy has so much energy."

Jan had been a godsend the last couple of years. She loved Remmy and always took good care of him. "Thanks again, Jan."

"Anytime. He's a great kid. He drew Addilyn some pictures in his tent. He loves her."

He wasn't the only one.

Once she was gone, I put my bag in my room before going to stand at Remmy's door and listen to them playing cars.

"Will you hum to me tonight, Addawin?"

"For sure."

"Good. Ms. Jan can't hum like you. She tries, but it's not very good. Don't tell her."

She laughed. "I won't say a word. You are so precious, Remmy."

"Does that mean you wuv me?"

"Yes, sweet boy, it does."

Slayed. I was fucking slayed. This is what I wanted to come home to every day.

Addilyn walked into the living room and curled up on the couch. We were going to watch an old movie but hadn't decided which one.

"You've bewitched my son."

"You jealous?" she quipped with a smile.

"Maybe," I joked back. But we knew I would never be jealous of my son's happiness.

She grabbed the envelope and opened it, saying, "What are we going to watch?"

"How about *The Maltese Falcon*?"

"Let me search the ending."

I laughed but froze as the blood drained from her face and her eyes shot to mine.

"Someone knows."

"Knows what?"

"About Remmy," she whispered.

I stood abruptly and took the piece of paper from her shaking hands.

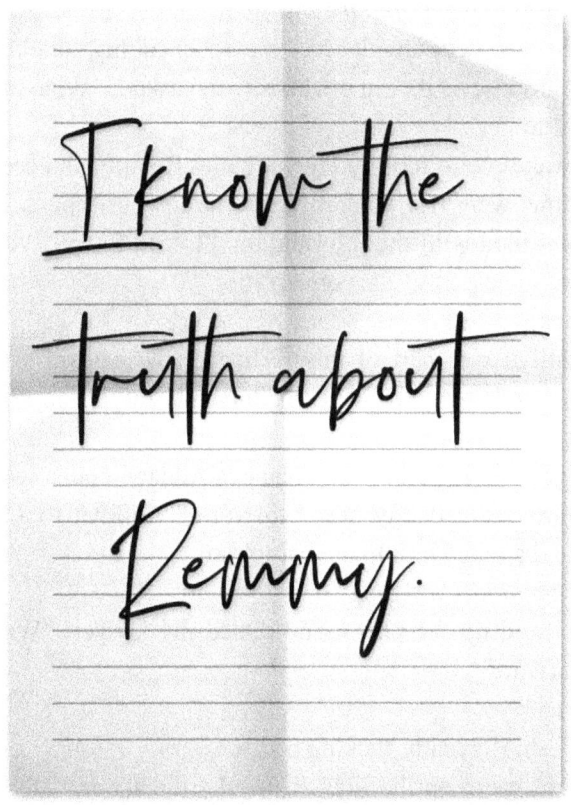

I was gripped with equal doses of fear and fury as I scanned the sloppily written note.

Addilyn sat on the couch shaking her head. "Why? Why would they contact *me*?"

"To send a message to me."

The anger boiled inside me, and it was hard to keep it contained.

"What message?"

"That they can fuck with everything I hold dear—my son and you."

I will find them. And they will pay.

Addilyn's eyes widened. She touched my hand, and I pulled her close to me. In a whisper, she asked, "What are you going to do?"

It was time to tell my lawyer about Remmy and see what my options were. He couldn't give me his best counsel if he was blindsided with the information. "I need to call Walt. Do you want to be part of the conversation?"

"Yes."

Addilyn was part of this. Whoever the bastard was had made sure of it. As we were heading into the office, Remmy came out of his room.

"I need to go bathroom. Then can Addawin hum again?"

"Sure. Your daddy needs to work." Addilyn took Remmy's hand and led him to the bathroom.

I cannot lose my son.

I picked up the phone and dialed my lawyer. "Walt, we have an issue."

"Bad?"

"Yeah, it's really fucking bad."

I laid it out on the line—Crystal's threats, the DNA test, and everything.

Walt gave his advice. "I suggest waiting to see if this person makes contact again. This may just be a fishing expedition, but based on what you said, probably not. We need to find out who they are and what they want, though I assume it's money. But if that's the case, why contact you through your girlfriend? Control? Mind games? Based on the information you have, do you think it could be the Martins?"

"I don't know."

"Well, Crystal is gone, and she had no close family. You didn't mention the DNA test to her, so it's likely she didn't know about it and therefore couldn't have told anyone. That leaves the Martins. Tread carefully with them, just in case; we don't want to piss anyone off unnecessarily. Do you think Addilyn would talk to them? Feel them out?"

"I can't ask her to do that."

"Well, you may need to reconsider that," Walt responded.

"I won't put her in the middle of this."

I squeezed my hand in a fist. The Martins would be sorry if they somehow found out about Remmy and thought they could use it against me.

"Even if it means saving you a lot of time and money plus a court battle you might lose, Lucian? You need to think this through. Feel them out. You can take the necessary precautions to make sure she's safe."

Losing Remmy wasn't an option. *He's mine, damn it.* I swallowed hard around the lump in my throat.

"I'll do it." Addilyn stood in the doorway, looking beautiful. She had changed into her pajamas and piled her hair on top of her head.

My head snapped up. "You don't even know what it's about."

"If it helps with Remmy, I'll do it."

There was no hesitation in her voice at all. *How did I get so lucky?* "I'll call you back, Walt."

"Sounds good."

I hung up the phone. "Addilyn, I can't ask you to reach out to your mother."

"My mother? What does she have to do with this?"

I leaned back. "They're our only lead at this time. They find out about you, you refuse any contact, and the threats begin."

"How would they know?"

"Maybe I wasn't as careful as I thought I was. Maybe they hired a detective who found it out. I don't know."

She sat as I caught her up on my conversation with Walt. "Of course I'll do it."

"Addilyn."

She remained resolute. "I'll do it. For you and Remmy. I'll do whatever it takes to keep from upsetting his life any more than it already has been."

Addilyn loved my child as much as I did. She and Remmy were my top priority. And I hated that I was about to upset her with the news I had. "There's more I need to tell you."

Shit.

She needed to understand what Walt and I had uncovered on the Martins before she agreed to anything.

Cautiously, she said, "Okay…"

I brought the file over to the couch in my office. "Two days ago, I got this. I was going to tell you, but I wanted our little getaway to be about us, nothing else."

"I get it. More than you realize." What does that mean? She swallowed hard. "What's in it?"

I took a picture out of the file. "Your younger half brother is sick. The Martins found out a few days before the charity event. He needs a donor. I imagine they want to ask you to test and see if you're compatible?"

Addilyn's head reared back like she'd been slapped. "What do they want me to donate?"

"Based on his disease, a kidney and part of your pancreas."

She took the picture, and tears welled in her eyes. "I-I-I can't give that to them."

"I would never ask that, sweetheart. I just wanted you to be aware of what they were potentially going to ask so you weren't surprised."

With the picture in hand, Addilyn stood and began to pace. "If they ask that of me, I can't give that to them. I cannot do that. What am I going to do?"

Her reaction seemed a little over the top. "I don't expect you to." Her pacing became more erratic, so I stepped into her path. "Addilyn, we'll figure this out."

Tears were streaming down her face. "I can't. I can't do that. Even if it means saving Remmy, I can't."

"Sweetheart, I get it." It had never crossed my mind that she would donate her kidney.

I tried to pull her to me, but Addilyn took a step back and shook her head. "No, no, no. You don't get it." Sobbing, she sat in the chair and cradled her face.

Now I was getting worried. "What's wrong? Did the doctor tell you something you haven't told me?"

"Lucian, I—I—" She could barely get the words out around the sobs.

She was nearing full-blown hysterics. I grabbed her face, making her look in my eyes. "Breathe with me." I rubbed my hands up and down her arms. "It was never even a thought— much less an expectation—that you would give up a kidney. Do you understand?"

I repeated my motions until Addilyn calmed down. I needed to find out what was going on. "Tell me what's going on."

"I'm pregnant."

The world fell away, and I blinked a few times, wondering if I'd heard her correctly. *Pregnant*? "W-what?"

She sobbed harder. "I found out at the doctor. I had no idea. And I still don't know how. I haven't missed my birth control. We used condoms every time, right? I just—I don't know how it happened. And I should have told you last night, but I wanted it to just be us. I needed to be away from it all for a while."

Addilyn is pregnant with my baby.

I reached out to touch her stomach where our baby was growing. *Our child.* I looked up at her, and she was getting worked up again. "I didn't do this on purpose. And we'll split all costs. I don't expect you to pay for everything."

"We're having a baby." I needed to say it. I needed to hear her say it again.

"Yes, I'm so sorry. I promise I don't expect anything."

I kissed her stomach, and Addilyn stilled as I touched her with both hands, whispering, "Our baby."

Addilyn frowned. "Yes." Then she put her hands on mine. "This baby is yours. You'll never have to worry about that."

My eyes shot to hers. "How are you feeling? What do you need?"

With a watery smile, she said, "I've been scared to death to tell you. I know what you went through before."

"Don't be scared. It took both of us to get here." And selfishly, I knew this would tie Addilyn to me.

She stilled, the tears drying up. "I expected you to—"

"Freak out?"

"Yes."

I should be freaking out. But fuck, I'm excited. "How far along are you?"

"I don't know. I need to go to the OB-GYN." She sniffed as the tears stopped.

"When is your appointment?"

She bit her lip. "I haven't scheduled it yet. I didn't want to go without knowing if you wanted to be part of it. If you do, I wanted us to pick out a doctor together. The doctor did a blood test confirming I was pregnant, but I was so freaked, I went to Wynter's. I peed on fifteen sticks. They all said I was pregnant."

Wynter knew. Based on everything we were going through, I understood why Addilyn went there. "I want to be there for every single second. I mean it. Every. Single. Second."

"Really?"

"Yes."

I stood and held out my hand. Addilyn took it, and I led us to my bedroom. Once there, Addilyn began to twist her fingers together.

"What's wrong?"

"I don't want you to feel obligated to stay with me—even because of our child. Ever."

Shit. Was that what she was afraid of? "I will stay with you because I've fallen in love with you. And I'm not just saying that because you're pregnant." To emphasize my point, I cradled her face. "You are not Crystal. You could never be Crystal."

"I'm so scared."

Addilyn threw her arms around me, and I held her tight. "We'll get through this together. But I will tell you I am over the fucking moon. I love you, sweetheart."

Sniffing, she pulled back and searched my eyes. "You really are?"

"I really am."

We got ready for bed, and it wasn't long before she was fast asleep. This explained why she'd been so tired lately. I kept my hand on her stomach, in complete awe. *My* child was growing inside her. *Mine.* Crystal had never allowed me to touch her or go to appointments with her. But I had loved Remmy from the first moment I held him. And I already loved this baby.

I had to figure out a way to get Addilyn to move in with me without her feeling like she was losing her independence. My goal was to always empower her. But I was certain that soon, Addilyn DeRoss would be my wife.

CHAPTER 29 ♥

Lucian

"Y ou sure you're up to this?" I whispered in her ear.

Nerves had her on edge. Addilyn took a deep breath and whispered, "Yes."

That morning Addilyn had been insistent about setting up something with her parents the same day. She wanted it over with prior to Thanksgiving. I hadn't slept through the night. Instead I spent it staring at the woman I loved with all my heart. I thanked my lucky stars she'd come into my life and now was pregnant with our child.

The waiter guided us to a private room at the back of the restaurant. Teresa and Dwayne were already seated, completely overdressed for lunch. *Assholes*. We'd decided to keep the news of Addilyn's pregnancy to ourselves—and Wynter and Kaysen—for a while. It was best until we worked out what our next steps would be. And if the prick who sent the letter wasn't one of the Martins, whoever it was might have tried to use Addilyn's pregnancy against us.

They stood when we arrived at the table. "Addilyn, Lucian."

The informal greeting was an obvious tactic to put us on friendly terms. "Dwayne, Teresa," I greeted back coldly, playing along with their game. Addilyn only nodded before taking her seat.

Looking at Teresa was like looking at an older version of Addilyn, although her features were sharper than her daughter's. Teresa motioned to the glasses. "Would you like anything besides water?"

"Who is my father?" Addilyn asked. I kept my eyes on the Martins to watch their reactions. Most liars had some sort of tell.

Teresa shook her head and took a deep breath. "You don't want to go down that road. Trust me."

"Why did you leave me?"

Teresa sighed. "Addilyn, that was so long ago. I think that is another road we shouldn't go down. I made so many mistakes."

Addilyn appeared calm and in control, but I saw the devastation in her eyes for a brief second before she shut it down. If her father had been a mistake, then Teresa thought Addilyn was a mistake, too. "I want to go down that road."

With a sugary smile, Teresa said, "Darling—"

Addilyn held up her hand. "Don't. You lost the right to use any term of endearment for me. I agreed to meet with you. Let's start somewhere else. Why did you insist on talking to me? It's obvious that I'm not going to let the press know I'm related to you. And you've had over twenty years to make contact with me."

The corners of Teresa's mouth turned down. I was still assessing her sincerity. "I'm so sorry for what I did."

That was a nonanswer. *What's their endgame?* Dwayne was watching me as Addilyn gathered her purse.

She stood. "I believe we're wasting our time."

Dwayne's nostrils flared ever so slightly. and Teresa's eyes widened. They needed Addilyn. That much was clear. So, if they knew anything about Remmy, this was the likely moment they would play their card.

I was surprised to see a tear trickle down Teresa's face. "I was so young. It was so hard. I needed to start over and reinvent myself. I just... I needed a do-over. So, I dropped you off at Mom's and left. It was for the best. Your father wasn't a nice man, and I just needed to distance myself. And then... too much time passed, so I let it be. I know Mom gave you a good life."

She said all the words and had the tears, but her whole display lacked any sort of emotion.

Addilyn took a sip of her water, completely calm. I admired her strength. "And you never thought to come back for me?"

"You were settled; you seemed happy. It was better not to rock the boat."

Or have articles appear in the paper and rock Teresa's socialite world. It made me sick to my stomach. Addilyn placed a trembling hand on my leg. To show support, I placed mine on hers.

"Why didn't you come to Grammie's funeral?"

"I did, but from a distance. I figured it would upset you if I made an appearance then. Please forgive me." She sniffled for dramatic effect.

Bullshit. This woman was a narcissist.

I squeezed Addilyn's hand. She set her jaw and pressed for more. "Who is my father?"

"His name was Jericho Hall. But I beg you, do not go down that path. It will only lead to trouble. I did you a favor. Dwayne has done you a favor by making sure he never knew about you." Teresa's eyes widened as if she realized she'd just slipped. Or maybe it was intentional to throw me off while she waved her hands about nervously. "Just let it be. I don't want to cause you more heartache. And I don't want him to even know you exist."

Addilyn blinked a few times. "You broke Grammie's heart when you left. She didn't deserve that. For years, she searched for you. But she was never going to find you because she was looking for Angela DeRoss, not Teresa Martin or whatever name you assumed."

Teresa seemed to be hiding something—or maybe not. Either way, it was likely we'd never get all the answers.

Addilyn straightened her shoulders. "Thank you, Teresa, for the information. Was there a specific reason you wanted to meet with me?"

Dwayne puffed out his chest but deferred to Teresa. That was the smart move. He was a secondary character in this little show. At least there was a biological connection between Addilyn and Teresa. "Your half brother needs a kidney and pancreas transplant due to complications from his diabetes. He's on the organ donor list, but I wanted to see if you would allow for a test to see if you are a potential candidate. Wade is anxious to meet his half sister. You have two brothers—Wade and Kent."

I began to doubt they were the people behind the letter about Remmy. It was possible I was wrong, but I just wasn't getting that vibe.

Addilyn remained silent. Teresa added, "We'll pay. I'll make it worth your time. You won't have to worry about money as you go about your life."

Without any connection to the Martins. Those were the words Teresa left unsaid. I sympathized with their son's condition. No parent or child should have to deal with that. However, they were assholes who didn't care about Addilyn's best interest.

"What do you think?"

Addilyn shook her head. "I can't. I'm physically unable due to my health."

The Martins looked at each other, clearly perplexed, before Dwayne said, "How much do you want?"

Addilyn reared back. "This is not about the money."

Teresa tried to smooth things over. "I know. And I should have contacted you sooner. But it wasn't the best timing with Dwayne up for a promotion."

Definitely a narcissist. There was one thing Teresa was right about; it had been for the best that she'd left Addilyn with Grammie. *Psychotic bitch.*

Addilyn stood, shocked. "Please don't ever contact me again."

If there was a Remmy card, this was their last chance to use it. I put my hand on Addilyn's back as we turned to leave the restaurant.

"I'll tell Braden Whitfield where you are," Teresa called out.

That's their big card?

Bringing Braden into our lives could complicate matters if he even still cared about Addilyn. But with Monique and Bridgette getting along, I doubted he did. But… that wasn't good enough for me. No one was going to threaten Addilyn.

Radiating with anger, I took a few steps forward and placed my hands on the table. "If you follow through on your threat, I will stop at nothing to ruin you. If Braden so much as even *visits* New York City, I will bury you."

"You have nothing on me," Dwayne spat.

I smirked. "Try me. Don't fuck with my family or my girl."

Dwayne crossed his arms over his chest. "God forbid your little boy ever got sick... it would be a shame if his treatment were delayed... or denied."

Enough. The threat was weak at best, but there was intent, which crossed way over the fucking line. This motherfucker was going to learn his place. I pulled out my phone and called Walt.

"Hello."

"Release the first batch to the media."

"Fuck. That bad?"

"Yeah. Do it. I'll be in touch." I hung up the phone.

Dwayne stood, red-faced. "What are you doing?"

"Like I said, don't fuck with me, my family, or my girl. This is just the beginning. You want to lose it all? Just keep going. I have more. I meant what I said. Don't contact Addilyn again, and you better make sure Braden Whitfield never steps foot in New York."

Teresa walked around the table, her hands held out in front of her. "Let's be reasonable."

"The time for being reasonable ended the second your husband threatened potential medical treatment for my child. Your selfishness as a mother lost you your relationship with the most amazing woman I know. Go fuck off and never cross our path again."

I took Addilyn's hand, and we left the restaurant. Jim was waiting at the curb. Once we were in the car, Addilyn asked, "What information did you release?"

"Proof of a malpractice suit Dwayne had covered up. His ineptitude cost someone their life. It should have cost him his license and position at the hospital, too. But he's got connections."

She gasped. "How did you find that out?"

"My investigators dug deep. I wanted to be prepared. The Martins aren't good people. Dwayne also skims money from his nonprofit charity. What I had leaked today should be enough to ruin him socially—possibly more than that. But he'll have a good lawyer, and he'll get a deal."

Addilyn worried her lip. "What will stop him from coming after us if you've taken all that from him?"

"Because if he comes after us, I'll ruin him financially, too. That's what will happen next. He'll know I'm not bluffing after this blow."

Unfortunately, we were no closer to knowing who'd sent the note about Remmy. Crystal had to have talked to someone. *But who?*

"Lucian?"

"Yeah, sweetheart."

"Can you have your investigators look into Jericho Hall?"

I'd known that was coming. And I understood the reason behind it. I worried that Teresa's threat about it causing Addilyn heartache might be real, but I agreed to look. She deserved to know. "Yes, if you'd like."

"Please. And if we don't like what they find, we don't ever have to contact him."

At least Addilyn was open to the concept that Jericho—if what Teresa had said was true—might not be a model citizen.

There was so much shit stacking against us. And now I needed to order a tail for Braden Whitfield just in case. At least the media attention had calmed down. "Keep an open mind when I ask this next question."

"Okay…"

"Will you move in? I don't mean the apartment downstairs, but with Remmy and me? It'll make me feel better. Keep your place, too, if you want. I'd like to be with you through every moment of this pregnancy."

"Yes."

I paused, waiting for more.

Addilyn tipped her head to the side and smiled. "You expected a fight?"

"I did. That was easier than I expected."

She sighed. "With everything going on, it makes sense. We have a stranger claiming to know about Remmy. Then there's my crazy bio mom, and you've just royally pissed off her husband. And now, I'm pregnant."

Shit was stacking against us.

I kissed the top of her head, thankful she was mine.

Now, we needed to find out who was sending the notes about Remmy.

CHAPTER 30

Lucian

" and as a result, Dr. Martin has been suspended pending an investigation of newly uncovered evidence of willful medical malpractice. Investigators aren't releasing the specifics, but inside sources say it could lead to a heavy fine, not to mention the loss of his medical license and position at the hospital. The board of directors at Hopeful Children, the nonprofit Dr. Martin started with his wife, Teresa, has suspended his position pending the investigation. Dr. and Mrs. Martin declined to comment."

I shut off the TV, glad that was done. In all likelihood, he'd hire a slimeball attorney and never serve a day for his crimes. In time, we would see if he was smart and stayed away. For now, I had someone tracking his movements.

It was Thanksgiving Day, and I wanted to put everything aside for Addilyn and Remmy. They had been cooking while watching the Macy's Thanksgiving Day Parade from the window. We'd put up the tree, decorated it last night, and Remmy's Elf on the Shelf had come to life this morning. I walked into the living room to find them hand in hand at the window. Mister Teddy was pressed against the glass so he wouldn't miss any of the parade.

"Addawin! Look! It's Darby!"

She waved at the giant elf balloon. "Hey, Darby."

"How'd he get outside?" Remmy was fascinated with the magical elf.

Before my phone call, I'd hidden the elf, so it looked to Remmy as if he'd left for the parade. "Addawin, that's really him. He grew so big!"

"That is so neat. Wave and yell his name so he knows you're watching."

Remmy grinned up at Addilyn. "Darby does silly things. You'll see."

"I can't wait, but he better stay out of my baking stuff."

Remmy giggled and covered his mouth. "I bet he gets in your baking stuff."

The two of them stood at the window, looking at the balloons as they passed by. My entire world was in this room, and I felt settled for the first time in a while. This was the life I wanted. *Would the person who knew about Remmy make contact again?* I hoped not. I wanted peace for my son, for my family.

I snapped a picture of their silhouettes.

"Daddy, Daddy, look! It's Darby."

I picked up Remmy and held him at the window. "I see. Wow, he got really big for the parade."

The door opened, and Wynter walked in. "Knock! Knock! I'm here." The front desk had buzzed me a few minutes before to let me know she was on her way up.

"Oh, good, you're here!" Addilyn went over to give her a hug. "You're just in time to make dressing.."

A few seconds later, Kaysen arrived. "Unkem Kaysum! You're here, too!"

Kaysen spun Remmy around then turned him into an airplane. "It's a bird. No, it's a plane. No, it's pilot Remmy taking over the sky."

"Whee!" With his hands out straight, Remmy made an airplane engine sound as Kaysen flew him around the room.

Addilyn called from the kitchen. "Remmy, did you want to help pour the ingredients in the bowl for the dressing?"

"Gotta go, Unkem Kaysum. Addawin needs my help."

"Okay, little man."

As soon as his feet touched the ground, Remmy was off. Kaysen walked over to me. "How are you holding up?"

I had called him the night before to tell him about the baby. "I'm good. Really good. We go to see the doctor next week."

Addilyn and I had researched OB-GYNs in the area and decided on one we both liked.

Kaysen gave me a one-armed hug. "I'm happy for you. You deserve this."

A few days ago, Addilyn told me that Kaysen was at Wynter's apartment when she blurted out her news. He'd never said a word, which I appreciated. I would have wanted to hear about the pregnancy from Addilyn and not someone else.

"Have you made any plans?" Kaysen asked.

I shook my head. "No, we're just taking it day by day."

"That's smart." He seemed a little distracted, looking out the window at the parade, and I let him be. Some ghosts were too painful to acknowledge. We'd known each other for years, and I never pushed.

I handed Kaysen his drink. "Someday you'll find happiness, too."

He took a few steps back and winked, but the pain was evident in his eyes. "That's not in the cards for me, but I'm good. Let me show you an app I've been working on.."

Typical Kaysen deflection. Wynter walked down the hallway, and Kaysen's eyes followed her. Whether he wanted to admit it or not, he had it bad for her.

But sometimes we ignored what was within our grasp. I'd almost gone that route with Addilyn. Hopefully, Kaysen made the right choice.

CHAPTER
31

Addilyn

"You're about five to six weeks pregnant."

Lucian looked at me, probably doing the math in his head as quickly as I was. It had been one of our first times together. "We'll see you again at ten weeks. Here's a quick guide to things you'll want to avoid for now. But for the most part, just continue life as usual."

The doctor handed us a bunch of pamphlets that Lucian took. Earlier, when we'd met with the nurse practitioner, I had barely gotten a word in edgewise because he'd had so many questions. I loved it. Lucian was truly plugged into this pregnancy. In some ways, it felt like he was experiencing this for the first time with me.

"Thank you, doctor," I said. I liked our doctor. She was older but had a great bedside manner. The reviews had been amazing, and she had experience handling high-profile clientele. Not that we were movie stars, but considering Lucian's status and the lingering interest in Crystal's death, the vultures would circle again if we gave them a reason.

Dr. Navara adjusted her glasses to the top of her head. "Helen will be in to finish setting up your account."

Lucian nodded. "Thank you."

"Of course. Congratulations. If any concerns arise before your next appointment, call the office. Just remember—lots of rest, eat healthy, and be active at the level you have been."

Maybe pregnancy wouldn't be as bad as I anticipated. I had built it up in my head like I needed to live in a bubble. "Thanks, Dr. Navara."

The door closed, and Lucian beamed at me. "July. We're having a baby in July."

I touched my stomach. "It's hard to believe. July seems so far away, yet so close."

The door opened, and Helen, the nurse who handled registering patients, walked in. "Okay, so we have two options. Our clinic has a base fee that isn't covered by insurance. You can choose to do a payment plan or pay it at once for a slight discount. After the baby is born, there'll be another bill for the amount not covered by insurance after your deductible is met."

Lucian took the bill without batting an eye. "Charge it to this card."

No, that wasn't the plan. "Wait, can we set up fifty percent on a payment plan?"

The nurse looked between us, holding Lucian's black credit card, unsure what to do. It was one of those cards with no limit. We'd agreed to split all the costs. Lucian asked, "Can you give us a few minutes, Helen?"

"Of course."

She left, and I raised my eyebrow. "I'm paying for fifty percent. We agreed to this, Lucian."

He took a deep breath and relaxed his posture. "Will you let me pay?"

"No, I want to split the costs." I stood from the chair and gathered my coat. "We agreed. I'll make payments and have it paid for by the time we have the baby."

Lucian thought for a second, and I knew he was strategizing his argument. "So, we were both equal partners in making this baby, right?"

I narrowed my eyes, wondering why he was helping my point. "Yes."

"And we both agree we should be equally responsible in this process."

"What are you up to?" I laughed. "I am paying for half of this, Lucian. Stop trying to negotiate."

He gave me his signature cat-ate-the-canary smile, letting me know that yes, indeed, he was up to something. "I'm asking questions. Humor me. We're both responsible, right?"

I rolled my eyes. "Yes, and paying for fifty percent gets us there."

"So, whose body is changing and who has to ensure everything she does is safe for the baby?"

"You. You can take on monitoring everything I do and eat," I quipped, raising my eyebrow.

Lucian chuckled. "As if you'd let me do that." He had a point, but I stayed silent. Lucian leaned back in his chair, and I knew he was giving a relaxed illusion to keep me calm. Surprisingly, it worked.

He continued. "Since you're the one carrying the baby and having to be careful, paying makes me an equal partner in this."

I rubbed my temples. "Lucian, I don't want you to feel obligated. I may not have the cash in the bank, but I can pay for it."

Lucian ran his thumb along my chin. "I know this, and I love you for it. I want to try to help as much as possible. If you're stressed about payment, then that's not necessary. You could do this on your own, but that's not necessary, either.. This is us working together to make this not stressful so we can enjoy the pregnancy of our child. Let's help each other where we can."

Again, he had valid points. And I had to give points to Lucian for not taking control. "Okay, you can pay for this." I held up a finger. "The only reason I'm agreeing is because you let us decide together."

He gave me a chaste kiss. "Then it's settled. Thank you."

After finishing the account setup, we took the employee elevator down to avoid being seen. In the car, Lucian answered a few emails on his phone. It was Friday, and there were a few critical meetings for him to wrap up. He had mentioned potentially going out of town for the company expansion. The investors wanted him there the week before Christmas. I'd offered to watch Remmy, but Lucian was torn about leaving us. "What are your plans today?"

"I'm going to the office to meet with Ria. With the app for Keller Industries, Ria and the team are swamped so I offered to help."

Since I'd stopped going to the office, the media had practically disappeared.

"I need to head into the office, too. I'll be on back-to-back conference calls. I'll have Jim drop you off first. When you're ready to be picked up, just text him."

Being chauffeured around was something I had accepted for now. It kept Lucian at ease, and it really wasn't so bad. "Okay."

At the curb in front of my office, Lucian kissed me before I got out. "See you tonight. Take care of our little one. Love you."

I smiled against his lips. "I will. Miss you and love you, too."

In my office, I booted up my laptop. I was on cloud nine. We were having a baby and doing it together.

Focus.

I pulled up the numbers for Keller Industries' app. The projections still looked great. The new rollout of the app had been received well from the users. The rating had improved from a 4.5 to a 4.8 out of 5. That was impressive. Things were moving in the right direction. It was weird being on the sidelines now. I had created the pitches, but part of me also felt a little irrelevant. Maybe I was torn. I wasn't sure.

Ria appeared at the door with her purse on her shoulder. "It's good to have you back in the office; I've missed you. With the piranhas gone, are you ready to come back?"

"Yes, for sure. When would you like me back?" Now that the words were out there, I realized how much I would be away from the baby if I worked away from home in seven or so months. *Do I want to come back?* It left an empty feeling in my chest. *Aren't I supposed to want to return?*

She smiled. "Fantastic! Now, take the next three weeks off. We'll start back after Christmas."

"Wait, what? I'm not taking off the next three weeks. I was just off for Thanksgiving."

"Girl, I checked your vacation, and you've only taken four days over the last two years. It's my Christmas gift to you. Go enjoy it."

I was speechless, which added to the guilt of my earlier thoughts. "Thank you."

Midge came to the door. "I have a Dave Dubster at the front desk. He asked for Addilyn specifically. He's a new account."

From the way Ria took her purse off her shoulder, I imagined she was about to take the meeting for me. "I'll do it," I said. "And if he turns out to be a viable client, I'll send you all the details."

"You're amazing. Thank you, Addilyn. Chuck is taking me away for the weekend. After having his parents here for Thanksgiving week, this girl needs lots of wine and a day at the spa."

I chuckled. "Have fun."

"Oh, I will."

A few minutes later, Midge showed Mr. Dubster into my office. The slicked-back dark hair and wrinkled suit didn't give off the professionalism I'd expected. First up would be to clean up his image—in a tactful way, of course. For this meeting, I kept it professional. "It's nice to meet you. I'm Addilyn DeRoss. Please have a seat. Would you like anything to drink?"

"Nah, I'm good, I guess."

His response was a little less professional than I was used to, but I took my seat and waited for him to say something. He simply looked around my office, so I started. "So, Midge said you asked for me specifically. What led you to me?"

"Lucian Black."

Okay. Something isn't right.

I sat up straight and stared at him, wondering what was going on. I placed my hand on my desk in front of the phone in case I needed to page Midge. "Can you expand on that?"

"Sure. I want to talk about my son."

This was either Remmy's father or someone who knew Crystal's secret.

Play it cool.

I tipped my head to the side. "And who is your son? Did we create a marketing campaign for your son? Is he a model? Did we meet at a function? I'm sorry, but I'm having a problem connecting the dots here."

The guy shook his head. "Baby, I know you're playing me. I'm Remmy Black's biological father."

Shit.

This man was not letting up. *Act stupid. Keep him talking.* I figured that was what Lucian would do. If I panicked, the truth would be out there. Unless he'd performed a paternity test, there was no way he knew for sure. "Remmy's adopted? I'm sorry, Mr. Dubster, but I was under the impression Remmy Black was Lucian Black's biological son. I'm not sure how I can help you. If you're a reporter looking for information about Crystal Black's death, I'm going to have to ask you to leave."

He shook his finger. "You're either very good or really don't know what I'm talking about." He leaned forward. "Doesn't matter. I need you to get a message to Lucian Black. Crystal told me I was the father and we'd be set. See, I've been fuckin' her since we were in high school. She was never able to say no to my dick. Then she landed herself a rich bastard, which didn't bother me none since she sent me money. Then she went and fucked it up good. Now, I have no use for a kid, but I imagine your boyfriend would fork over a few million for him."

It made me sick to my stomach to hear him disregard Remmy as if he was nothing more than an item to be bought and sold. My voice broke, but I cleared it. "I do not appreciate your tone, Mr. Dubster. I'm going to have to ask you to leave or I'll call security."

"Well, baby, I don't appreciate Lucian not paying to keep my son." He stood and adjusted his cheap suit. The stench of stale cologne wafted through the air. The evil glint in his eye sent goose bumps along my skin. *Why would Crystal ever cheat on Lucian with him?* It had to have been some sick, codependent relationship. Dubster strutted to the door then came back. I thought I might be sick.

He sneered. "I'll be in touch. The bitch may be dead, but I still want my payout. She said she was going to talk to him. If he wants to keep my son, it's going to cost him. I'll go to court just to prove a point and make his life hell. Tell your guy to get his checkbook out."

I stood. "Mr. Dubster, I'm asking you one last time to leave. I don't appreciate you coming to my office and disrupting my day. Your threats mean nothing. Go try to scam someone else."

I saw the doubt for a second. So Dubster wasn't a hundred percent sure. I picked up my phone. "Midge, please have security escort Mr. Dubster out of the office."

He winked before walking out and meeting the security guards.

I sat there stunned, unsure what to do. If I left the office immediately, it looked suspicious after my speech. I had to stay until closing time.

Midge poked her head in. "Everything okay?"

"Yeah, I'm going to go get a snack from the break room. Do you want anything?"

"I'm good. Thanks, Addilyn."

Before going to the break room, I dashed into the bathroom, where I was violently sick. This wasn't good. It wasn't good at all. *Remmy.* The man was a sleazeball and wanted nothing to do with his son—if he was, in fact, the father. He just wanted a paycheck.

I grabbed some crackers before pacing my office for the next two hours. My heart felt like it was in a vice. If I called Lucian, he'd leave and come. And if Dubster was watching for my reaction, this might play right into his assumptions. From his reaction, I had been successful in planting doubt.

When it was nearly five, I texted Jim, who was five minutes away.

I had to get myself together before I stepped outside. In my gut, I believed that this Dubster guy could actually be Remmy's father. He had dark hair like Lucian and the same build. It made me sick.

"I'm headed out, Midge."

"Me, too. I was hoping to get out of here a little sooner. I'm meeting friends at Madison Square Garden for a concert."

Midge was only a couple of years younger than me and loved to party.

That was on the way to Lucian's office. "Let me drop you off."

"Really?"

"Sure."

If I had someone with me, it might not appear that I was running to Lucian, just having a girls' night out. Maybe. Or maybe I was crazy. For the chance it might help sell my story, it was worth it.

My legs felt wooden as I walked to the car. Jim lifted a brow but said nothing as we climbed into the back seat. I kept a smile on my face and managed to laugh as if I was having a good time. Midge talked ninety miles an hour, which helped hide the fact that I said little. It was a relief when we dropped off Midge. She was nice, but I wanted Lucian.

"Is everything okay, Addilyn?" Jim asked from the front seat.

"I… Can you take me home?" That was the only thing that came to mind.

A few seconds later, my phone rang. "Is everything okay?" Lucian asked. "Jim said you seemed a little off."

What am I supposed to say? "I… uh…"

"What's wrong?"

"I need to see you."

"Jim's going to bring you to my office."

"Okay," I managed to whisper.

It took everything I had not to break down in tears. My mind raced with every detail from the meeting with Dubster. I knew I had lost the calm facade I'd worn when I left the office. "Can you bring me to the parking garage and let me take the elevator up?"

"Of course."

We pulled into the garage, and Lucian stepped out of the elevator to meet me at the car. "What's going on, sweetheart?"

"Your office." My voice cracked again. I was about two seconds from breaking down.

Once in his office, he walked over to the bar and grabbed me a bottle of water. "What's going on? Is the baby okay?"

The baby. I should have reassured him on the phone. I'd been so focused on Remmy. I nodded. "Yes, I'm sorry. The baby is fine. Is there anything recording?"

That comment put Lucian on high alert. He unplugged the device he used to record meetings for Nancy to summarize. "You're pale. Drink some water."

I took a few small sips, afraid I might be sick again. I asked, "Are you sure it's safe?"

"Yes."

Finally releasing a sob, I said, "A man came to the office today claiming to be Remmy's dad."

He paled and took a few steps back, before regaining his composure. Then his eyes narrowed, and anger radiated from him. For the first time since I met Lucian, I sensed fear. "Tell me everything."

I launched into the story, brushing away tears as they streaked down my face. Lucian's hands were fisted so tight they were white. "He wants money in exchange for Remmy."

"Done."

I shook my head. "You can't. You need to talk to Walt. See if there's anything that can be done. But if you pay him, it leaves a trail, gives him more to use against you."

"I can stop this if I just give him what he wants."

When I'd still been in shock and pacing my office, I'd thought this too. But it wasn't the answer. "You'd be giving him a reason to blackmail you for the rest of your life. It won't end with one payout. And you know that. Think rationally, Lucian, instead of reacting. How will this end if you pay him right away?"

"He's my fucking son. I don't care about blood. I don't care about money. I won't lose Remmy to an asshole who couldn't give two shits about him." Lucian abruptly stood and began to pace.

I reached out for his arm and stopped him midstep. "Of course you won't. But it won't do Remmy, our unborn child, or me any good if you aren't here. You play by the rules; you always have. Don't start going down a different path now." I'd been doing my best to hold it in, but I began to cry. "I'm scared, too. But we can't just react. That's what he's counting on. Take two minutes and think about it. Right now, if I managed to act as well as I hope I did, Dave Dubster is second-guessing whether Crystal played him."

He paced a few more times. "I won't have a legal right."

"You've raised him as yours—that has to count for something. And you need to find out who this guy is. If he's not a good person, that works in your favor. Lucian, this is a game, and you are smarter. Outmaneuver him."

A renewed determination seemed to take over Lucian. "He's picked the wrong man to fuck with."

CHAPTER 32

Lucian

"Lucian, if there were ever a time for you to listen to me, it's now." I remained silent on the other end of the line. "Do *not* pay him. That would be like admitting Remmy is not your child."

Dave Dubster was a piece of filth con artist. I stared at the picture Walt had had couriered over in a file early that morning. One stint in prison for theft, two arrests for public intoxication, and one arrest for domestic abuse, although those charges had been dropped. There was also a yearbook picture of him and Crystal together.

If the man had been decent, I could have understood that he had rights. But he only wanted money in exchange for Remmy. There was no love there. If someone told me I had a son, I would go straight to the source to work it out. The court would take the child's best interest into consideration.

"Lucian, do you understand what I'm saying?"

"Yes," I gritted out. I knew Walt and Addilyn were right. When I initially found out, my emotional, gut reaction had been to pay him. But I knew that was the wrong way to go.

"Based on his record, we have a good chance of fighting this. But if he truly is Remmy's biological father and pushes the issue, we will have to do the legal dance. His lawyer will paint Dubster as the victim. We'll have to show he's unfit." Walt continued when I said nothing. I needed a few minutes to think. "Dubster wants you to react. Addilyn's lack of reaction was smart. No one jumped and panicked. And I'm guessing he waited and watched because he's not one hundred percent sure now, either."

I agreed, having already come to a similar assessment. Addilyn had handled the previous day exceptionally well, although it should have never happened. Today she had dark circles under her eyes, which meant she hadn't slept, and that wasn't good for her or the baby. "I'm not paying him, and I won't contact him. I get it."

He took a deep breath. "You also need to think about going to court. Since Addilyn knows everything, she can be asked to testify unless…"

"I know." Her testifying against me would be a nonissue if things went according to plan. But I wanted to make sure Addilyn never thought the two were tied together because they weren't.

Walt shifted gears. "Can the test you had done be traced back to you in any way?"

"No."

"Good. I have a guy tracking Dubster's whereabouts. We haven't located him yet."

The asshole was probably perched somewhere close, watching us. "Let me know as soon as you do. And no, I won't contact him when you do. But he knew when Addilyn arrived at her office because he requested her by name from what Midge told her. I doubt he's going away."

"I agree. We'll talk soon."

I hung up the phone and leaned back against the couch where Addilyn had set up camp. Underneath some other papers, I saw the words *Baby Budget*. Curious, I picked it up.

There were estimates for cribs and furniture, day care costs, clothing allowances, and other baby supplies. Under each section was a total that was divided by two. This was another issue I had to navigate. It was unnecessary for Addilyn to be stressed about money. I had more than enough for all of us, and with the additional stress from Dubster, Addilyn didn't need more to worry about.

I heard Remmy giggling in the other room.

Addilyn said, "The tickle monster is going to get you."

"Oh, no! I run fast."

"Here I come!"

I put the sheet back under the notebook and walked to Remmy's bedroom door, where I leaned against the jamb. Remmy was running circles around his room as Addilyn tried to catch him.

Aunt Taryn would have loved Addilyn.

"Daddy! Daddy! Save me!" Remmy had a huge grin on his face as he ran to me. I swooped him up.

I kissed his cheek. "Is the tickle monster after you?"

"Yes!" He giggled.

"Maybe we should chase the tickle monster and tickle her."

"Yes! Daddy! Yes!"

Addilyn shook her head. "You can't catch the tickle monster."

"Yes, we can," Remmy said, waving his hands in the air.

I set him down and the chase ensued. Addilyn ran through the house, just out of Remmy's reach. I came out around the side of the island and picked her up, eliciting giggles from both.

"Daddy! You got her!"

We moved to the couch and Remmy started tickling her. Addilyn went with it, laughing up a storm. I had never been happier in my life. Now, I needed to find a way to ensure I didn't lose Remmy.

"What are you working on?"

I'd just put Remmy to bed and joined Addilyn. She sat on the couch in my bedroom with bundles of yarn, knitting what looked like a blanket. "I'm making Remmy a blanket for when we tell him about the baby. I was thinking maybe Christmas. I don't know. But whenever we do, I thought it would be special for him to have one identical to his baby sister's or brother's."

"He'll love it."

Addilyn's fingers flew as she knitted, but I sensed she was nervous about something. "What's on your mind?"

"I don't know when I'm going to tell Ria. She wants me back in the office first of the year. How long will I have off for maternity leave? I need to start looking at day cares we can afford but are safe at the same time. And what happens when a meeting runs late? And if I want to breastfeed, how would that work?"

There was more to it than what Addilyn was saying, but I saw that she wanted it. And I wanted her to have it. "Do you want to stay home with the baby?"

Addilyn's eyes grew wide. But with the surprise, I saw the longing. She shook her head. "No. I mean, yes, but no. I'll go back to work. I'm just trying to sort it all out in my head."

"Okay." It wasn't the time to push. Addilyn needed the security and knowledge that she could survive on her own. I knew she'd never ask, but I wanted her to be able to stay home with our baby, as well. The last thing I wanted was for Addilyn to be worried about money. "What color are you making the baby's blanket?"

"I figured I'd make them matching so Remmy would feel connected. I don't know— maybe it's stupid." She shrugged, and her lower lip quivered.

Something was off. I touched her hands where they furiously worked the knitting needles. "What's wrong, sweetheart?"

Her hands stopped. "We can't lose him. I know I've only been in his life for a millisecond, but I love him, Lucian. And… I don't know. What if the court takes him from you? From us? I… I just—" She put her hand to her mouth to stifle a sob.

I took the knitting out of her hands and hugged her. "I know. We're not going to lose him. I'm going to fight with everything I have to make sure that never happens."

"I'm so afraid."

Me, too. But I didn't give voice to that thought. Instead, I said, "We'll make it through this."

And hopefully that means he's never tainted by Crystal's decisions. I held Addilyn, too afraid if I spoke again, I might show the fear lurking just beneath the surface.

CHAPTER 33 ♥

Lucian

"**F**ucking A."

I stared at my calendar for the morning where the name Dave Dubster appeared. Nancy had been given a heads-up that he might schedule an appointment, and I'd told her to fit him in. I picked up my phone. "Walt, he's meeting me here in two hours."

"You have the paperwork to sign?"

"Yes."

"Make sure he signs every part of it."

"I will."

I hung up the phone. Walt had devised a plan to have Dave sign a waiver. In all the legal jargon, it allowed for recordings while at Black Media. It was a "new policy at Black Media for training purposes" we had implemented for the time being. Walt said because New York was a one-party consent state, it was likely the recording could be admissible in court to show extortion. And if a judge listened to it or not, the seed would be planted.

Walt was worth his weight in gold.

I paged Nancy. "Make sure Dubster signs each piece of the form for the new protocol."

"No problem, sir."

The next few hours dragged on. It was like time stood still. When I thought I was going to lose my mind, Nancy walked in, quietly closing the door behind her. "Mr. Dubster is here. All the forms have been signed. Rosa is with him, but wanted to make sure everything was in order for this new protocol."

Nancy handed me the forms, and I checked over the signatures. Each one appeared the same and *Dave Dubster* was legible. *Stupid fuck.* Probably hadn't read a word. "Thanks. Please show him in."

I checked to ensure the recorder was going before taking my seat again. The smug bastard walked in and took a seat. "Nice digs you got here. Crystal hit the jackpot with you. I always knew my girl could do it."

Piece of shit. Remain calm and unaffected. "I'm sorry, I don't believe we've met."

Dubster sat taller and stared me in the eye. "I'm Dave, Remmy's father."

The words still hurt like a son of a bitch. This man wasn't a father. A father would never use his child as a bargaining tool to get ahead in this world.

I tilted my head. "I'm not sure what kind of scheme you're running here, but I can assure you, Remmy Black is my son."

The guy put his feet up on my desk, sending a message of absolute confidence. "Well, I guess we can go to court and find out. Or we could settle it out of court."

"What kind of dealings did you have with my ex-wife?"

He flashed his yellow teeth when he smiled. "I was the man she loved. You were the mark."

All along I'd been played. Crystal was sicker than I ever imagined, and I was a stupid fuck for falling for it. Remmy was worth it all in the end.

"Can you clarify what you mean by 'settle it out of court'?"

He put his hands behind his head as if he had not a care in the world. "Ten million dollars."

He threw the number out there as if he were talking about ten dollars. From the reports I'd read, this man was lucky to have ten thousand dollars.

"Let me get this straight. You want me to give you ten million dollars to go away so I don't have to go to court and prove my son is my son?"

It was only a second, but it was there... doubt. Addilyn was right. Dave Dubster was not one hundred percent sure he was the father. "Ten million dollars and you bought yourself your son. I'll fade away, and that'll be it."

"And why do you think Remmy could possibly be yours?"

He gave me a shit-eating grin. "Because I was fucking Crystal long before you came into the picture. And continued to fuck her afterward. She told me that Remmy wasn't yours and you'd pay big for him after you fucked her over during your divorce."

I leaned forward and steepled my fingers. "I assure you Crystal was wrong. She was out of money and desperate. You must know that if you were fucking her behind my back all that time. However, my late ex-wife was committed for a bipolar disorder. Remmy Black is my son. You won't see a dime of my money or *my* son."

"Then I guess I'll see you in court. See, I've got myself a lawyer who says I got a right to damages and shit."

Fucking scum. His lawyer was probably salivating at the chance to be connected to my name in the media. *Stay the course and don't react.* I remained seated and kept a calm, cool demeanor. "My lawyer isn't cheap, and I'll be expecting you to reimburse me for his time in the counterclaim we file."

The arrogant ass rose. "Remmy Dubster. Has a nice ring to it, don't you think?"

"And when you have a son, you should name him that. Good day, Mr. Dubster. Security will show you out."

"Think it over. If you don't want the hassle, I left my number with the gal outside your office."

Security was waiting for him, and I heard, "All right. All right. I'm leaving," as they escorted him out.

I shut off the recording device and banged my fist on my desk. "Fucker. Motherfucker."

Dubster wasn't walking away. He smelled easy money and was willing to take the chance that Crystal hadn't been lying about Remmy being his child.

Damn it all to hell.

Crystal, you're a fucking bitch, and I hope you're already rotting in hell.

CHAPTER 34

Addilyn

"So, have you talked to Lucian about how you're feeling?"

I finished dusting one of the tables in my apartment. It had been a while since I'd been there, and the place needed some TLC. "Yes. No. Maybe. No... I don't know."

Wynter sat cross-legged on my couch while I therapy cleaned. "So... you didn't?"

"No, but what do I say? Hey, yeah, I want to leech off you and stay home with the baby." I sat on the bed in a huff.

Wynter had the patience of a saint as my emotions bounced all over the place. "One, you're not a leech. Two, if that's what you want to do, then talk to him. All he can do is say no. But I don't think that's the issue."

"What do you think is?"

Wynter came to sit beside me. "That you're scared of giving up your independence. You feel guilty walking away from a career you worked so hard for. And after Braden, you're afraid to be dependent on another man." I played with my fingers but stayed quiet. She added, "Well, think about it. You are not Crystal, and Lucian is not Braden."

Lucian had proven time and time again he was nothing like Braden. "I'm so scared."

"What's really bothering you?"

"I just… I don't want to pay someone else to raise my baby. But I…" I trailed off, unsure how to respond. I'd been working on the budget, and it was overwhelming. Just half of the baby's basic needs exceeded my monthly budget. I'd worked it several times, and each time I ended up in the hole.

"Is anything else going on?"

I thought back to my earlier conversation with Lucian. "There isn't any news on my real dad. I think my mom lied. Or Lucian's investigators haven't been able to find him yet. He's going to keep looking. It's just… I don't understand why my mother is so cold. Why did she leave me all those years ago?"

"Fuck her and her expensive-ass designer shoes. In the end, she's ruined. I know you'd rather reconnect than have a bitch mom, but bravo to Lucian for laying down the law. Sometimes people are selfish bastards and that's the only explanation that makes sense."

True. "Thanks. I don't know why I feel so out of sorts. It's like a ping-pong back and forth with everything. And I just… I don't know."

Wynter sat next to me. "Sweetie, you need to talk to Lucian."

"He shouldn't be expected to pay for everything. I was just as much a part of making this baby as he was. The sole responsibility doesn't fall on him."

She patted my hand. "I know. What about marriage?"

I loved Lucian and wanted to be with him, but I would never make him feel obligated to marry me. "Neither of us has mentioned it. I don't want to get married because of a baby."

"I get that, too. Speaking of the baby, how are you feeling about the pregnancy?"

I touched my stomach. "It's hard to describe, but I love this little person with all my heart. And good grief, I'm an emotional basket case. I've tried to keep it together, but there are times I want to burst into tears. I was watching a commercial before you got here and bam! Waterworks."

"Those are called hormones."

"Well, they suck."

There was a knock at the door, and Wynter turned to me with a smile. "I wonder who that could be?"

I was a little nervous. Unannounced guests had been a bad thing lately. Wynter popped a pretzel in her mouth, unconcerned. "Open the door."

She knew who it was. "Who is it?" I asked.

"You'll see."

With a raised eyebrow, I walked over to the door.

Remmy stood there in a tiny tuxedo. "Addawin, will you join me?" He handed me a rose.

"Where are we going?"

"It's a secret." He put his finger to his lips. "I can't tell you."

"Okay, I—"

Wynter handed me my purse. "I'll lock up here. Off you go."

She gave me a little shove, and I turned back to her, clearly clueless. "What's going on?"

"You have a date with Remmy. Go."

Remmy held my hand, and I wondered where Lucian was. Jim stepped around the corner and pushed the elevator button. "This way, Addilyn."

In the car, Remmy sat in his car seat, a ball of energy.

"You seem excited," I said.

He zipped his lips and shook his head. Jim chuckled in the front seat.

"How long until we get there?" I asked. Remmy zipped his lips again, not saying anything.

He silently kicked his legs, and I thought he might burst from how happy he seemed.

"So, you aren't going to tell me anything?"

His lips were turning white he had them pressed so tightly together.

After a short ride, Jim pulled the car in front of Tavern on the Green. It was a beautiful New York City landmark, and I'd mentioned wanting to eat there when Lucian and I had our first date at my apartment.

"Are we eating dinner?"

Remmy nodded before covering his mouth like he'd said something wrong, and then he shook his head. Jim opened the car door, and Remmy held my hand as we approached the door. A man wearing a top hat greeted us. "Ms. DeRoss. Mr. Remmy."

"Good evening," I responded.

Remmy started pulling me inside. "We gotta go find daddy! Come on!"

"Okay."

The place was empty except for a few staff members. Remmy directed us as if he knew where Lucian was hiding. We rounded the corner and entered the glass solarium. A

Christmas tree stood in the middle with Lucian standing beside it in jeans and a long-sleeved blue shirt.

"I did good, Daddy! Not a peep. I zipped my lips." He gave Lucian a high five and whispered something. In response, Lucian nodded.

I took a step into the room. "What's going on?"

Lucian said, "Well, Remmy and I had a long chat today."

My heart sped up. "About?"

"You."

I smiled, loving this game. "Well, I hope it was a good chat."

Remmy nodded and whispered, "It was, Addawin. Don't worry. It's why I got my tux."

Lucian took a step toward me. Remmy covered his mouth with his hand, but I still heard a few giggles.

"Addilyn, Remmy and I wanted to ask you something."

"What's that?"

Lucian knelt on one knee, and I gasped. Remmy mimicked the pose beside him. From Lucian's grin, I doubted they'd rehearsed that part. I covered my mouth and tears welled in my eyes. "I want to be your forever. Will you do me the honor of becoming my wife?"

I nodded, filled with excitement. "Yes. Oh my gosh, yes!"

Lucian stood and put a ring on my finger. It was a beautiful yellow diamond nestled in an antique setting. "This was my Aunt Taryn's. She gave it to me and asked that I give it to the woman I could never imagine spending my life without. You are that woman."

I began to cry and Lucian pulled me close.

"Daddy, why Addawin crying?"

I knelt on the floor with Lucian and hugged Remmy. "Because I am so thrilled. I get to be with you and your daddy forever."

Remmy hugged me. "I wuv you."

"I love you, too. Remmy. More than you'll ever know."

CHAPTER 35

Addilyn

"What are you doing over there?" I awoke to find Lucian smiling at me from the chair beside the bed.

I stretched against the satin sheets of our hotel room bed, easing the soreness in my limbs. After dinner at the Tavern on the Green, Lucian and I had gone to a five-star hotel and spent the night making love while Wynter stayed with Remmy at the apartment.

"Watching you. You're beautiful."

I turned onto my side and tucked my hand under my head. "I think you're biased."

"That may be the case, but you're mine just the same. And I love seeing you wear my ring."

And I loved wearing Lucian's ring. He hadn't said it, but I knew he hadn't given it to Crystal because he knew she wasn't his true love. "You sure know how to make a girl feel special."

"And I'll always try."

The happiness on Lucian's face wiped away any doubt about the reason he'd asked me. Lucian Black loved me and wanted to spend his life with *me.*

I asked, "What were you thinking about for the wedding?"

"That's up to you. Do you have something in mind?"

I gave it a thought. "I want it to be small. Like super small. I don't want a fuss."

Lucian raised an eyebrow. "Why small? Is this about cost?"

"No." I sat up and pulled the sheet up with me. "It's not. Promise." I shuddered, thinking about a big affair. "All those people staring at me. The amount of preparation that goes into it seems exhausting. And I'd rather spend all the planning time making memories, not worried about flowers."

"So when do you want to get married?"

The night before had been a blur, but I remembered the Christmas tree and the fleeting thought I'd had when I saw it. "What would you say if we got married at your apartment, by the Christmas tree, in pajamas on Christmas Eve? Keep it the three of us, and then on Christmas morning, we tell Remmy about the baby."

"Love it. We'll work on getting everything done together."

That would be perfect. Intimate and family oriented. Lucian leaned over and gave a quick kiss. "I want to show you something."

He walked out of the bedroom. I grabbed my robe and followed him out into the living room where an array of food was displayed for breakfast. There was a stack of paperwork at the end. "Are you hungry?"

"I'm pregnant. I'm always hungry."

Lucian smiled, then sat. After fixing my plate I joined him on the couch, nibbling on some fruit. "What's going on?"

"I'd like to discuss something. I want you to listen to what I'm saying before you respond."

This seemed heavy for so early on a Saturday morning. "What's on your mind?"

Lucian grabbed my free hand. "I know you want to raise our baby and stay home with him or her." I went to speak, but he gently pressed his forefinger to my lips. "Please let me finish. I'm not demanding anything. I want to get my whole thought out there for you to think about. If you aren't ready to respond today, that's okay."

I nodded, a little nervous.

"And I know that you feel fifty percent financially responsible. And even with getting married I would assume you'd still feel the same way."

It was hard not to interject, but I remained quiet and nodded.

"I get Braden screwed you over and left you to start over. I get it. I truly do. You know I've wrestled my own demons when it came to Crystal."

Where was he going with this? He grabbed the paper. "There is five million dollars in an account for you." I gasped and shook my head. But Lucian kept going. "It's in funds you can access. If for any reason you left me, the funds are yours without question. There is enough in this account that you should feel secure knowing you and our child would be taken care of. There is not going to be a prenup. My lawyers, of course, advised against this avenue, but I won't start this marriage with a contract that says things might end. The funds I'm giving you are a gift. That's it. I want you to feel secure that you can raise our child. I want to make your dreams come true.

If you want to stay home and raise our baby and Remmy, I will do whatever it takes to make you feel comfortable in doing so."

My throat tightened. "I don't want the money, Lucian. I just want your heart."

"And you have that. I don't want you worried *if* you decide to quit your job. That is *your* choice. But I want you to have the choice free without financial worries. I don't want you worried about paying for half a stroller, Addilyn. I want you to buy a damned fleet of whichever ones you want."

This was too much. "Lucian, I can't—"

"Then what will make you feel secure that you can make choices without the burden of finances? I support your choices. If you want to work, that's fine. But I want it to be what *you* want."

"But what about you? What do you want?"

"For you and Remmy to be happy. And when this next little boy or girl comes, I want them to be happy, too." Lucian was patient as he watched me struggle with this offer to make my dreams a reality. "My only goal in this is to make you feel secure so you aren't stressed."

Trust. I had to have trust. And Lucian was willing to throw it all away for a child that wasn't his. He loved with his whole heart. And that heart belonged to me. In a moment of self-awareness, I made my decision. "I don't want the account. But I want to stay home and raise this baby. I want to be there with Remmy. The thought of having a nanny be with the baby most of the time just doesn't feel right to me."

Love was never a guarantee. But a life without love was no life at all. Life was giving Lucian and myself a second chance at happiness.

Lucian kissed me and whispered against my lips, "Then be with our baby. Be there with Remmy. Be there with me."

CHAPTER 36 ♥

Lucian

"Lucian, Dubster's lawyer sent me a motion. They're going for custody and plan on filing tomorrow."

"Fuck." I knew this was coming.

Walt took a deep breath. "They asked if we wanted to settle out of court. That was the reason they claimed to send it before filing."

Bastards just wanted an easy payday. "What are our options?"

"You said you're getting married Christmas Eve?"

"Yes."

I knew Walt had been relieved to hear Addilyn and I were getting married sooner rather than later—from a legal standpoint. I'd also been upfront with Addilyn and assured her the two weren't related. I never wanted her to doubt my intentions. My fiancée's trust was important to me, and I didn't want to lose it.

"I'll get it stalled until January with some motions I'll come up with. That way you'll be married and Addilyn won't be able to testify against you about any knowledge of Remmy... just in case it comes to that."

I scrubbed a hand down my face. "Hopefully, it doesn't make it that far."

"Let's hope, but prepare for the worst."

We hung up and I stared at the latest investor proposal for my expansion overseas. If I went through with it, Black Media stood to make a fortune. But what would be the cost? I pushed the contract aside, not ready to commit. Nancy came over the intercom. "Mr. Black, Ms. DeRoss is here."

"Send her in."

Addilyn walked in with a bag. "I thought you might be hungry. Nancy said you had about thirty minutes free for lunch today so I thought I'd swing—" She stopped. "What's wrong?"

"Dubster's lawyer reached out to Walt. We'll be at trial after Christmas."

Addilyn gasped. "No, no." She shook her head. "No."

I remained calm on the outside. With her condition, situations easily set her off. This was serious, but I needed Addilyn to not be stressed. "It's being delayed until after Christmas so you can't testify against me. We'll be protected as husband and wife."

She nodded. "Will it come to that?"

Walking around to the front of the desk, I brought her to me. "I hope not. But Walt wants to be prepared for the worst. And remember we have the tape. And the fact Remmy knows me as his father."

"We can't lose him. I'll do whatever it takes, Lucian."

"Me, too, sweetheart."

CHAPTER 37

Lucian

"Walt, that is horseshit and you know it!" I was fucking pissed as I stared at the court order.

"I know, Lucian. It was unexpected."

Unexpected.

I fisted my hand and slammed it on my desk. "What the fuck? We're straight to DNA testing?"

"I called the judge to get it moved until after January. She wanted to put this to bed quickly when we convened. She told me the easiest thing was a DNA test. Before she decides if this goes to trial, she'll read the results to us. In her eyes, you're the father and this saves time. If I argued... well, you know how it would have ended, Lucian."

"Fuck."

"Yeah, our hands are tied. You refuse, it'll raise eyebrows. You need to be shocked to hear you aren't the father when that time comes. In the meantime, take Remmy down to the lab so you can be tested."

"When?"

"Judge has asked for today or tomorrow. She wants it done before the weekend. Dubster's lawyer already sent me an email stating he was already on his way."

"Shit. Shit. Shit." There weren't any options. I'd hoped we'd be able to get through Christmas without worrying about this. Unfortunately, the test would be looming over our heads the entire time.

"Listen, just get it done. We'll have a hearing on the third of January and go from there. Practice being shocked."

"Understood."

This was going to be the worst day of my life.

"That tickled," Remmy giggled. They took the saliva sample from Remmy and put it in a tube next to mine.

Addilyn had quit her job with High Impact Marketing earlier that morning. I knew it had been emotionally hard for her, but she was here for Remmy and me. From what she'd told me, it had gone well and Ria had been expecting it. She was genuinely happy for Addilyn.

Addilyn hovered around the tech. "And you're sure these samples won't be tampered with?"

The young guy smiled at Addilyn, loving the attention from a beautiful woman. "Yes, Ms. DeRoss. See this number right here? It's being logged as Lucian Black. And this number will be logged as Remmy Black. And this number is for…" the tech looked at Remmy and then continued discreetly, "the other person. It's all logged into the tablet, and we have the best security. Nothing will happen."

"Oh, wonderful. It makes me feel better that there won't be a mix-up."

"I want to do that again." Remmy said. The tech had been great. He brought another swab over. "I'll let you get your own this time to take home. You can even take a plastic tube, too."

Remmy excitedly took it. When I turned, Addilyn's expression was oddly neutral. I quirked my brow at her and she gave me a confused look. I knew this was hard for her. When I called to tell her about the appointment today, she'd been near panic. Her odd calm was confusing.

"How about we go get ice cream before we go home?" I asked.

"Yay!"

As we left the laboratory, Addilyn checked her phone. "Oh no. I forgot I'm supposed to meet Wynter for lunch. How about you boys go and we'll have a special dinner tonight?"

I leaned over and kissed her cheek. "Take the car. Remmy and I will walk over to Dylan's Candy Bar."

"Yay! I love Dylan's."

Addilyn kissed us good-bye. "See you at home. Bring me some candy."

We waved good-bye and Remmy held my hand like a big boy.

Please don't let me lose him. I can't lose my son.

CHAPTER 38

Lucian

"I now pronounce you husband and wife."

I was the happiest man on earth as the pastor pronounced Addilyn was my wife. I stared into her eyes. "I will love you for the rest of my life, Addilyn."

"And I'll love you the rest of mine."

I leaned over to kiss Addilyn in the glow of our Christmas tree while Remmy hugged our legs. "Addawin, now you never have to leave."

She smiled against my lips, and I savored this perfect moment. Addilyn knelt to hug Remmy, and I nodded to the pastor and his wife as they discreetly left. The pastor's wife had been our witness.

Addilyn hugged Remmy to her. "I know. I am so excited to be part of your family."

My son clutched Addilyn and whispered, "Can we have those cookies now?"

We laughed as we moved to the window, where Addilyn had set up the milk and cookies for us to enjoy after the wedding. At first, I had been skeptical why Addilyn wanted to keep the wedding simple, but I realized we needed this. Our lives had been too chaotic. And since the details didn't matter, Addilyn had made Remmy very much a part of the decisions. Earlier that afternoon, he and Addilyn had baked the cookies.

He took a bite. "Mmm-mmm, we baked good."

Addilyn ruffled his hair. "Yes, we did."

My life was complete.

This was peace.

Somehow, we'd managed to push aside the trouble with Dave Dubster for the last few days and live in the moments we had.

Remmy sat in Addilyn's lap in his reindeer PJs. She kissed his cheek. "It's almost bedtime. Are you excited for Santa to come?"

"Yes! And I know what I want! I changed my mind."

Over the past few weeks, Remmy had been consistent about what he wanted. I responded, "I thought you told him a new fort and a car."

He shook his head. "Not anymore. I want something else."

I saw Addilyn's eyes widen, and I'm sure she mirrored my hope that it was a request that could be fulfilled. Christmas Eve, and everything was closed.

Hesitantly, she asked, "And what do you want now?"

"A baby brudder or sister."

Our eyes met and we shared a secret smile.

"I wanna play with dem. And we can make cookies with dem. I'll be the best big brudder ever."

Addilyn kissed the top of his head. "I think it's almost time for bed."

I picked up Remmy. "We'll see what can be done about that. But for now, we need to get to sleep so Santa can come. Otherwise, he might miss our house."

Remmy laid his head on Lucian's shoulder and pretended to snore. "I go to sleep real fast."

We laughed and made our way to his bedroom where he hugged Mister Teddy to him. Addilyn kissed his cheek. "I love you so much, Remmy. Thanks for letting me join your family."

"Wuv you, too, Addawin. I told you Daddy wuved you."

"Yes, you did."

Addilyn began to hum, and it brought me back to the first time she met Remmy. The moment I walked in and saw her racing cars on his rug, I'd known I was in love. She loved Remmy, truly loved him as if he were her own.

After a few measures of the song, Remmy fell asleep. He'd been so excited about today that he'd woken up extra early.

I held Addilyn's hand as we went to our bedroom and I locked the door. Addilyn walked to the fireplace and turned my way, unbuttoning her white silk pajama top.

My cock hardened at the sight of her lingerie underneath. She had on a white teddy that hugged her every curve. I stalked over to her, taking off my pajama top. Addilyn licked her lips. The moment I was close enough, I jerked her to me, eliciting giggles.

"Is someone impatient?"

"Very."

I captured her mouth. and she moaned into mine.

"You are mine." I led her back to the bed and laid her down. "Say it, Addilyn. Say you're mine."

"Yes, Lucian. I'm yours. I'll always be yours."

CHAPTER 39

Addilyn

"**M**erry Christmas, wife."

Lucian's words warmed me all over. I stretched, exhausted from our night. His hand cupped my breast under my shirt as he kissed my neck.

"Lucian, we can't."

His lips caressed my skin. "I know, but I can't stop touching you."

At some point, if everything went according to plan, we would sneak off for a couple of days for a honeymoon. But given the current situation, neither of us wanted to be away from Remmy. "I can't believe we're married."

"This is one of the best days of my life. The other being when Remmy was born. And the third will be the day our child is born."

Tears filled my eyes, and Lucian quickly wiped them away. "I hope those are happy tears."

"They are. So happy."

His hand rested on my stomach. "Looks like Santa granted Remmy's wish after all."

I giggled and kissed Lucian. "I can't wait to tell him. We need to get ready. He's going to wake up at any second."

We got dressed, unlocked the door, and Lucian turned up the electric fireplace to give the place a warm, cozy feel. Through the night, it had been a soft glow as we made love.

"What would you think if I turned the apartment downstairs into my office and maybe a media room for family time? When the baby gets here, I'm going to be home for a bit as we adjust. That way, I can work and be close by."

"Really?"

He nuzzled my nose. "Yes, really. Do you like the idea?"

"I love it."

After kissing me, he pulled back. "I have something for you. Stay right there." I was so excited for Christmas. I pulled out Lucian's present from underneath the bed and laid it on the bedspread. He raised his eyebrow. "What's that?"

"I have a gift for you, too."

I loved staring at Lucian in his black silk pants as he walked shirtless to the fireplace.

He came back with a small box. "Merry Christmas."

I pulled off the lid and found a beautiful glass jar filled with pieces of paper. "What's this?"

"Three hundred and sixty-five reasons why I love you are in the jar. Over the next year, I want you to see through my eyes all the reasons I love you, so that on even the rough days, you'll know."

"Lucian." My throat was tight. "This is beautiful."

"Open one today."

I grabbed a piece of paper and read it out loud.

I love the way you love my son.

"I do love him so much. If—" I choked up and nearly lost it.

Lucian put his finger on my lips. "No sad thoughts today. None. We're going to have faith this works out."

I prayed that was true. "Open your gift."

Lucian opened the box and pulled out two albums.

"I've been scouring your photos for pictures of you and Remmy and pieced this together from his birth until this year. The second is for our baby. There are places to leave notes for them and give your children pieces of wisdom. Then, on their eighteenth birthdays, you'll give it to them so when they're grown and out on their own in the world, they'll never forget how much their daddy loves them."

He leaned over to kiss me. "This is the best present I have ever received."

"Daddy! Daddy! Santa came." The door flew open and Remmy ran in. "Come! Come! He brought me my fort!"

Lucian picked up Remmy and walked toward the living room. "I thought you were going to get us first."

"Too excited! He came!"

Children were the most precious gift. I placed the piece of paper back in the box, wanting to keep track of all the reasons why Lucian loved me. I walked into the living room and found Remmy running around to his different toys. He looked frustrated.

"What's the matter?"

"I thought there'd be a baby out here. I told Santa I wanted a baby brudder or sister."

I pressed my lips together before explaining, "Well, Santa doesn't deliver real babies."

His shoulders slumped. I looked at Lucian, and he grabbed the present I'd wrapped a couple of days ago. "Open this present first. It's something Addilyn made you."

"You *made* for me?" Remmy cocked his head toward me.

"Yes, just for you."

Paper flew off the box, and he ripped the lid off. "What's this for?"

"Well, it's a blanket I made for you and…"

Lucian pulled out the two blankets and finished. "There's one for you… and this one's for your baby sister or brother."

"I'm getting a baby? Santa gave me my wish!" Remmy jumped up, holding his blanket.

"Yes, you are. There is a baby in Addilyn's tummy."

Remmy ran over to my stomach and yelled at it. "I wanna play cars, okay? Come play."

Lucian chuckled and scooped him up. "Well, the baby won't be here until summer. But once he or she gets big enough, I bet they'll play cars with you."

"Why did Santa put the baby in Addawin's tummy?"

"Because it has to grow. Then when the baby is grown, you'll have a baby brother or sister."

None of this made sense to Remmy, and we had to tiptoe around some answers. As the morning progressed and he opened gift after gift, Remmy kept his blanket close to him. "I gonna teach my baby brudder or sister how to do this." Remmy raced around the living room.

Lucian wrapped his arm around my shoulders, and I focusing on branding every moment into my mind. Life was too short to let the moments rush by.

CHAPTER 40

Lucian

"Mr. Black, Mr. Dubster, I appreciate you meeting me informally with your attorneys." The judge sat behind her desk in her chambers.

This meeting was a nightmare in the making. When the judge read the results, all hell was going to break loose. I readied myself to play the part of a shocked father. The entire thing made me sick as I watched Dave Dubster's ambulance chaser of a lawyer speak quietly to his client. Addilyn squeezed my hand but otherwise appeared to be perfectly calm.

Before the judge could say anything further, Dubster's attorney said, "I'd like to—"

Judge Mateas cut him off. "I'd like to look at these results, and then we'll decide what the next steps are. But I'm warning you, Mr. Thatcher, I am not a fan of frivolous lawsuits."

"Understood. I—"

She held up her hand, silencing him. The judge opened a sealed envelope and pulled out the paperwork. Her eyes scanned all the reports, her brow pinching. *Fuck.* I readied myself. Addilyn watched the judge. I was two seconds from flying out of my chair and beating the shit out of Dave fucking Dubster.

The judge looked to the other side of the room. "Mr. Dubster, why, may I ask, do you believe you are Remmy Black's father?"

He waited for his lawyer to nod. "Because I was fu— sleeping with Crystal Black before she married Lucian Black. I kept sleeping with her after."

The judge didn't even try to hide her disgust. "So, you've known that Remmy Black existed—and was potentially your child—these past nearly four years?"

"Yes." The attorney looked at Dubster in disapproval.

The judge asked her next question. "Why come forward now?"

This time Dubster waited for his lawyer to nod again. "His mother is dead. I want to be his father. Kid needs a father."

"I see."

Fuck. This was where the ball would drop and the war would begin. She set the papers aside. "Mr. Dubster, go waste someone else's time. Lucian Black is the father of Remmy Black. And I will have this entered into the public record to stop any more nonsense going forward."

"But she said!" Dave shouted.

The judge folded her hands on her desk. "Well, Mr. Dubster, Crystal Black misinformed you. There is no need to proceed with a trial. Good day, gentlemen."

What.

Just.

Happened?

I knew I wasn't Remmy's father. Yet the judge had stated I was. I kept a neutral face, as if that was the verdict I had been expecting. Walt stood and motioned for me to join him. I gave a nod to the judge and put my hand on Addilyn's back to guide her out of the room.

When we were in the limo, Walt looked at me. "I thought you said—"

"I thought so, too."

I knew so. The original test had been done meticulously. I wasn't going to argue with the judge, but I was worried what might happen next.

Walt scrubbed his graying hair. "Well, thank fuck you were wrong."

"Yes."

But I wasn't. I knew I wasn't.

Walt poured himself a drink from the bar of the limo. "So, that's over with. Now that the judge has that recorded, we won't have to worry about any other scum coming out of the woodwork. Shit, Lucian, be thrilled. We won without having to go to war."

"I am thrilled. Beyond thrilled. Thank you, Walt, for everything."

"You're welcome. I'm going to take the rest of the day off. Call me if you need anything."

"I will."

After we pulled up to his building and let him out, Addilyn smiled at me, tears in her eyes. "It's over."

"Yes, it is."

I rolled down the partition window. "Jim, can you swing by my office?"

"Yes, sir."

We rode to my office, and I was quiet, trying to figure it out. *Did I read the report wrong?* No, I hadn't. I was thankful, but wary at the same time, needing to understand if there was another player in this game. A player so powerful they had control over DNA test results.

When we arrived, I closed my office door and turned on the privacy setting for my windows. "This makes little sense."

I went to the locked safe and pulled out the report.

0.01% chance of paternity.

"What is that?"

I handed it to Addilyn, who took and read it. Then she walked over to my recording device and unplugged it. Intrigued, I followed her into the bathroom, where she turned on the fan and locked the door. Then she held the report over to the sink, grabbed a matchbook from her purse, and lit it. When the report caught fire, she dropped it into the sink.

"What are you doing?" I asked, perplexed.

"Finishing this."

What?

Stunned, I watched the report burn. Addilyn had arranged this. Somehow, she'd ensured we'd never lose Remmy. I lifted a brow and she mouthed, *"Not here."*

Once the paper was charred beyond recognition, she swept the ashes into a plastic bag from her purse and added water.

Holy shit.

Addilyn had arranged to dispose of this evidence.

"Addilyn?"

"Don't. It's done, and I'd do it again in a heartbeat."

I grabbed her hand. "Come on."

There were answers I needed, and I needed them now.

CHAPTER
41

Addilyn

"You had the tests switched?" Lucian asked as soon as we walked through the door of the beach house.

I placed my purse on the table and flopped on the couch. Lucian had brought us here because it was a safe place to talk. "Yes, I did."

His confusion was written all over his face. "How?"

"After today, we will never mention this again. But you need to know that I did it for you and that little boy I love with all my heart." He nodded. "The day we had the tests done, I noticed everything was digital. There was no paper trail. I took a picture of the screen with your, Remmy's, and Dave's file numbers and went to see Wynter."

I watched the expression on his face as he put the pieces together. "Keller Industries supplies the security software to the laboratory. You had Wynter switch the tests."

"Yes. I knew it was a risk since we weren't one hundred percent sure Dubster was the father. We knew you weren't, which means the judge would know as well, opening up a hell neither of us wanted. And I know it's illegal. And I knew it would piss you off. But it will never come back to us. You, me, and Wynter are the only ones who know or will ever know what happened. No one else."

I could feel myself becoming emotional, but I continued. "That man only wanted money for our precious boy. I saw a way to make sure Remmy stayed safe, and I took it. I know you're going to be mad at me, but that's a chance I was willing take, Lucian."

He stopped and walked to me. I waited for his reaction. In a swift movement he pulled me to him. "Oh, sweetheart, come here. It was a huge gamble, but you are the bravest woman I know." Lucian looked me in the eye. "So, Dubster really was the father."

This was the part that would hurt forever. "Yes, biologically." I put my hand over Lucian's heart. "You are Remmy's *real* father. Being connected by blood doesn't make someone a parent, their love for the child does. If Dubster could have been a good father, I would never have done this. I want you to know that. It would have ruined Remmy—losing his mother first and then being taken from the only father he'd ever known and forced to go with someone who would have sold him for money."

"I know."

Lucian kissed me fiercely, as if his life depended on it. He picked me up and carried me to the bedroom. Never again would we speak of Dave Dubster or what had been done to protect our little boy. It would be a secret we would take with us to the grave.

CHAPTER 42 ♥

Addilyn

"Addawin, when can I meet the baby peanut?"

At the last ultrasound, we'd shown Remmy pictures of the baby. He thought it looked like a peanut, so the term stuck. "Not until the summer, remember?"

Remmy huffed on the couch. "I shoulda told Santa I wanted a ready baby. I don't like it has to cook."

Explaining pregnancy to an almost four-year-old was complicated when details had to be vague. So, my tummy was an oven for the baby to cook in. I laughed and pulled the lasagna out of the actual oven.

"Are you sure it's in your tummy? It doesn't look fat."

I pressed my lips together to keep from laughing. Most of my clothes were too small. "I'm positive. My tummy will grow soon."

Lucian stepped out of the elevator. "Dinner smells amazing. Did you wash your hands, Remmy?"

He jutted out his lip and walked down the hall. Lucian's brow lifted. "What's his deal?"

"He's a little sad Santa didn't bring him a ready-made baby. And he wants me to be fatter so he knows there's a baby in there."

Lucian laughed, coming up behind me to wrap his arms around me. "I like the changes and can't wait for your stomach to show our baby inside."

"I hadn't noticed."

"Hmm… then I'm not doing my job right."

"Probably should up your game."

He nipped my ear. "Game on, Mrs. Black."

I shivered at the dark promise but tucked all that away when Remmy bounced back into the kitchen. We ate dinner, and I treasured every moment of our family time. I loved being home with Remmy during the day, and I believed he loved it just as much.

After dinner, I picked up the toys in the living room and straightened up the place while Lucian put Remmy to bed.

"I'm going to order Remmy a countdown timer for his room," he said as he walked back into the living room.

"For the baby?" I laughed, and he nodded. "He'll love that. How did your call go?" Lucian had been working to finalize the expansion overseas.

"I've put the brakes on expansion."

I stopped cleaning and turned to Lucian. "What? Why?"

"It was going to require extensive travel, and that's not in the best interest of my family at the moment."

That surprised me. He'd been working toward the expansion since before we met. "Lucian, we'd—"

"I'm not missing a moment of this pregnancy. After the baby arrives and life settles down, I'll look at it again. I've been the one stalling this deal for about the last month or so. Yes, the company would stand to make a lot of money from this deal, but we have more than enough. Someday, I'll expand. That day just isn't now."

"Well, as long as that's what you want."

"It is."

After dinner we settled in our bedroom. Lucian was taking a shower after I feigned being tired. Well, I was tired, but never too tired for Lucian. Quickly, I changed into a little teddy that showcased the tiny baby bump I'd noticed earlier. It was like I had popped overnight.

Lucian walked out of the bathroom, scrubbing a towel over his head. "You know—" He stopped and stared at me. In the next second, he was on his knees in front of me. "When did this happen?"

His strong hands caressed my stomach. "Today. I woke up and suddenly, nothing fit."

"I love this."

The dark storm was there full force. "Tonight, you're going to ride my cock."

My legs shifted together. As Lucian's hand drifted up my leg, I laid back, letting him own me mind, body, and soul.

CHAPTER 43

Addilyn

"Oh my gosh! I love your little pooch." Wynter put her hands on my stomach when I stepped out of the dressing room. "It's crazy how fast it came. My clothes fit for a few weeks… and then they don't." I looked in the mirror at the black dress with the high waist. "Do you think this will work for events?"

It was elegant and still had a sexy edge but would grow with me as my stomach expanded.

"It looks beautiful."

I reached for the price tag, but Wynter shooed my hand away. "Lucian's orders. Get what you like. No looking at price tags."

"We need to be sensible." I raised an eyebrow.

Wynter raised her eyebrows. "Or enjoy a man who wants to dote on you. Plus, you can pay him back by stuffing his sausage."

"Oh gosh, that is not a good analogy for a pregnant woman. But still…" Wynter gave me the look and I conceded. "Fine, no price tags. But promise me you won't let me buy a cotton T-shirt that costs four hundred dollars."

She gathered the yes pile, which was quite large already. "Promise. Once we're done, how does lunch sound?"

"Amazing."

It was nice having a girls' day. Yesterday, I'd gone to lunch with Ria. She had a new person starting, and I was going to help onboard her three days a week for a couple of hours. Ria had been wonderful to me, and I was happy to help. When she offered to pay me, I offered my services for free. It was because of her company I found the love of my life.

And I found it was just as important to schedule adult time as well as activities for Remmy.

We found a table at Rex, and it brought back memories of when I'd first found out who Mister Mystery was. Marty had gotten to know me pretty well since Lucian and I frequented this spot. A man walked in and I froze, recognizing him immediately. It was Kent Martin, the older of my half brothers. He stood at the pickup line.

I told Wynter, "I'll be back."

I took my drink over to the pickup line where Marty stood. "Can I get a refill?"

"Absolutely, Addilyn."

Kent didn't appear to know who I was. I hadn't heard from or seen the Martins since our uncomfortable lunch meeting. It was like they'd vanished after the news broke about them. Not once had my siblings reached out. This might be a bad idea, but I needed to know if they knew who I was.

"Order up," Marty said.

With his tray in hand, I said to Kent, "That looks delicious. What was that listed as on the menu?"

"Turkey on rye. It's my favorite. I think it's the number four." He looked me straight in the eye, but there was no recognition.

I smiled but felt a little hurt inside. "Thanks, have a great day."

"You, too."

He had no idea who I was. Teresa Martin had lied. Kent wasn't excited to meet me. I'd often wondered if my half brothers hadn't reached out because of Dr. Martin's malpractice scandal. He likely had no clue I even existed.

Marty handed me back my drink, and on stiff legs, I walked back to Wynter. Inconspicuously, I watched Kent. He had my dark hair. We had similar features, but Dwayne's influence made us different enough with his broader shoulders and fuller face.

Wynter nudged my foot. "What are you staring at so hard?"

I broke the connection and looked at the food I'd barely touched. "That's my half brother, Kent Martin."

Wynter gasped. "You're kidding me."

"No, I'm not."

Wynter knew the entire story. "Want me to do some recon?"

It was hard not to look, but I stopped before I became obvious. "I… uh…"

"You do." She pulled out some cash to leave on the table. "Have Jim pull the car up and wait around the block."

This seemed like a bad idea, but I was curious. "You sure? Wynter, please be careful."

"It's a café full of people. I'm not following him down a dark alley. I got this."

I walked out and met Jim at the curb. Once I was in the car, I instructed him on where to wait. Fifteen minutes went by before the door opened, letting a gust of cold air in with it as Wynter sat next to me.

"Are we good, Mrs. Black?"

"Yes, Jim, thank you."

The car pulled away from the curb. Wynter shook her head to get rid of the few rain droplets. "Well, I asked if he was Kent Martin because I recognized him from his parents' charity. He said he was and looked worried I was going to bring up their latest transgressions. I deflected and said I loved what they do for the community, insinuating I hadn't heard."

"And?"

"I asked how his family was. He skirted around his parents… surprise, surprise. And then he said his brother had gotten a kidney transplant last week. He was on his way to check on him."

I sagged back in my chair, relieved that Wade had found a donor. I didn't want anyone to suffer.

Wynter added, "But no, I don't think he recognized you. He never acted weird."

That hurt more than I'd expected it to. "Why does it bother me?"

"Because it means your bio mom really is a bitch. And she's a narcissist like Lucian said. It's hard when there isn't a black-or-white answer."

That was true. Now that I wasn't of use to them, she had no use for me. It was hard for me to wrap my head around ever treating my child like this. She loved her sons, but not me. It hurt. Lucian still had investigators searching for my dad, too. I had questions I might never get answers to. I shrugged, "I guess so." I tried to shake off the gloom. "Thanks for coming with me today."

"It was fun. I will gladly spend Lucian's money any time. And I got some things today that will bring you-know-who to his knees."

While we'd been shopping, I'd taken a call from Jan, and Wynter had stepped into a different store. I figured that was when she'd bought the lingerie. "How are you and…" I lowered my voice. "…you know who?"

There was a little shift in her expression, but Wynter hid it well. "We're fine. I've been holding out on him some. Or maybe a lot."

"Why?" I laughed.

She shrugged. "I like to drive him wild. It's good for him to have to work for it."

I laughed but sensed there was more to what she was saying. "Poor, poor guy who shall not be named."

"Or poor me. I'm the one who has been orgasm-less for a week."

We looked at each other and said, "No, definitely poor, poor Nipple Man."

CHAPTER 44

Lucian

I stared at the report as I waited for Addilyn to get home from training with Ria. I'd asked Kaysen if he could take Remmy for ice cream.

"Honey, I'm home."

I stood, dreading this conversation. Addilyn placed her purse on the table and looked around. At eighteen weeks pregnant, she had a definite baby bump I couldn't stop touching. "Where's Remmy?"

"He's with Kaysen."

"What happened?"

"Come sit down."

Addilyn sat. "You're scaring me, Lucian. Is everything okay with Remmy?"

"He's fine. I received some information today, and I need to share it with you. I think we located your father."

Addilyn's eyes widened. "Are you serious? Where is he?"

"He's alive, but Teresa was actually right. He's a card shark and swindler."

I knew Addilyn had hoped for a happily ever after with her father. She wanted the connection she'd missed with her mother. But this man was trouble.

Addilyn's shoulders dropped. "Are you serious?"

"Unfortunately so. They've tracked him to Brooklyn."

She gasped. "He's here? I'm surprised he hasn't tried to contact my mother."

I slid a picture toward Addilyn. "This was what your mother looked like around the time of her meeting with Jeb Jericho Hallis."

"She altered his name? Or she didn't know his real name? Maybe it was a one-night stand and he doesn't remember her. Or maybe he doesn't know I exist. It's so confusing."

There were details about what drove Teresa Martin that we would never know. "I don't know."

For a second, Addilyn looked at the picture of her mother, who looked completely different with blond hair and plain clothes. "I want to see him."

"Addilyn…" The man had been in prison more than he hadn't. He was more crooked than a three-dollar bill.

Addilyn turned my way. "Not meet him, just see him from a darkly tinted car window. I need it for closure."

She deserved that much, even if it meant taking her to see the scum bucket.

"Okay, let's go. I'll get a location on him."

The drive to Brooklyn was quiet as Addilyn read over the information I had acquired. Teresa altering his name had thrown my investigators off. Jim pulled up to a curb and we waited.

About thirty minutes later, a greasy-haired man in a cheap blue polyester suit walked out of a bar like he owned the place, holding a bottle of beer. Then he staggered and took another swig of his beer.

Addilyn asked, "That's him, isn't it?"

"Yes."

The man pushed another man out of the way as he approached a group of women that looked like prostitutes. We weren't in the best part of Brooklyn, but Jim and I were armed. And this was better than Addilyn trying to find him on her own.

She turned to me. "I've seen enough. Let's go."

She was quiet the rest of the day. So quiet that at one point, I started to worry. Kaysen offered to keep Remmy at his apartment overnight, which gave Addilyn time to process.

Later that night, she stood at the window, staring out into the city.

"How are you doing?" I asked.

"It's been a strange day. It's weird, but part of me wishes I never found out Teresa Martin was my mother. It was easier knowing my mom had left for my own good and not her own selfishness. I will do everything I can so that Remmy never knows that feeling—even if it means lying about Crystal."

I wrapped my arms around her. "What can I do?"

"After tonight, I'm never going to let them occupy my thoughts again. My father appalls me, and I guess I'm fortunate my mother kept him out of our lives. My mother... I'll never have the answers, and I'm okay with that. She chose money over her daughter, and that's her loss. As far as Remmy and the baby are concerned, I want them to believe that my mother left me when I was little, and I never found out who she was. The truth dies with us, Lucian. Neither of the kids need to be tainted by something that cannot be changed."

I turned Addilyn around. "We create our own world, Addilyn. And we'll create our own happily ever after, as well. I cheated and looked at the ending. We're going to get that second chance at love you always wanted."

She gave me a small smile. "Did you just ruin the story?"

"I think I made it better."

CHAPTER 45

Addilyn

"Why doesn't she play, Addawin?"

We'd been home from the hospital for only a few hours. Remmy had been anxious for us to return. He hated having to leave the hospital each night for the last few days. I kissed the top of our daughter's head, smitten with her. "Well, she has to grow just like you did."

Remmy scrunched his nose while looking at his baby sister. Lucian held Remmy on his lap. Taryn cried, and I shifted her. "It's okay, baby girl, Mommy has you."

Being a mother was the best thing in the world, and I considered myself blessed to have two amazing children. Remmy's face looked a little sad, and I touched his cheek. "What's going on? Why do you have a sad face?"

Since meeting Taryn in the hospital, I knew Remmy was excited, but there seemed to be something bothering him. He pulled Mister Teddy closer. "Is Tawen gonna call you Mommy?"

That question shocked me a little, but it clicked what was going on. Now that I had a baby, Remmy was scared I wouldn't love him the same as I loved Taryn. His mother had abandoned him, so it was probably in his little mind that I might, too. I sat Taryn in her bassinet and turned my attention to Remmy. It was important he felt equal to his sister. "Yes, she will call me Mommy."

His little lip quivered. "Why can't I call you Mommy?"

My heart broke, and my eyes shot to Lucian, unsure how to answer the question. Lucian faced Remmy toward him. "Do you want to call Addilyn Mommy?"

"Yes. I wanted to for a long time. My mommy was sick, so she died. Now I don't have a mommy."

Lucian looked at me and nodded. I reached my hands out, and Lucian gently put Remmy on my lap. "Then you can call me Mommy. I consider you my son. You can have two mommies, Remmy. I have wanted you to call me Mommy, too."

Remmy's face lit up, and he got off my lap to stand beside the bassinet. "Tawen, I have the same mommy as you. Addawin is a good mommy. You gonna wuv her." Leaning down, he gave Taryn a small kiss.

Lucian caught Remmy midjump and set him back on my lap. It was hard for Remmy to remember he had to be gentle with me and his sister. He hugged my neck so tight. "I wuv you, Mommy."

"I love you, too, son."

Taryn began to cry, so Lucian picked her up and cooed to her. "Oh, my sweet girl, I think you need a diaper change." He paused a beat. "Is that so? Well, let me ask your big brother." Lucian looked at Remmy while rocking the baby. "Taryn wants to know if you'll hold her hand while I change her. She gets a little scared during a diaper change."

Remmy puffed out his chest. "I'm Tawen's big brudder. I make sure she not scared."

Lucian winked as they left the room. They were my entire world, and I knew I had gotten the happily ever after Lucian saw.

A week after we got home, Remmy and Taryn were asleep. At the same time. It was an absolute miracle. Remmy was back to his normal self and loved calling me Mommy. My heart was full.

I found Lucian in his old office on our floor, working. Next week, he was going to work in the renovated office downstairs, but this week, he had been with me every step of the way, helping. He was my better half in every way.

He looked up and stopped working. "How are you feeling?"

"Tired, but loving it at the same time. Are you still okay with me taking Remmy to Dylan's Candy Bar tomorrow for some one-on-one time?"

Lucian smiled. "For sure. Remmy's already planned out what he wants to order at the restaurant." This week Lucian had taken Remmy to the park for some father-son time, and I believed it helped Remmy's confidence. After that, we decided for the time being to make sure Remmy got at least an hour or two alone time with one of us every day since Taryn needed so much.

"Good. Every time he calls me Mommy, I want to cry. It's the sweetest thing in the world that he chose me."

Lucian looked down for a second and took a deep breath before meeting my eyes again. There was a new vulnerability there I hadn't seen before. "How would you feel about adopting Remmy?"

My throat tightened. "Really?"

"Yes, really. In his eyes, you're his mom now. And I'm awed how you keep Crystal painted as a good mother for him. After what she did, I know it's hard, but I also see the good it does. There's no reason to paint an ugly story when it only causes more hurt. I talked to him tonight, and he wants you to adopt him. He wants to make sure he belongs to you like Taryn does."

I started sobbing and took off toward Remmy's room, not caring that it was past his bedtime. When I opened his door, he flew across the floor into the bed and closed his eyes.

"Remmy."

He fake-snored. "I asleep, Mommy."

I knelt beside his bed. "Can you wake up so I can tell you something?"

Remmy flew up. "I awake."

With my hands on his face, I made sure I looked him in his eye. "Your daddy and I talked. I want you to know I want to adopt you, too. I want you to be my son."

"Really, Mommy?"

"Yes, my sweet, sweet son. You never have to worry you don't belong, Remmy. I love you as much as I love Taryn. There is room in my heart for everyone."

He put his tiny hands around my neck, and I held him tight. "So, if I ask Santa for anudder baby brudder or sister, you love us all?"

Lucian chuckled behind me. "Well, we might have to tell Santa to wait a little bit."

"Rats. I want a grown baby who plays."

Lucian came to sit on the bed. "Taryn will grow fast. Just wait."

CHAPTER 46♥

Lucian

It was late when I finished work and came upstairs to find my wife. Addilyn stood in front of the fireplace in our bedroom, humming and rocking Taryn. The reason I existed was for my family. Taryn was six weeks old. Remmy had turned four a week ago, and we had finalized the adoption on his birthday. Thanks to my selfless wife, my little boy would have the childhood I'd always dreamed for him. Everything I ever wanted was here in my home.

Addilyn turned my way and smiled. "She's finally asleep."

"Let me put her to bed."

I held my little girl and kissed her forehead. *Thank you for this life.* Not too long ago, I wondered if I was going to lose everything I ever cared about. Then, in the most unexpected way, I'd found love.

After I laid our sleeping daughter in her bassinet, I grabbed Addilyn's hand. "Dance with me."

"There isn't any music."

"Don't you know? We make our own music. We always have."

I brought Addilyn to me and thanked my lucky stars. Our unexpected love was the best thing I could have ever dreamed of.

EPILOGUE

Complicated Love

"Where have you been?"

I nearly jumped out of my skin at the sound of his voice as I entered my apartment. "Geez, you scared the shit out of me."

The light flipped on, and there was Kaysen, sitting in his favorite chair and staring at me.

I deflected, already on edge. "What are you doing here?"

"Wondering where you were."

Stay calm.

Normally, I avoided Kaysen for a day or two after I returned from *that* trip. The one I took three or four times a year to make sure my walls remained intact. There was no way I could keep up my façade when I was fragile, ready to crack from the ghosts of my past that haunted me.

Kaysen stood, and I swore he saw right through me. He took a few steps closer and asked again, "Where have you been?"

For a second—a very weak second—I almost told him. I *wanted* to tell him. I wanted Kaysen to tell me everything was going to be okay. I wanted him to hold me. I wanted him to tell me I'd made the right decision. I wanted more than just a fuck buddy. But I shoved all that away and buried it.

If I told Kaysen, he'd never look at me the same way again.

"Where were you, Wynter?"

I flicked my wrist. "I was just around. Did you miss me?"

"Wynter, you skipped town three days ago with only an 'I'll be back on Sunday.' Same as you do every two or three months."

Why isn't he letting this go?

We were friends with benefits. Some might have said best friends. And we never pried—it was what made us work. "I needed to handle some stuff."

I was just a question or two away from breaking down and telling him everything. So, I pulled my sweater over my head, and Kaysen's eyes zeroed in on my body. He pulled me to him and crushed his mouth to mine. The kiss was rough, needy, as if his ghosts were trying to take over him, too. This was why we worked. We made each other forget. For just a few minutes, we were free of our sins.

I needed him.

He needed me.

Kaysen's lips moved to my jaw and then to my ear. He whispered roughly, "I know what you're doing, baby. It's what you always do when I get too close."

His rough words shocked me, and I took a step back.

Shit, I was messed up in the head.

But so was Kaysen.

That was what made us perfect for each other in every way.

It was what made us... complicated.

Complicated Love, Wynter and Kaysen's story,
is coming September of 2019.

Visit www.authorkristinmayer.com
to stay up to date on the latest news.

While you wait for *Complicated Love*, if you haven't,
check out my Alaskan series.

Each book is a standalone within an interconnected series
that follows the Foster brothers:
Drake, Hayden, and Kane.

INTOXICATED
by YOU

An Exposed Hearts Novel

KRISTIN MAYER

Prologue

Alexa

The last few days had been a blur. One moment, my father was alive, and the next, Drake called to tell me he'd died. I'd spoken to him only three hours before he passed. And now he would never pick up the phone again when I called.

Something had seemed off the last few times we'd spoken. Like there was something he'd wanted to tell me but hadn't. *What's wrong?* When I'd asked, he'd deflected, which only made the anxiety of what it might have been worse.

Will I ever find out?

My dad was my rock—the person I could go to with anything. And now I would never be able to ask for his advice or make furniture with him when something was on my mind.

At least I still had Drake. Together, we would find our way.

Through it all, the love of my life had been by my side. Drake had been there for me in every way imaginable. He was my soul mate.

But inside, I was numb, and my mind was a mess as I tried to process the loss of my father. It felt like I was a stranger in my own skin. And I hated that feeling. Normally, I was self-assured and ready to tackle the world. But since my dad died, I was simply lost and not sure what my next step would be.

If only my dad could guide me.

My hands trembled as I opened the letter—the last piece of communication I would receive from my dad. After the reading of his will, his lawyer had given me the letter and said Dad had brought it by a couple of weeks ago.

Alexa.

As I traced the familiar handwriting, my throat tightened. That afternoon, I had slipped away to the pond behind my parents' house to read the letter by myself. The ground was thick with snow and it was bitter cold, but I didn't care.

A slow tremor started in my hands as I prepared myself. Maybe this was the guidance I needed to keep moving forward. Maybe fate had impressed upon Dad to bring this letter to the lawyer, knowing his time here on Earth was limited. I was a firm believer that everything happened for a reason.

I slipped my finger under the flap of the envelope and opened it.

The first line drew a sob I wasn't aware I'd been holding back.

My darling Alexa…

Dad would never say those words to me again. We'd never make any new memories ever again. I closed my eyes and tried to calm down. *I can do this. I can read this letter.*

Taking a deep breath, I focused on my dad's words.

My darling Alexa,

You have always meant the world to me. I've been struggling with something that I need to tell you. I couldn't find the words while we talked on the phone. I hope to take you to the cabin and tell you during your next visit. But if that time doesn't come, I've written this letter. I have to protect my little girl.

I know you love Drake, but you need to listen to me.

Drake is not the right man for you. I know this comes as a shock, but I need you to trust me on this. As your dad, I implore you. End things with him. It will be for the best. I know this doesn't make much sense, but I need you to do as I ask. Do this one thing for me. In time you'll understand why. This may be the last piece of fatherly advice I can give you.

I love you, Alexa, with my whole heart.

Dad

When I reached his signature, my world imploded. My heart shattered into a million pieces, and nothing made sense.

How can I give up Drake?

How can I not *listen to my dad?*

CHAPTER
One

Alexa

"Answer your phone," I whispered, peering into the window. The entire town of Skagway was in the Red Onion Saloon, celebrating Mayor Richmond's reelection. I'd arrived in Skagway two days earlier and so far had managed to go unnoticed, which was quite a feat for such a small town. But I wasn't going to go unnoticed today. Oh no, Teagan had insisted I meet her there to get the keys for the property I'd bought. Why she took them in the first place still perplexed me.

The real estate agent, Nancy, had driven to Ketchikan for a convention. I'd gotten a text saying she'd given the keys to Teagan. I'd never asked Teagan to get them and couldn't get a straight answer why she had. The previous night, I texted her to say I was just going to have a locksmith come open it up for me. Magically, I got a response to meet her at the Red Onion

Saloon to get my keys.

I'd gotten the place for a song, which worried me. Something felt off about the whole situation. But things with Teagan normally did. And I needed to start cleaning up the soon-to-be clinic as soon as possible.

Inside the bar, people cheered while the mayor stood on a chair in the middle of the room. Drake was inside—I could feel it. Whenever he was near, my body came alive and excitement danced along my skin.

But I wasn't ready to see him. I'd hoped these feelings would have disappeared over the last two years. But if my current state of awareness was any indication, they hadn't in the slightest. Which sucked. Drake Foster was the one person I couldn't be with. Ending things with Drake had been my father's last request before he died.

Teagan knew this. She *knew* it.

Drake had probably moved on, but I'd refused to ask. If he'd found someone else, I didn't know if I could face it. The thought caused my chest to ache. I knew at some point it would be necessary to see him. Face what I had done. But not today. *Not today.* I needed to get myself grounded and face other demons from my past.

Facing Drake would happen, of course. I'd returned to my small hometown to open a clinic with my friend Hollis. *Well, technically, he's Dr. Hollis Fritz.* Skagway didn't have its own doctor. For major medical crises, the injured had to be airlifted to another town with a doctor. It cost thousands of dollars after insurance; that alone could put severe financial stress on a family here. Waiting for transport delayed treatment for critical cases. And if the weather was bad enough, even airlifting wasn't possible.

That was the reason my father had died two years ago after a logging incident. There was too much ice, and the chopper couldn't get to my dad in time. With a focus I'd never had before, I'd gone back to college my sophomore year and buried myself in my studies to finish my nursing degree in record time.

My phone vibrated, and I crouched down lower to answer Hollis.

Hollis: *Decided to come up a day early. I'll be there later today.*

Me: *Want me to pick you up?*

Hollis: *Nah, my car is being delivered to the airport. I'll get settled at the hotel. We can meet up tomorrow. You still going to the clinic?*

Hollis had always been a bit of a loner. That was why we'd clicked two years ago. He was a trust-fund baby who wanted a break from the leisurely life of the rich and famous. Our little town of Skagway, Alaska, would provide that escape.

I hunkered down a little lower to ensure my head wasn't visible above the windowsill.

Me: *Yeah, that's the plan. I'm currently standing on a crate outside the Red Onion trying to get Teagan to give me the keys. She's holding them hostage.*

Hollis: *Umm… is that normal for Skagwayians?*

That made me laugh. Hollis and Alaska were going to be an interesting combination. His mother was livid he even considered wasting his talents up here. He'd graduated first in his class. We'd met during clinical while he was working on his residency. Even though he was four years older, we'd hit it off as friends instantly.

Me: *No... not really.*

Hollis: *Oh... well good luck with that.*

Me: *I need to go. My calves are starting to hurt.*

Hollis: *Just talk to him.*

I put my phone away, not answering his text. Hollis thought I should tell Drake everything. For two months after I left, Drake had tried to contact me. Finally, I'd changed my number and moved to a different location in New York so I would be unreachable. Otherwise, I knew I'd have gone back to him.

I am such a bitch.

Drake hadn't deserved that. He was a good guy—the best. Before the logging incident, I'd planned to spend the rest of my life with him. I'd loved him. I still loved him. But Dad had known something. He would never have led me astray.

I rang Teagan again and held the phone up to my ear. "Come on, Teagan. Pick up. I'm not in the mood to play your games today."

Voice mail again. *Damn it.* I wasn't sure why I had a soft spot for her. Her selfishness and games drove Drake nuts. But I knew it was Teagan's way of protecting herself. Her parents had been as shitty as they came. If I had been in her spot, I hoped someone would try to help me—a true friend.

When I asked if I could stay with her, she'd been hesitant at first but then agreed. Since I arrived, though, I'd only seen her the one time when I arrived. Then she'd taken off with Donnie.

That meeting had been awkward, almost strained. I needed to find another place to stay. Maybe I'd go to the hotel.

Inside the bar, the crowd cheered. I felt like a serious creeper, standing on a shaky wooden crate with my head just above the windowsill, watching. Teagan was in the back with her boyfriend, Donnie, who had rubbed me the wrong way since day one—nearly three years ago—and rang a ten on my creep-o-meter. I'd have to walk through the whole bar just to get to her. *She's doing this on purpose. Or maybe she's just being Teagan.* The thing was, with Teagan, I never knew. With a frustrated sigh, I blew out a breath.

"Hey, Lex. Who are you spying on?"

The deep voice took me by surprise, and I jumped with a scream and fell off my perch. Pain shot through my ankle. "Ouch!"

Why me? Why?

The circumstances looked much worse than they were— an innocent situation gone terribly wrong. All I'd wanted was to avoid the man who still affected me in more ways than he should. And now that man was standing less than two feet away. My skin danced with the familiar electric current that left my head buzzing.

Be strong.

The crate had given me a nasty scrape on my calf. *Damn it.* It was superficial but bleeding nevertheless. I knew I shouldn't have worn shorts that day, but the weather was unseasonably warm. I looked around to make sure no one else had heard my shriek, buying some time to pull myself together. Judging by the racket inside, I had most likely escaped additional embarrassment.

I gave another quick scan around us to make sure no one else was there. Skagway had a local gossip newsletter that went out on a weekly basis via email. The Twiner sisters ran it like world-class paparazzi. Sometimes, for *red hot* news, there were even special editions. They had a knack for being in the "worst" place at the "best" time.

Every. Single. Townsperson. Was. On. The. Subscription. List.

The people of Skagway enjoyed the gossip. Hell, even *I* read it. When my email pinged with the newsletter each week, it called like a beacon.

Jean-clad legs I was all too familiar with stepped closer. "Need a hand?"

The deep timbre of his voice still made me weak in the knees. It was deep and husky and took *manly* to a whole new level. Already my resolve was weakening. I would have to read my father's letter again to reinforce my walls. I carried the note around with me in case I ever felt the need to call Drake, which was often.

The men in New York City were nothing like Drake. They were too refined, lacking the edge—the wildness—Alaska infused in the men who lived here. Drake was savagely protective, romantic, strong, and loving all wrapped up in one ridiculously hot package.

I glanced up, meeting those warm chestnut eyes I remembered all too well. His dark hair was still short like I remembered. I swallowed and said, "Drake." My voice cracked.

Yeah, I sound nervous. Stay calm. Drake knows you. He knows you better than anyone.

I cleared my throat. "I wasn't creeping. I was waiting for Teagan."

"Why not come in? She's inside with Donnie."

That was the million-dollar question. "Umm... I... You know..." I gave up and stood. Immediately, I felt the blood trickle down my leg.

Ugh. I need to get this cleaned up.

Drake leaned against the post and crossed his right leg over his left. He was all muscle. "Let's get you fixed up. I've got a first aid kit upstairs at my place. We can take the back stairs."

I took a step back. "I'll be fine. I can walk."

Drake looked at my leg. "Ol' Man Rooster is talking with the Twiner sisters out front. If you go that way, you'll pass right by them." He shook his head. "I'm sure that'll give them something to talk about for a while. You'll be the star of the weekly Twiner Tellings newsletter."

His smirk caused me to take a deep breath. He knew I hated being in the newsletter. Hated it. And in the two years I'd been gone, Drake had only been in it once—for something inconsequential. I'd secretly scoured it for any news about him. Was he seeing someone? *Don't think about that. It doesn't matter.*

Lurking outside the Red Onion was not how I wanted the Twiner sisters to find out I was back in town. The rumors would be rampant. And if truth be told, now that I had him near, I wasn't ready to be without him again.

Just a few minutes. I want to be near him for just a few

more minutes. Then I'll leave. I'll go read the letter and re-mind myself why I stayed away for so long.

"Lead the way."

Drake handed me a towel from his back pocket. When working at the bar, he always had one tucked there. "It's clean. Hold it to your cut, and I'll carry you. We don't want you leaving a trail of blood up the stairs."

Without an argument, I took the towel. Drake's strong arms wrapped around me, and he easily picked me up.

I yelped. "It's—"

"I don't remember you being this jumpy."

I clamped my mouth shut. I was a nervous wreck around him. *What do I say?* Any kind of explanation would only make the situation look worse than it was. "I promise I wasn't lurking."

"Then why not come inside to see Teagan? You nervous to see me?"

Of course, Drake was straightforward. He always had been. We'd known each other since we were babies. When I was a senior in high school, he'd stopped to help me change a flat tire on the side of the road. From there, we started hanging out. With my father's blessing, Drake took me out on our first date. He was two years older and had wanted my father's approval since I was still in school.

Why did Dad change his mind?

Drake shifted his hold on me as he climbed the stairs, which brought my thoughts back to the oh-so-familiar feeling of being in his arms. Goose bumps formed along my skin where he touched me. Two years apart from him had done nothing but amp up my desire for him.

He paused at the door. "Why are you nervous, Lex?"

Lex. He was the only one who ever called me Lex, and it still did things to me—made me feel like I was still his.

Outside his door, we stared into each other's eyes. "You know why I'm nervous. It's been two years since we saw each other, spoke to each other."

"Don't be. I'm still just me. The same man I was two years ago."

Not according to Dad.

Regret surged through me, and I blinked a few times. "Yes, of course. I figured facing a large crowd would be awkward after what I did. I deserve it if you hate me."

It was too much; I had to break eye contact. If he hated me, I wouldn't be able to stand it. *Why does it feel so right to be near him?* In just mere minutes, my world felt fuller than it had for the last two years. This was why I had to cut off all communication. Drake Foster consumed me.

Shifting his hold on me, he was able to open the door without putting me down. I'd forgotten how strong he was. "I could never hate you." The softness in his voice brought me up short, and I blinked several times to clear my thoughts. Gently, he set me down. "Let me get the first aid kit. It's in my room."

"Thanks."

My body instantly missed his touch. *If only I could be back in his arms.* He deserved to know what happened two years ago. But the knowledge that my dad hadn't approved of him might hurt him more. Drake had loved my dad. They'd been close. Which was why my father's last letter telling me to end things with Drake had gutted me. How could I even consider spending the rest of my life with a man my father didn't approve of? When I'd first read the letter, I hadn't been myself. I'd felt like a stranger in my own skin. And now that I was in Drake's presence again, I felt doubt at my father's words for the first time.

Did I make the wrong choice?

I shook my head and tried to get my thoughts straight. Drake's place was just as I remembered—masculine. The furniture was solid wood—handmade by Drake's father, Ike. Things were tidy-ish, as usual. The shirt he wore yesterday was on the back of the couch where he probably removed it to watch TV. A lone beer bottle sat on the table. I had so many memories of us here together—cuddled on the couch as we watched a scary movie, making love by the fireplace, celebrating when I'd been accepted into college with a nearly full scholarship.

It had taken me three years to save up enough money to go to college to study nursing at twenty-one. The scholarship supplemented my savings so I hadn't needed a loan. It had been a blessing. Being a nurse had been my dream since I was a little girl.

Drake reappeared in the doorway and paused while our eyes met. Time had been good to him, and he looked fit as ever. His T-shirt hugged his muscles and showed off how broad he was.

With a quick shake of his head, he snapped out of it and brought the first aid kit to me. Quickly, I set to work cleaning the cut and putting a Band-Aid over it. "Good as new. Thanks, Drake."

"Anytime."

A few moments passed as we stared at each other. I knew I should leave, but I couldn't bring myself to do it. I wanted more time.

Finally, Drake said, "Mom told me about the clinic."

The mention of his parents caused pain to shoot through me. I missed them so much. Weakly, I smiled. "Yes, Skagway is going to finally have a doctor. Hollis is amazing."

Something shifted within Drake, and he expelled a breath, taking a few steps back while raking his fingers through his hair. "It's a good thing you're doing."

My throat grew thick. "Thanks. Maybe Dad... well, you know."

He grabbed my hand, and the fierce protectiveness I always associated with Drake came rushing back. "I know. He'd be proud."

I had made a terrible mistake leaving Drake Foster.

CHAPTER
Two

Drake

I dragged a hand down my face as the door closed. Lex was back. And I still fucking loved her. Hell, I never stopped. When she came home to bury her father, I thought we were okay. I had been there for her in every way I could be. At least I thought I had. Replaying our time together, I still had no idea what I'd done wrong.

Then the morning she left, everything changed. She ended things between us. Something had happened, and she'd shut down… completely.

Hollis fucking Fritz.

The name itself made me see red. I hated the fucker, and I'd never met him. After Lex had left, I'd kept trying to reach out to her. She wouldn't return my calls, emails, letters. Nothing. I'd hoped she would work through whatever was bothering her and then reach out. But that never happened. Finally, I went after her. She was mine. The problem was when I got there two months later, she was running into that bastard's arms.

So, I left and buried myself in the Red Onion and the town. I joined the city council, started playing cards with my buddies every other week, got nominated for an Alaskan business board, and helped my dad build furniture on the side. Anything to keep my mind off what had happened. And I thought it had worked. I thought I'd managed to pick up the pieces and move on... until today.

I felt sick to my stomach as I opened the fridge and cracked a beer. For a mere moment with her in my arms, I'd forgotten she had a boyfriend. So, I would keep my distance from now on. Cheating wasn't something I condoned. Never had. Never would.

In the two years she'd been gone, she'd only gotten more beautiful. Her blonde hair was a little longer, but other than that, nothing else had changed. Lex's petite body fit perfectly in my arms. With that thought came the realization that trying to forget Lex was a waste of energy. There was no forgetting her.

I am so screwed.

That night I was going to Moochie's house to play cards with some of the guys. We'd all been friends since school and got together when we could. They were all married with kids—or kids on the way. I'd be bringing an extra case of beer for sure. The distraction would definitely help.

Lex being back was going to fuck with my head, especially since her boyfriend was coming back with her.

But if she needed something, I would be there for her. I'd made a promise to her father that I had to keep. It was what he whispered to me as he was dying.

Take care of my Alexa. She's going to need you.

Besides losing Lex, the day Lloyd passed away was the worst day of my life.

From the time we started dating, when Lex was in high school, I knew she wanted to be a nurse. I'd supported her going away to pursue those dreams. I thought our love would last. All that shit they say about distance making the heart grow fonder was utter bullshit. If that was the case, we'd still be together.

There was a soft knock on the door. *Damn it.* I needed to be alone and gather my thoughts and control before I went back to the bar. Snapping at customers wasn't good for business. Lex being back in town and bringing that jackass city boy changed everything.

How do I not punch the fucker?

I opened the door, and Lex stood there, still beautiful as ever. She twirled a piece of her blonde hair where it spilled over her shoulder, and she chewed on her lip.

Is she as messed up as I am about this situation?

"Sorry, I forgot my phone."

Remain calm. Neutral. Unaffected.

"Come on in. Want a beer?" I opened the door wider to let her in.

Her sweet smile nearly did me in. "No, thanks. Maybe another time. I got the keys from Teagan. Finally. And I need to go check out Doogle's place. I'm hoping to open the clinic within a week. I know it needs some TLC, but with a little elbow grease, it should be fine. At least that's what Nancy said."

Without a team of people, there was no way she'd make that date. Nancy drove me fucking nuts, too. She would say anything to make a sale. But she was the only realtor in Skagway. And she only did it part time. She also helped coordinate tours for tourists during the season.

Lex picked up her phone and put it in her back pocket. The way she tapped her fingers against her leg told me she was nervous. And I imagined that was from the thought of going out to the Doogle place by herself. My grip tightened on the bottle at the mere thought of Hollis being in Skagway, but I couldn't let her go by herself. *Where is the bastard?* I already hated him. "Do you want some company?"

She paused for a second, her hand relaxing. And there was another gorgeous smile on her face. "That would be nice. Empty old houses creep me out. Teagan can't come. She's headed somewhere with Donnie. They're always heading somewhere, it seems. I haven't seen her but for a couple of minutes since I've been home."

Sometimes Teagan didn't think things through. More than once, I'd had to pick Lex up because Teagan had abandoned her for some random hookup. Pissed me the fuck off.

"Let me get my keys."

"Oh, I'll drive. I have a bunch of stuff in my car. Or you can follow me. It's up to you. But you don't have to. I don't want to wreck your afternoon." Her eyebrows crinkled as she rambled.

Yeah, this is hella confusing to me, too, sweetheart.

What I wanted was to understand what happened. Closure. For me. Maybe then I might be able to move on. Because, honestly, it made zero fucking sense. Lex was it for me. I knew this, but I'd have to figure out something.

We made our way down the stairs, her peach scent taunting me. "You sure you don't need to go back to the bar?"

"Yeah, I'm sure. Crete has it under control."

I pulled out my phone to let him know.

Me: *Won't be back until later.*

Crete: *No problem.*

Crete was a good kid. He helped support his mom and two sisters. His dad had been involved in the same accident as Lex's. It had rocked the town when the three loggers lost their lives by some freak malfunction in the logging equipment.

I followed Lex to the car and saw the Twiner sisters leaning around a pole, watching us. There was no escaping them. We'd be in this week's newsletter for sure. During the tourist season, they dressed up in gear people wore to do gold mining. They thought it added to the impression of the town.

They. Were. Crazy.

Lex blew her hair out of the way. "The Twiners've made us."

"They have?" I glanced again at the dark-haired twins.

"I wonder if we'll make a special edition?"

She isn't worried about Hollis? Do I ask about him? I decided to keep it surface level for now. If I started asking about her boyfriend, things would get awkward. I commented back, "Probably. I think Elvira had her camera out."

"Oh, we're for sure making a special edition. Shit, I hate being in that stupid thing."

It was hard to suppress my laugh, but somehow, I managed. Lex's leg bounced from nerves as she drove. I stretched my legs out in her dad's old red Chevy truck. "Your dad's truck still runs good. I've been going over to the storage unit and cranking it from time to time."

When she glanced my way, Lex had that look I remembered getting anytime I did anything for her. Her adoration made me feel like a fucking king.

"Thank you. I appreciate it. Makes me feel like I still have a piece of him."

"I know."

We turned into a driveway on the outskirts of town and got out of the truck. From there, it was obvious the place was run down. A lot of the deck needed to be replaced, and the yard was overgrown and filled with branches. I imagined inside would be the same.

We walked up to the door. It was hot as hell today, and I wiped the bit of sweat that had formed on my brow. "Did you hire anyone to fix up the place?"

"No." She stepped on one of the broken boards. "Before I bought the place, I asked Mom to take a look. She didn't have time but said it was in decent shape the last time she saw it. And… umm… you know how she can be."

Yeah, I knew how she could be. And supportive of her daughter's ambitions wasn't an example. Irene and I had a rocky relationship, to put it mildly.

Touching one of the broken railings, Lex blew out a breath. "I think I'm going to have to push back the opening. It's a little different in person. I guess it's true… the saying. You get what you pay for."

I kept my mouth shut. Things between Irene and me were strained at times. For the most part, she tended to favor Raquel, Lex's sister. A parent should never show favoritism to one of their children over another. My parents never did between my two brothers and me.

Lex unlocked the door. Everything was covered in dust and smelled musty. I rubbed the back of my neck. Yeah, it needed a lot of work. "Maybe Fred can squeeze you into his schedule."

Around this part of Alaska, Fred was about the only option for repairs, which meant he stayed busy.

"Yeah, I'll call him." Lex kept walking through the room. Pausing, she took a deep breath and pointed to the front area. Something changed, and her face brightened. "Can't you see it? Patients come in here. There's exam rooms over here. Offices. Upstairs can be a residence. It's going to be wonderful."

Her excitement was contagious. It had always been that way with her. "Yeah, I can see it. It'll be great."

She got that sweet look in her eyes. "Thanks, Drake. I know you get how important this is to me."

"I do."

Things shifted between us, and I took a step back. *She has a boyfriend.* "What did you need help with? I need to get back to the bar."

Was that hurt that flashed across her face? After this was over, I was going to need a stiff drink. Maybe two. Or three. A case of beer wasn't going to do at Moochie's. I was going to need whiskey and a lot of it.

"Oh yeah. I'm sorry. I forgot. Can you help me take some measurements of the rooms? I need them to create a layout for when all the equipment comes. I'm going to take pictures, too. This way I can make a budget of what needs to be done."

I picked up one of the tape measures from her bag. "I'll start upstairs."

"Thanks."

Again, things felt awkward, or maybe it was what was left unsaid between us. *Just ask her what happened.* But the words died in my throat. Instead, I walked upstairs and took all the measurements and noted them in my phone. The second floor was just as bad as the first. Maybe worse. Some of the drywall needed to be repaired, and the plumbing looked shot.

I could hear Lex cursing as the measuring tape retracted, making a racket. *So damn cute.* She was impatient and had a temper to match. Another snap of the measuring tape made me smile and drew me to her.

I trotted down the stairs. "How's it going?"

"Stupid thing is trying to kill me." She threw it down on the floor and stomped on it.

"I think you've effectively killed the tape measure."

We smiled at each other and then laughed. I had to fight the urge to sweep her up in my arms and kiss her until we couldn't breathe. Her lips were addictive. I could happily drown in her touch. Instead, I cleared my throat. "Upstairs is done. I'll finish downstairs if you want to take pictures of the upstairs."

In no time, we were done and headed back to the Red Onion. Lex pulled up to the front and said, "I'll let you out and go park."

I chuckled. "This time, try not to lurk outside the window."

"I will try. I can see how it might become a habit. Lex the Lurker."

"Definitely has a ring to it." Laughing, I got out of the truck and walked inside, unable to wipe the pussy-ass grin off my face.

The bar had slowed down some. Most of the party had left, leaving a few locals. I waved and chatted for a minute before going behind the bar.

A new guy was here; had to be a tourist. From the looks of his loafers, he was a city boy. Lots of those came here thinking they'd tame the wild. If I were a pussy and rolled my eyes, this would be the time to do it as I watched him, imagining his thoughts. People like him drove me crazy.

Two of the local girls—Samone and Jane—had saddled up close to him. Those women would sleep with anyone. The city slicker smelled of money, which meant those two girls would be after him.

"Oh, Hollis, it's going to be so nice to have a doctor in town," Jane said.

My head snapped up and I stared at the guy. There was no fucking way this was a coincidence. This was Skagway, for shit's sake. The guy gave Samone a smile, and I felt rage shoot through me. Lex didn't deserve this. No rich asshole was going to cheat on the woman I'd give my right arm to still be with.

Jane slid him a piece of paper. "Call me."

He took the piece of paper, and I lost it.

Intoxicated by You is available now
at your favorite online retailer!

Other Books by Kristin Mayer

Available Now

The Trust Series
Trust Me
Love Me
Promise Me

Full-length novels in the TRUST series are also available in audio from Tantor Media.

An Exposed Heart Series
Intoxicated by You
Wrecked for You
Changed by You
Wrecked by You

Full-length novels in the EXPOSED HEARTS SERIES are also available in audio from Audible.

The Effect Series
Ripple Effect
Domino Effect

The Twisted Fate Series
White Lies
Black Truth

Timeless Love Series
Untouched Perfection
Flawless Perfection
Tempting Perfection

Stand Alone Novels

Innocence

Bane

Whispered Promises

Predestined Hearts

Coming Soon

Play Me—Joint Collaboration with Kelly Elliott—
Coming March 2019

Complicated Love—Coming Fall of 2019